*New York T*___ of over four
dozen rom___ ___ntemporary
'Animal Magnetism' a___ ___ITA for *Simply*
Irresistible and is a t___ ___ winner as well.
Co___ct with Jill on he___ ___iishalvis.com for a complete book list
and ___ read her daily ~~blog~~, where she recounts her Misplaced City Girl
adv___tures, or visit her at www.facebook.com/jillshalvis or @JillShalvis for
oth___news.

Pr___ for Jill Shalvis:

'Pa___ d with the trademark Shalvis humor and intense intimacy, it is definitely
a m___read . . . If love, laughter and passion are the keys to any great romance,
the___novel hits every note' *Romantic Times*

'He___arming and sexy . . . an abundance of chemistry, smoldering romance,
and___ious antics' *Publishers Weekly*

'[S___ s] has quickly become one of my go-to authors of contemporary
ron___. Her writing is smart, fun, and sexy, and her books never fail to leave
a s___on my face long after I've closed the last page . . . Jill Shalvis is an
aut___ot to be missed!' *The Romance Dish*

'Jil___halvis is such a talented author that she brings to life characters who
mal___you laugh, cry, and are a joy to read' *Romance Reviews Today*

'W___ I love about Jill Shalvis's books is that she writes sexy, adorable
heroe___ . . . the sexual tension is out of this world. And of course, in true Shalvis
fashi___n, she expertly mixes in humor that has you laughing out loud' *Heroes*
and Heartbreakers

'I always enjoy reading a Jill Shalvis book. She's a consistently elegant, bold,
clever writer . . . Very witty – I laughed out loud countless times and these
scenes are sizzling' *All About Romance*

'If you have not read a Jill Shalvis novel yet, then you really have not read a
real romance yet either!' *Book Cove Reviews*

'Eng___ zing writing, characters that walk straight into your heart, touching,
hilar___us' *Library Journal*

'Wi___, fun, and sexy – the perfect romance!' Lori Foster, *New York Times*
best___'ling author

'Ri___ing suspense laced with humor and heart is her hallmark, and Jill Shalvis
alwa___delivers' Donna Kauffman, *USA Today* bestselling author

'Hu___or, intrigue, and scintillating sex. Jill Shalvis is a total original' Suzanne
Forster, *New York Times* bestselling author

By Jill Shalvis

Lucky Harbor Series
Simply Irresistible
The Sweetest Thing
Head Over Heels
Lucky In Love
At Last
Forever And A Day
It Had To Be You
Always On My Mind
Once In A Lifetime
It's In His Kiss
He's So Fine
One In A Million

Merry Christmas, Baby & Under The Mistletoe
(A Lucky Harbor omnibus)

Animal Magnetism Series
Animal Magnetism
Animal Attraction
Rescue My Heart
Rumour Has It
Then Came You
Still The One

Jill
SHALVIS

always
on my mind

headline
ETERNAL

Published by arrangement with Forever,
a division of Grand Central Publishing.

First published as an ebook in Great Britain in 2014
by HEADLINE ETERNAL
An imprint of HEADLINE PUBLISHING GROUP

First published in paperback in Great Britain in 2015

ISBN 978 1 4722 2288 6

Offset in Times by Avon DataSet Ltd, Bidford-on-Avon, Warwickshire

Printed and bound by CPI Group (UK) Ltd, Croydon, CR0 4YY

MIX
Paper from
responsible sources
FSC® C104740

HEADLINE PUBLISHING GROUP
An Hachette UK Company
338 Euston Road
London NW1 3BH

www.headlineeternal.com
www.headline.co.uk
www.hachette.co.uk

To all the real-life firefighters out there,
you are true heroes.

And to the people in the field who gave me so much help
on the research (and shared some amazing stories!),
I'm forever grateful:

Mississippi Commissioner of Insurance and State Fire
Marshal Mike Chaney
The Mississippi State Fire Marshal's Office
Chief Deputy Fire Marshal Ricky Davis
Deputy James "Jimmy" Jackson, Fire Marshal Supervisor
State Deputy Fire Coordinator Brad Smith

always
on my mind

Chapter 1

♥

Saying that she went to the annual Firefighter's Charity Breakfast for pancakes was like saying she watched baseball for the game—when everyone knew that you watched baseball for the guys in tight uniform pants.

But this time Leah Sullivan really did want pancakes. She also wanted her grandma to live forever, world peace, and hey, while she was making wishes, she wouldn't object to being sweet-talked out of her clothes sometime this year.

But those were all issues for another day. Mid-August was hinting at an Indian summer for the Pacific Northwest. The morning was warm and heading toward hot as she walked to the already crowded pier. The people of Lucky Harbor loved a get-together, and if there was food involved—and cute firefighters to boot—well, that was just a bonus.

Leah accepted a short stack of pancakes from Tim Denison, a firefighter from Station #24. He was a rookie, fresh from the academy and at least five years younger than her, but that didn't stop him from sending her a wink. She took in his beachy, I-belong-on-a-Gap-ad-campaign appearance and waited for her good parts to flutter.

They didn't.

For reasons unknown, her good parts were on vacation and had been for months.

Okay, so not for reasons unknown. But not wanting to go there, not today, she blew out a breath and continued down the length of the pier.

Picnic tables had been set up, most of them full of other Lucky Harbor locals supporting the firefighters' annual breakfast. Leah's friend Ali Winters was halfway through a huge stack of pancakes, eyeing the food line as if considering getting more.

Leah plopped down beside her. "You eating for two already?"

"Bite your tongue." Ali aimed her fork at her along with a pointed *don't mess with me* look. "I've only been with Luke for two months. Pregnancy isn't anywhere on the to-do list yet. I'm just doing my part to support the community."

"By eating two hundred pancakes?"

"Hey, the money goes to the senior center."

There was a salty breeze making a mess of Leah's and Ali's hair, but it didn't dare disturb the woman sitting on the other side of Ali. Nothing much disturbed the cool-as-a-cucumber Aubrey.

"I bet sex is on your to-do list," Aubrey said, joining their conversation.

Ali gave a secret smile.

Aubrey narrowed her eyes. "I could really hate you for that smile."

"You *should* hate me for this smile."

"Luke's that good, huh?"

Ali sighed dreamily. "He's *magic*."

"Magic's just an illusion." Aubrey licked the syrup off her fork while managing to somehow look both beautifully sophisticated and graceful.

Back in their school days, Aubrey had been untouchable, tough as nails, and Leah hadn't been anywhere in the vicinity of her league. Nothing much had changed there. She looked down at herself and sucked in her stomach.

"There's no illusion when it comes to Luke," Ali told Aubrey. "He's one-hundred-percent real. And all mine."

"Well, now you're just being mean," Aubrey said. "And that's my area. Leah, what's with the expensive shoes and cheap haircut?"

Leah put a hand to her choppy auburn layers, and Aubrey smiled at Ali, like *See?* That's *how you do mean...*

Most of Leah's money went toward her school loans and helping to keep her grandma afloat, but she did have one vice. Okay, two, but being addicted to Pinterest wasn't technically a vice. Her love of shoes most definitely was. She'd gotten today's strappy leather wedges from Paris, and they'd been totally worth having to eat apples and peanut butter for a week. "They were on sale," she said, clicking them together as if she were Dorothy in Oz. "They're knockoffs," she admitted.

Aubrey sighed. "You're not supposed to say that last part. It's not as fun to be mean when you're nice."

"But I am nice," Leah said.

"I know," Aubrey said. "And I'm trying to like you anyway."

The three of them were an extremely unlikely trio, connected by a cute, quirky Victorian building in downtown Lucky Harbor. The building was older than God, currently owned by Aubrey's great-uncle, and divided into three shops. There was Ali's floral shop, Leah's grandma's bakery, and a neglected bookstore that Aubrey had been making noises about taking over since her job at Town Hall had gone south a few weeks back.

Neither Ali nor Leah was sure yet if having Aubrey in the building every day would be fun or a nightmare. But regardless, Aubrey knew her path. So did Ali.

Leah admired the hell out of that. Especially since she'd never known her path. She'd known one thing, the need to get out of Lucky Harbor—and she had. At age seventeen, she'd gone and had rarely looked back.

But she was back now, putting her pastry chef skills to good use helping her grandma while she recovered from knee surgery. The problem was, Leah had gotten out of the habit of settling in one place.

Not quite true, said a little voice inside her. If not for a string of spectacularly bad decisions, she'd have finished French culinary school. And not embarrassed herself on the reality TV show *Sweet Wars*. And…

Don't go there.

Instead, she scooped up a big bite of fluffy pancakes and concentrated on their delicious goodness rather than her own screwups. Obsessing over her bad decisions was something she saved for the deep dark of night.

"Jack's at the griddle," Ali noted.

Leah twisted around to look at the cooking setup. Lieutenant Jack Harper was indeed manning the griddle. He was tall and broad shouldered and looked like a guy who could take on anything that came his way. This was a good thing, since he ran station #24.

Fire Station #24 was one of four that serviced the county, and thanks to the Olympic Mountain range at their back, with its million acres of forest, all four stations were perpetually busy.

Jack thrived on busy. He could be as intimidating as hell when he chose to be, which wasn't right now since he was head-bopping to some beat only he could hear in his headphones. Knowing him, it was some good, old-fashioned, ear-splitting hard rock.

Not too far from him, leashed to a bench off to the side, sat Kevin, a huge Great Dane. He was white with black markings that made him look like a Dalmatian wannabe. Kevin had been given to a neighboring fire station where he'd remained until he'd eaten one too many expensive hoses, torn up one too many beds, and chewed dead one too many pairs of boots. The rambunctious one-year-old had then been put up for adoption.

The only problem was that no one had wanted what was by then a hundred-and-fifty-pound nuisance. Kevin had been headed for the Humane Society when Jack, always the protector, always the savior, had stepped in a few weeks back and saved the day.

Just like he'd done for Leah more times than she could count.

It'd become a great source of entertainment for the entire town that Jack Harper II, once the town terror himself—at least to mothers of teenage daughters everywhere—was now in charge of the *latest* town terror.

Another firefighter stepped up to the griddle to relieve Jack, who loaded a plate for himself and stepped over to Kevin. He flipped the dog a sausage, which Kevin caught in midair with one snap of his huge jaws. The sausage instantly vanished, and Kevin licked his lips, staring intently at Jack's plate as if he could make more sausage fly into his mouth by wish alone.

Jack laughed and crouched down to talk to the dog, a movement that had his shirt riding up, revealing low-riding BDUs—his uniform pants—a strip of taut, tantalizing male skin, and just the hint of a perfect ass.

On either side of Leah, both Ali and Aubrey gave lusty sighs. Leah completely understood. She could feel her own lusty sigh catching in her throat, but she squelched it. They were in the F-zone, she and Jack. *Friends.* Friends didn't do lust, or if they did, they also did the smart, logical thing and ignored it. Still, she felt a smile escape her at the contagious sound of Jack's laughter. Truth was, he'd been making her smile since the sixth grade, when she'd first moved to Lucky Harbor.

As if sensing her appraisal, Jack lifted his head. His dark, mirrored sunglasses hid his eyes, but she knew he was looking right at her because he arched a dark brow.

And on either side of her, Ali and Aubrey sighed again.

"Really?" Leah asked them.

"Well, look at him," Aubrey said unapologetically. "He's hot, he's got rhythm—and not just the fake white-boy kind either. He's also funny as hell. And for a bonus, he's gainfully employed. It's just too bad I'm off men forever."

"Forever's a long time," Ali said, and Leah's gut cramped at the thought of the beautiful, blond Aubrey going after Jack.

But Jack was still looking at Leah. Those glasses were still in the way, but she knew his dark eyes were framed by thick, black lashes and the straight, dark lines of his eyebrows. And the right brow was sliced through by a thin scar, which he'd gotten at age fourteen when he and his cousin Ben had stolen his mom's car and driven it into a fence.

"Forever," Aubrey repeated emphatically. "I'm off men *forever*." Leah felt herself relax a little.

Which was silly. Jack could date whomever he wanted, and did. Often.

"And anyway," Aubrey went on, "that's what batteries are for."

Ali laughed along with Aubrey as they all continued to watch Jack, who'd gone back to the griddle. He was moving to his music again while flipping pancakes, much to the utter delight of the crowd.

"Woo-hoo!" Aubrey yelled at him, both she and Ali toasting him with their plastic cups filled with orange juice.

Jack grinned and took a bow.

"Hey," Ali said, nudging Leah. "Go tip him."

"Is that what the kids are calling it nowadays?" Aubrey asked.

Leah rolled her eyes and stood up. "You're both ridiculous. He's dating some EMT flight nurse."

Or at least he had been as of last week. She couldn't keep up with Jack's dating life. Okay, so she *chose* not to keep up. "We're just…buddies." They always had been, she and Jack, through thick and thin, and there'd been a lot of thin. "When you go to middle school with someone, you learn too much about him," she went on, knowing damn well that she needed to just stop talking, something she couldn't seem to do. "I mean, I couldn't go out with the guy who stole all the condoms on Sex Education Day and then used them as water balloons to blast the track girls as we ran the four hundred."

"I could," Aubrey said.

Leah rolled her eyes, mostly to hide the fact that she'd left off the real reason she couldn't date Jack.

"Where you going?" Ali asked when Leah stood up. "We haven't gotten to talk about the latest episode of *Sweet Wars*. Now that you're halfway through the season and down to the single eliminations, the whole town's talking about it nonstop. Did you know that there's a big crowd at the Love Shack on episode night?"

Yes, she'd known. At first she'd been pressured to go, but she couldn't do it. She couldn't watch herself if anyone else was in the room.

"You were awesome," Ali said.

Maybe, but that had been the adrenaline high from being filmed. Leah had pulled it off by pretending she was Julia Child. Easy enough, since she'd been pretending that since she'd been a kid. After the first terrifying episode, she'd learned something about herself. Even as a kid who'd grown up with little to no self-esteem, there was something about being in front of a camera. It was pretend, so she'd been able to break out of her shell.

The shocking truth was, she'd loved it.

"And also, you looked great on TV," Aubrey said. "Bitch. I know you were judged on originality, presentation, and taste, but you really should get brownie points for not looking fat. Do you look as good for the last three episodes?"

This subject was no better than the last one. "Gotta go," Leah said, grabbing her plate and pointing to the cooking area. "There's sausage now."

"Ah." Aubrey nodded sagely. "So you *do* want Jack's sausage."

Ali burst out laughing, and Aubrey high-fived her.

Ignoring them both, Leah headed toward the grill.

Jack flipped a row of pancakes, rotated a line of sausage links, and checked the flame. He was in a waiting pattern.

The status of his life.

Behind him, two fellow firefighters were talking about how one had bought his girlfriend an expensive purse as an apology for forgetting the anniversary of their first date. The guy thought the present would help ease him out of the doghouse.

Jack knew better. The purse was a nice touch, but in his experience, a man's mistakes were never really forgotten, only meticulously cataloged in a woman's frontal lobe to be pulled out later at her discretion.

A guy needed to either avoid mistakes entirely or get out of the relationship before any anniversaries came up.

"Woof."

This from Kevin, trying to get his attention.

"No more sausage," Jack called to him. "You know what happens when you eat too much. You stink me out of the bedroom."

Kevin had a big black spot over his left eye, giving him the look of a mischievous pirate as he gazed longingly at the row of sausages. When Jack didn't give in, the dog heaved a long sigh and lay down, setting his head on his paws.

"Heads up," Tim called.

Jack caught the gallon-sized container of pancake batter with one hand while continuing to flip pancakes with his other.

"Pretty fancy handiwork," a woman said.

Leah.

Jack turned and found her standing next to Kevin, holding a plate.

Jack gave Kevin the *stay* gesture just as the dog would have made his move. Great Danes had a lot of great qualities, like loyalty and affection, but politeness was not one of them. Kevin lived to press his nose into ladies' crotches, climb on people's laps as if he were a six-pound Pomeranian, and eat…well, everything. And Kevin had his eyes on the prize—Leah's plate.

Jack gestured Leah closer with a crook of his finger. She'd shown up in Lucky Harbor with shadows beneath her forest-green eyes and lots of secrets in them, but she was starting to look a little more like herself. Her white gauzy top and black leggings emphasized a willowy body made lean by hard work or tough times—knowing Leah, it was probably both. Her silky hair was loose and blowing around her face. He'd have called it her just-out-of-bed look, except she wasn't sleeping with anyone at the moment.

He knew this because one, Lucky Harbor didn't keep secrets, and two, he worked at the firehouse, aka Gossip Central. He knew Leah was in a holding pattern too. And something was bothering her.

Not your problem...

But though he told himself that, repeatedly in fact, old habits were hard to break. His friendship with her was as long as it was complicated, but she'd been there for him whenever he'd needed her, no questions asked. In the past week alone she'd driven his mom to her doctor's appointment twice, fed and walked Kevin when Jack had been called out of the county, and left a plate of cream cheese croissants in his fridge—his favorite. There was a lot of water beneath their bridge, but she mattered to him, even when he wanted to wrap his fingers around her neck and squeeze.

"You have any sausage ready?" she asked.

At the word *sausage*, Kevin practically levitated. Ears quirking, nose wriggling, the dog sat up, his sharp eyes following as Jack forked a piece of meat and set it on Leah's plate. When Jack didn't share with Kevin as well, he let out a pitiful whine.

Falling for it hook, line, and sinker, Leah melted. "Aw," she said. "Can I give him one?"

"Only if you want to sleep with him tonight," Jack said.

"I wouldn't mind."

"Trust me, you would."

Coming up beside Jack to help man the grill, Tim waggled a brow at Leah. "I'll sleep with you tonight. No matter how many sausages you eat."

Leah laughed. "You say that to all the women in line."

Tim flashed a grin, a hint of dimple showing. "But with you, I mean it. So...yes?"

"No," Leah said, still smiling. "Not tonight."

"Tomorrow night?"

Jack spoke mildly. "You have a death wish?"

"Huh?"

"Rookies who come on to Leah vanish mysteriously," Jack told him. "Never to be seen again."

Tim narrowed his eyes. "Yeah? Who?"

"The last rookie. His name was Tim too," Jack deadpanned.

Leah laughed, and Tim rolled his eyes. At work, he reported directly to Jack, not that he looked worried.

"I'll risk it," he said cockily to Leah.

Jack wondered if he'd still be looking so sure of himself later when he'd be scrubbing down fire trucks by himself. All of them.

Leah yawned and rubbed a hand over her eyes, and Jack forgot about Tim. "Maybe you should switch to Wheaties," Jack said. "You look like you need the boost."

She met his gaze. "Tim thought I looked all right."

"You know it, babe," Tim said, still shamelessly eavesdropping. "Change your mind about tonight, and I'll make sure you know *exactly* how good you look."

Jack revised his plan about Tim cleaning the engines. The rookie would be too busy at the senior center giving a hands-on fire extinguisher demonstration, which every firefighter worth his salt dreaded because the seniors were feisty, didn't listen, and in the case of the female seniors, liked their "hands-on" *anything* training.

Oblivious to his fate, Tim continued to work the grill. Jack kept his attention on Leah. He wanted her to do whatever floated her boat, but he didn't want her dating a player like Tim. But saying so would be pretty much like waving a red flag in front of a bull, no matter how pretty that bull might be. She'd give a stranger the very shirt off her back, but Jack had long ago learned to not even attempt to tell her what to do or she'd do the opposite just because.

She had a long habit of doing just that.

He blamed her asshole father, but in this case it didn't matter because Leah didn't seem all that interested in Tim's flirting anyway.

Or in anything actually.

Which was what was really bothering Jack. Leah loved the challenge of life, the adventure of it. She'd been chasing that challenge and adventure as long as he'd known her. It was contagious—her spirit, her enthusiasm, her ability to be as unpredictable as the whim of fate.

And unlike anyone else in his world, she alone could lighten a bad mood and make him laugh. But her smile wasn't meeting her eyes. Nudging her aside, out of Tim's earshot, he waited until she looked at him. "Hey," he said.

"Aren't you worried you'll vanish mysteriously, never to be seen again?"

"I'm not a rookie."

She smiled, but again it didn't meet her eyes.

"You okay?" he asked.

"Always." And then she popped a sausage into her mouth.

Jack got the message loud and clear. She didn't want to talk. He could appreciate that. Hell, he was at his happiest not talking. But she'd had a rough year, first with the French culinary school disaster, where she'd quit three weeks before graduation for some mysterious reason, and then *Sweet Wars*.

Rumor had it that she'd gone pretty far on the show, outshining the best of the best. He knew she was under contractual obligations to keep quiet about the results, but he'd thought she'd talk to *him*.

She hadn't.

Jack had watched each episode, cheering her on. Last night she'd created puff pastries on the clock for a panel of celebrity chefs who'd yelled—a lot. Most of Leah's competition had been completely rattled by their bullying ways, but Leah had had a lifetime of dealing with someone just like that. She'd won the challenge, hands down. And even if Jack hadn't known her as well as he did, he'd have pegged her as the winner of the whole thing.

But she wasn't acting like a winner.

Had she quit that too?

Because the truth was that she tended to run from her demons. She always had, and some things never changed.

She met his gaze. "What?"

"You tell me. Tell me what's wrong."

She shook her head, her pretty eyes surprisingly hooded from him. "I've learned to fight my own battles, Jack."

Maybe. But it wasn't her battles he wanted to fight, he realized, so much as he wanted to see her smile again and mean it.

Chapter 2

The next morning, Leah walked to the bakery. From her grandma's house, downtown was only a mile or so, and she liked the exercise, even at four in the morning.

Maybe especially at four in the morning.

Lucky Harbor sat nestled in a rocky cove between the Olympic Mountains and the coast, the architecture an eclectic mix of old and new. She'd been to a lot of places since she'd left here, but there'd been nowhere like this small, cozy, homey town.

The main drag of Lucky Harbor was lined with Victorian buildings painted in bright colors, housing everything from the post office to an art gallery. At the end of the street was the turnoff to the harbor, where a long pier jutted out into the water with its café, arcade, ice cream shop, and Ferris wheel.

Right now, everything was closed. Leah was the only one out on the street. She loved the look of Lucky Harbor on sleepy mornings like this, with the long column of fog floating in from the ocean, the twinkle of the white lights strung along the storefronts and in the trees that lined the sidewalks.

Like a postcard.

And all of it, right down to the salty ocean air, evoked a myriad of memories. So did the bakery as she unlocked it and let herself in. It was warm already, and for now, quiet. Later, Riley would show up. Riley was a Lucky Harbor transplant who'd made her way to town as a runaway teen and then had been taken under the wing of Amy, a friend of Leah's. Riley had grown up a lot in the past few years and was now a part-time college student who worked a few hours a week at both the local café and the bakery. At the moment, though, Leah was alone. She flipped on the lights, and as always, the electricity hummed and then dimmed, fighting for enough power before settling. The cranky old building needed a renovation in the worst way, but Mr. Lyons was so tight with his money he squeaked when he walked.

So tight that he had the building in escrow. No word yet on what the new owner might be like, though he'd promised everyone that he'd honor their leases. This left them safe for the rest of the year at least.

Leah turned on the ovens. They were just as temperamental as the old building. She had to kick the broiler plate twice before hearing the *whoomp* of the gas as it caught. One more day, she thought with some satisfaction. The bakery was going to hold together for at least one more day.

Her grandma Elsie had been baking for fifty-plus years, but she hadn't experimented much in the past few decades. Leah had pretty much taken over, updating the offerings, tossing out the old-fashioned notion of frozen cookie dough, taking great joy in creating all new, all fresh every morning.

It was a lot of work, but she welcomed it because there was something about baking that allowed her to lose herself. Several hours later, she might have had to kick the ovens no less than twelve more times, but the day's offerings were looking damn good. Bread, croissants, and donuts…not exactly the fancy fare she'd gotten used to creating at school or on *Sweet Wars*, but she loved it anyway. And she'd done it all in spite of the equipment.

After that, she shelved her freshly made pastries in the glass display out front and dreamed about finishing culinary school someday. She stopped daydreaming when the bell over the door chimed for the first time that morning. Forest Ranger Matt Bowers strode in mid-yawn.

Leah automatically poured him a Dr. Pepper on tap and bagged up two cheese danishes—his morning special.

"Enjoyed *Sweet Wars* the other night," he said. "You're the best one."

If you can't be the best, Leah, don't bother being anything at all.

Her father's favorite sentence. His second-favorite sentence had been *Christ, Leah Marie, don't you ever get tired of screwing up?* And then there'd been her personal favorite. *You're going to amount to nothing.*

She knew there were people who'd had it far rougher than she had growing up, but his words had always sliced deeply, and her mother's halfhearted attempts to soften the blows with "he means well" or "he loves you" hadn't helped. Instead, they'd left her confused, hurt, and feeling like she could never please.

As a result, she wasn't very good with praise. It made her uncomfortable, like there was a standard that she couldn't possibly live up to.

"Tell me the truth," Matt said. "You won the whole enchilada, right?"

She handed him his breakfast. "I can't say," she told him. "Contractual promises."

Matt took a big bite of the first danish and sighed in pleasure. "Oh yeah. You totally won."

When he was gone, Leah sampled her danish and had to admit he was right about one thing at least. The danish was good.

The bakery door opened again, this time to one of the finest-looking cops in all the land—Sawyer Thompson.

"You're pretty good on that show," he said while she bagged up his favorite, a chocolate chip roll. "You win?"

"Not allowed to say," she said, starting to feel grateful for the contract she'd signed, the one that said keep her mouth shut or else. She handed him his bag.

He took a big bite of the roll and sighed. "You so won."

In spite of herself, Leah flushed with pleasure as he smiled at her, paid, and left.

"Seriously," Ali said from behind Leah, having come in the back door, undoubtedly for her midmorning donut. "You get all the hot guys. It's so unfair."

"You sell flowers," Leah told her. "I sell sugar. Do the math." She gave Ali a bag of donut holes to go and put it on her tab.

And so went the morning. People coming in, buying her stuff—which was good—and asking about *Sweet Wars*—which was bad.

If you can't be the best, Leah, don't bother being anything at all.

"Get out of my head," she said and went back to work. By noon she was ready for a nap, and she still had two more hours to go before Riley would show up. Leah still had to take her grandma for her physical therapy appointment, then grocery shopping for dinner, and then, if Leah was very lucky, she'd catch some sleep. She was going to be thirty this year, and she was already fantasizing about naps. Maybe she should try to get into the senior center...

But she knew it wasn't the hours making her tired. She was used to hard work. Nor was it being displaced, living on a futon in her grandma Elsie's tiny house for the duration of her rehabilitation. Leah was good at the wanderlust, nomadic lifestyle. She should be. She'd hit four colleges in four years, trying out premed, poli-sci, even journalism before going back to her first love.

Baking.

But coming back to Lucky Harbor had thrown her a bit. Elsie's knee surgery had been unexpected. Leah was grateful for how well her grandma was getting around, but the meds made it hard for Elsie to get up early in the morning and handle the baking. So Leah had come to help out for a week or so.

Except she'd passed the one-month mark and she was still here.

The door chimed again, and Dee Harper entered the shop, smiling at the man holding the door open for her.

Her son, Jack Harper.

Kevin was outside, his leash hooked around the wrought-iron bench beneath the picture window. Nose to the glass, the dog was eyeing the display cases like he hadn't eaten in a week.

Jack pointed at him. Kevin licked his chops but sat on his haunches, and then Jack's broad shoulders filled the doorway as he gently nudged his mom to the front counter.

"Hey," he said with a smile at Leah as he sniffed appreciatively. "Smells amazing in here."

"Thanks." She drank in the sight of him. His hair had been cut short again. More for the ease of care than style, she knew. He'd always been way too good-looking for his own good, and that hadn't changed. If anything, time and hard-won experience had only made him more drop-dead gorgeous.

Which wasn't really fair.

But more than his physical prowess was his incredible charisma and easy charm. The joke was that he could coax a nun out of her undies. But that natural magnetism was missing today.

"Anything, Mom," he said to Dee, gesturing to the wide display of choices spread out before them. "Everything. Whatever you want."

"Honey, I told you. I'm not all that hungry."

Jack's eyes were shadowed, his jaw rough with at least a day's growth. "The doctor said to eat, remember? He said if you want to walk through the castles of Scotland like you told him, then you have to build up your strength. And you love Leah's pastries."

Dee smiled at Leah.

Leah smiled back, working hard at not letting her sympathy or worry show. Dee Harper was fighting breast cancer. The chemo was the worst of it, and it was kicking her ass. Leah held out the plate of pastry samples she had on the counter. "Here, try one of my fruit tarts. They're something new I've been working on, but I'm still not sure I got them right. What do you think?"

Dee's expression said that she knew Leah was full of it. They both knew Leah never put out anything that wasn't as perfect as possible. Her father's legacy again—be perfect or be nothing at all. Mostly it was easier for Leah to be nothing at all, but baking was one of those things that she had to do. Like...breathing.

Dee took a bite of a tart. Her clothes were a little loose, and she wore a handkerchief to hide her hair loss. Leah saw the bandage around her forearm and knew they'd just come from the doctor. Jack pulled out a chair for his mom and waited until she sat before he limped very slightly back to the counter. Jaw set, he eyed the selection. "One of everything."

"Go sit," Leah said. "I'll bring it to you."

He didn't sit. He stood there at the counter, shoulders tense, his mirrored sunglasses shoved up on top of his head, saying nothing as he stared into the display.

Heart aching for him and for Dee, Leah poured two glasses of sun tea and brought them to the table. Dee had pulled a ball of yarn and two knitting needles from her bag and appeared to be working on a scarf. She made beautiful blankets too and sold her wares at various local art and craft fairs as her health allowed. When it didn't, friends sold them for her, as Leah had done last weekend.

Leah went back behind the counter and put together a tray of assorted goodies, bringing that to the table as well. Dee stopped knitting to squeeze her hand in thanks and made a token effort to eat some more of the tart.

Leah made her way back to Jack, still standing there at the counter. He shifted, the motion stirring the air with the scent of male skin and laundry soap.

"You okay?" she asked quietly.

"She needs food, and she won't eat. I thought your stuff would be irresistible."

"I meant your knee." Leah wiped her hands on her apron and took a step back to eye his long legs. He'd been a Hotshot for years, one of the rural firefighters who jumped out of planes to fight fires in the mountains and on the plains, until a knee injury five years ago had side-lined him. He'd taken a job working for the Lucky Harbor Fire Department. Not nearly as exciting, she knew. "What happened?"

He shrugged dismissively. Guy code for "nothing."

"Did you go see a doctor?" she asked.

He gave another shrug and turned to face her. "I need you to get her to eat."

His voice was low and a little raw. But that's not what got her. He'd asked her for something, for help, and he never asked lightly. Though it made Leah want to comfort him with a hug, she did an about-face and went back to the table. Sitting next to Dee, she nudged the plate of goodies closer to her as Jack's phone rang.

"I've got to take this," he said and strode out of the bakery.

The minute he did, Kevin leaped on him, tall enough on his hind legs that man and dog were nearly nose to nose. Jack ruffled Kevin's big head and gave him a push.

Kevin slid to the ground and rolled over on his back, exposing his belly. Obliging him, Jack squatted low, stroking the dog into ecstasy as he spoke into his phone.

Leah did her best not to look at his ass through the window, but it was hopeless. He had a great one.

Beside her, Dee set down the tart. "It's like old times, the two of you."

Not quite, but Leah knew what she meant. Back then, as the new girl, she hadn't fit in, and Jack had been the only one to tolerate her. He'd allowed her to tag along after him and his friends, though he'd always sent her home well before they'd gotten themselves into trouble.

And oh, how she'd resented that. She'd loved trouble. She'd loved *him*, the way he had of making her forget her miserable home life, or how he'd make her laugh. He'd been far more than an escape from a rough childhood for her. He might have been two years ahead of her in age and light-years ahead of her in experience, but he'd been her best friend.

They'd kept in touch over the years with texts and emails. They'd talked when she'd needed a familiar shoulder to cry on. Jack had always been far more stoic though, but he'd done his own fair share of calling her just to "make sure she hadn't fallen off the deep end." Leah had usually interpreted this to mean he needed to vent, and she'd drag out of him whatever was on his mind. She'd treasured those calls the most, being needed by him. They'd come all too rarely because Jack didn't like to need anyone.

"It's nice," Dee said.

Leah reached out and squeezed Dee's hand. "It's nice to be back."

"You're concerned about me. Don't be. I'm going to be okay."

"I know," Leah said, and hoped to God that it was true.

Outside, Jack rose, one hand holding the phone to his ear, the other resting on Kevin's head, which came up to his hip.

"I really didn't want anything to eat," Dee said. "But he wanted me to so badly."

"He's worried about you."

"Well that makes us even, because I'm worried about him too. Did he tell you? He needs another knee surgery, just like what your grandma had, but he's too stubborn to get it done."

"No," Leah said, her gaze roaming back to Jack's broad shoulders. "He didn't mention that."

"He pushes himself too hard."

"You know why," Leah said softly.

"Yes," Dee said. "I know why."

Everyone knew. Jack's dad had been a firefighter. He'd lived and breathed the job. And then he'd died on that job, becoming a local hero. What else was the boy of that hero supposed to do except become a firefighter as well and do his best to live up to the legend?

"I ruined him," Dee said.

"What? No," Leah said emphatically. "*No.* Dee, you raised him well. You—"

"I fell apart when his daddy died." She nodded at Leah. "Don't you pretend otherwise. I fell apart, and Jack watched me. And now he doesn't do relationships."

"Dee," Leah said, managing to find a laugh. "Your son has had more relationships than I have shoes. And we all know how many pairs of shoes I have. Too many to count."

Jack had always been irresistible to the opposite sex. Maybe because he'd always been tall and built with that protective, chivalrous air. Or maybe it was that spark in his rich caramel eyes, the one that said *I'm trouble and worth every minute of it.*

In any case, Jack had had a way of getting himself into, and then smoothly out of, any so-called relationship with a girl without it ever getting ugly. He was what Leah jokingly labeled "a picker." There was always some reason that he couldn't take his relationships to the next level. Too clingy. Too ostentatious. Too crazy. She'd long ago decided not to obsess over what excuse he'd use to dump her, knowing there were too many to worry about.

Dee was shaking her head. "I'm talking about a *real* relationship, Leah. One that lasts long enough for him to bring her home to meet me. He avoids doing that." She paused. "Well, except for you, honey."

Leah's stomach tightened. She and Jack hadn't ever really gone there.

Except that once. That *almost* once.

"He'll find the right woman," she said quietly. "It only takes one."

"But when?"

"Maybe he's working on it."

"He's not." Dee's brow was creased in worry, and her voice wobbled. "He's not working on it at all. And he's going to end up alone, as I have. And who could blame him? Ever since his dad died, it's all I've shown him."

"Dee—"

"It is my fault, Leah. He won't get too attached. I taught him that. I have to undo it before it's too late."

Her words grabbed Leah by the throat and held on. She wanted to say something, *anything*, like "it's not too late" or "there's lots of time," but looking into Dee's eyes, she knew that might not be true. Leah had a lot of faults, big, fat faults like running tail when the going got tough, pretending everything was okay when it wasn't, and sometimes, late at night when no one was looking, she even ate store-bought cookies.

But she didn't lie.

"I want to make this right for him," Dee said quietly. Desperately. "I need to make this one thing right at least."

Jack was a black-and-white kind of guy and not all that complicated when it came right down to it. He hated closed spaces—an endless source of amusement to his co-workers. He hated snakes. He hated green toenail polish.

And yet Leah could bank on the fact that he'd date anything blond and stacked, even if that stacked blonde lived in a small closet filled with snakes and wore green toenail polish.

She also knew he was the most stubborn man on the planet. He'd argue the sky wasn't blue, and it took an Act of Congress for him to admit when he was wrong about anything. But above all else, he was extremely careful not to share his heart. Which meant that Dee *couldn't* make this right. And yet there she sat, looking so worried and so heartbreakingly ill.

From the other side of the window, still on the phone, stood Jack, his posture giving away nothing.

But Leah knew he was worried sick too.

Kevin, now sitting on Jack's big boot, was also looking worried. Worried that there wasn't any food in his near future.

But Jack...

Damn. "He's okay," she said, hoping like hell that was really true.

"But how do you *know*?" Dee asked.

"Because..." And that's when it happened, when Leah's brain disconnected from her mouth. "We're together."

Dee went still.

So did Leah, still with shock at her own words.

"Wait," Dee said slowly. "You and Jack...*really*?" she asked, as if she didn't trust her own hearing.

"Uh—"

"Oh my goodness, honey." Dee was looking like she'd just found out it was Christmas morning and Santa had come. "Oh my goodness!"

For someone who didn't lie, this was a hell of a way to jump into the pool. Not a lie, Leah corrected.

A fib.

A fib told in order to give Dee the one thing Leah had to offer—a little peace of mind. Jack wouldn't care. Probably.

Okay, he was going to care.

Unless...unless he never found out. Was that too much to hope for?

"You and Jack," Dee repeated, a slow, warm smile creasing her face. A *real* smile, one that seemed to light her up from within. "I've hoped," she said, "oh how I've hoped. But he's always got some silly woman in his sights, and you're never here, and plus you're both so damn stubborn—"

The bakery door opened, the bell dinged, and Dee whirled around to face her son. "Oh, Jack! Oh, sweetheart, I'm *so* happy."

This clearly surprised the hell out of Jack. He stood there taking in his mom's expression, obviously trying to figure out what had happened in the span of the five minutes he'd been outside that could have changed her mood so drastically.

And also her appearance, Leah realized. Because Dee was…glowing.

"You should have told me," Dee said, practically vibrating. "Did you think I wouldn't have been thrilled to hear that you and Leah are together?"

Jack's gaze locked on Leah, brow raised.

Okay, so maybe he was going to find out.

Chapter 3

♥

You and Leah are together... Jack's mom's words bounced around in his head like a Ping-Pong ball as he stared at Leah for an explanation.

She had a hell of an explanation if her blush was any indication. "It just sort of came up," she said, nibbling on her lower lip.

He recognized the tell. She nibbled on her lip whenever she stepped in the proverbial pile of shit. "It just sort of came up," he repeated, nodding like this made perfect sense to him. But then he shook his head because it made absolutely no sense at all. He knew he was off his game big-time, crazy with worry over his mom, but this was not computing. "What exactly *sort of* came up?"

"Why, you and Leah, silly," his mom said with a delighted laugh.

A laugh.

Jack hadn't seen her so much as crack a smile in weeks.

Maybe months.

And here she was, laughing. Had it been only a day
ago that she'd been lying on her couch in her Sunday best,
arm poised dramatically over her eyes, as she told him
that she was just going to die quietly and try not to make
a mess "so don't mind me."

"Me and Leah," he said slowly, aware that he was starting to sound like a parrot. "What?"

"Honestly, Jack." His mom was still smiling easily,
like she had in the old days. The *very* old days, before his
dad had died. "I'm the shaky one today," she said. "Turn
on your brain." She was beaming with joy.

And Jack got his first real sense of doom. It started
deep in his gut and ended up dead center between his eyes
as a tension headache.

Back in the spring, when they'd first gotten his mom's
diagnosis, his summer goal had been simple—get his
mom through it. The goal was now in sight, the light at
the end of the tunnel visible. It was August and she was
beating the cancer, though granted the treatment was now
the one endangering her.

But he should have known nothing was ever as simple
as it looked.

"It's so wonderful," his mom said, hands clasped together. "I was just telling Leah that I'd always secretly
hoped, but you two seemed so set on ignoring all the
chemistry between the two of you. Remember back when
Leah graduated high school, sweetheart? You were home
from college for the summer, just before she left town.
Remember how much she loved you back then?"

Leah made a sound of embarrassment and started to turn
away, but Dee smiled at her. "It's true, honey, you know it

is. You used to do his homework for him, remember? He was perfectly capable of doing it himself, except that he hated English and history. He needed to keep his GPA up for that scholarship and you…well, you remember."

Yes, it was clear by the look on Leah's face that she remembered exactly. Two grades behind him, she'd managed to save his ass *and* keep up with her own school load—and since her father had required straight A's of her, not to mention the hours of filing and other administrative work she'd had to put in every day at his dental practice as well—this had been quite the feat.

"And then when Jack Senior died," Dee said, "and he fell apart, you were there for him."

Jack opened his mouth but closed it again. What was he going to do, remind his mother in public that she had been the one to fall apart? That it'd been all he and his cousin Ben could do to keep the house and their lives together? The doctors had eventually been able to treat her depression, but her bouts of anxiety had never abated.

"No one else could console him," Dee said to Leah. "Not Ben. Not me. No one." She paused. "Only you, Leah."

Admittedly, Jack had grieved and grieved hard. He'd been a teenager who'd lost his father unexpectedly, and then he'd grown up in the shadow of his dad's legend.

But there were worse things.

And yet his mom was right about one thing. Leah had been there, no matter what she faced in her own home life. She'd found time to make them meals, do his homework, cover his ass however it had needed covering.

She'd done that for him. She'd been his rock.

"I really thought the two of you would go for it back then," Dee said, and Leah sucked in a breath.

Jack did his best not to react because he wasn't willing to admit that he'd thought the same. That he'd thought it up until the day Leah had walked away.

Always running.

"You're right, Dee," Leah said, her gaze on Jack. "The chemistry finally got us."

"Did it?" Jack asked her softly.

"Yes." There was a long, indefinable beat when something seemed to shimmer between them, and then suddenly Leah was a study of movement, hustling to put some space between them. "I was about to tell your mom that it's not a big deal," she said, very busy wiping down the other tables, way too busy to meet his gaze. "And that we'd like to keep things under wraps."

"Under wraps?" Dee asked.

"Yes," Leah said. "Because as you know, Lucky Harbor doesn't keep its secrets very well. We'd rather no one knew yet."

His mom looked so disappointed. "So this is…new?" she wanted to know. "This relationship between you?"

Leah did glance at Jack then, two spots of color on her cheeks as, unbelievably, she deferred the question to him. He crossed his arms and blessed her with his you've-got-to-be-kidding-me expression.

"Um," she said, blanching a little bit. "Sort of new, yeah. A little bit."

Dee processed this. "I bet it happened at the music festival on the pier, right? I saw you two dancing that night. So romantic, so sweet."

The festival had been a month ago. Jack remembered that he and Leah had shared one quick dance and then he'd been called into work. And if he'd enjoyed it a little too much, the way Leah's skirt had twirled around her thighs, how she'd felt against him, he'd told himself he'd gotten caught up in the moment.

"Yes," Leah said. "It happened at the music festival. We had late-night brownies at the café afterward, and that was that."

"But Jack was called to work that night on a suspicious fire," Dee said. "I remember because he called me from the station at midnight to make sure I got home okay."

"Late, *late*-night brownies," Leah corrected.

"Don't you make your own brownies?" Dee asked.

"Once in a while I cheat," Leah said, sounding a little strained.

No wonder. Lying was damn hard work.

Jack moved around the counter to face her. She was wearing jeans and a long halter top that had some flour on it.

He was six feet two, but they were still nearly nose to nose thanks to a pair of strappy, high-heeled sandals. How she worked in her seemingly endless supply of shoes he had no idea, but they were sexy as hell.

This was confusing too. When had she become sexy as hell? And why? They were friends. Nothing more. She'd made that evident a long time ago. "Why do you wear shoes like that to work?" he asked. "You're going to break an ankle."

"Aw," Dee said, delighted.

He looked at her. "What?"

"You noticed her shoes! Jack, do you know what that means?"

That he'd gone over the deep edge? He put a hand to his head. Was the world spinning? He felt a little dizzy.

"Listen," Leah said. "Forget my shoes. About the other thing. About…us." She swallowed. "Your mom was worried about you." Her eyes were desperately trying to communicate something to him.

Probably that she was crazy.

Which he already knew.

Jack turned to his mom. "Mom, we've talked about this. I don't want you wasting your energy worrying about me. You need to be focusing on yourself right now."

Oh, Christ. Suddenly this was all making sense, the chain of events that had led to Leah's proclamation that they were a "thing."

Not that it mattered, because this wasn't going to happen. They were not going to lie to his mom.

"It haunts me at night, Jack," Dee said.

Ah, damn. He loved his mom, more than anything. But if she gave the "I've had a good life and all I want is for you to meet a great girl so I can die happy" speech he was going to burst a blood vessel. "Mom—"

"It's all my fault, Jack. Don't you see? After your dad died—"

"No," he said firmly. "*Nothing* about that was your fault."

It really hadn't been anyone's fault, which of course had made it all the harder to accept. Jack knew he wouldn't have made it through that time without Ben or Leah—something he'd never told her but should have.

Which meant that he couldn't kill her for this latest stunt.

"I never showed you it was okay to move on from grief," Dee said. "That's why you never have any meaningful relationships with women."

Jack opened his mouth to say he didn't have the life-style for that right now anyway, just as the power blinked out and then back on. Then something sizzled, and this time, when the lights flickered and went out, they stayed out.

"Crap!" Leah said. "My soufflé." And she vanished into the kitchen.

"You okay?" Jack asked his mom.

"I'm great, actually."

She was still smiling. *Jesus*. "Wait here," he said and followed Leah into the kitchen.

She stood in front of one of the ovens, staring gloomily into the small window.

"Don't start with me," she said. "Do you have any idea how long it takes to make a great soufflé? And now it's all going to be ruined. Dammit! I knew better. The power's been going on and off for days. Mr. Lyons looked at it and replaced the fuses. They should've lasted longer than this."

Jack frowned. "This has been going on for days?"

"Weeks, actually. Maybe longer. At first, I thought maybe Grandma had forgotten to pay the bill, but I made sure it got paid on time this past month."

Jack strode out the kitchen door to the back alley, moving along the wall to the electrical panel. Just as he opened it, the flower shop's back door opened too, and out came a harried-looking Ali.

"Jack," she said in surprise, a pair of clippers in one hand, a rose in the other. "Did you turn off the power?"

"No." He looked inside the electrical panel and swore. The wiring was a mess, crisscrossed and frayed. The building was so old that they still had fuses behind the wiring, and he could see two right off the bat that were blown.

The entire downtown commercial row of Lucky Harbor was quaint and historical, but not necessarily practical, since most of the buildings were a hundred-plus years old. This building, one of the oldest, was in serious need of a big renovation, but the historical society—currently run by Max Fitzgerald—had a pretty restrictive rein on the county building department and the permits, all in the name of protecting history.

But what they were *really* doing was unintentionally preserving Jack's—and all the other firefighters'—jobs because this was a disaster waiting to happen.

Leah had followed him out. She stuck her hand into her pocket and came out with a palm full of fuses.

"Look at you with all the preparedness today," he said dryly.

She winced. "The fuses keep blowing," she said quickly, clearly choosing to ignore their situation, and they did have a situation. "I have to be prepared," she said, "or I ruin whatever I'm cooking."

Their gazes met. Aware of Ali standing within hearing range, Jack said none of what he wanted to say. Which was along the lines of: *What the fuck, Leah?* Instead he said, "We need to find out what's wrong with the wiring and why the fuses are blowing."

"Oh, we know why," Ali offered. "The place is falling apart."

"What about the new guy?" Jack asked. "The one who bought this place?"

"He's got the money," Leah said. "But the inspection didn't go well, and he's been making a stink about the hidden problems and condition of the place. He wants the price reduced. But Mr. Lyons says he sold the place as is and he doesn't give a rat's ass about the problems and that Mr. Rinaldi can cry him a river. So the sale might fall through."

"Why is Lyons selling in the first place?"

"He wants to retire and get a 'chickie.' And I'm pretty sure he doesn't mean a chicken," she said with a shudder.

Jack took the fuses from her and began to change them out. "We have something else to discuss," he said.

Leah glanced at Ali, then back to Jack. She bit her lip again. "Later."

Oh, there was going to be a later.

"There you kids are," Dee said, coming out with the plate of pastries that Leah had made for her. Jack ground his teeth and kept working on the fuses as Dee offered the plate to Ali, who happily partook.

"Oh my God," the florist said with a moan as she took her first bite of a pastry. "So good. Did you know that her grandma swears that Leah somehow makes these with restorative powers? You'll feel like a million bucks after you eat her stuff, Dee."

Dee smiled. "I already feel like a million bucks, but it's not the food. It's thanks to Jack finally getting his head on straight and being with Leah."

Ali stilled, and then, eyes wide, turned to Leah.

But Leah was now choking on a scone, and probably, Jack thought with grim satisfaction, a good amount of guilt as well. She pointed to her throat, indicating she couldn't talk.

Ali pivoted and looked at Jack.

Jack peered deeply into the electrical panel, wishing it would ignite. Where was a fire when he needed one?

"Big news, right?" Dee asked Ali happily.

"Leah dating my boyfriend's BFF? Yep," Ali said. "That's big news all right. The biggest."

"They didn't want anyone to know," Dee said, completely oblivious to the fact that Leah was behind her back making a knife-across-her-throat gesture at Ali.

"Silly kids," Dee said. "As if you can keep a secret in this town."

"Silly kids," Ali agreed, smiling widely at the still-motioning Leah. "They should know better."

"Yeah, well, I have to go," Leah said. "Stuff." She gestured vaguely to the bakery. "In the oven." And with one last glare at Ali, she vanished back inside the bakery.

Dee beamed at Jack and then followed after her.

Jack got the last fuse back in. The power came back on. He turned and nearly plowed into Ali, who was still grinning. "What?" he said.

"Nothing." But she laughed.

He gave her a steely-eyed stare, which didn't appear to intimidate her in the least. In fact, she laughed again, obviously delighted. "It's just that you spent most of last month watching me squirm as Luke and I fell in love," she reminded him.

"Yeah?" he said. "So?"

"So," she said, and poked him in the chest, "it's going to be fun watching you squirm for a change."

"It's not what you think."

"No, Jack," she said, heading back into her shop. "It's not what *you* think."

He stared at the door as she shut it gently in his face. "What the hell does that mean?" he asked.

But the door didn't answer him.

Chapter 4

When Jack returned to the bakery, Leah was in the kitchen, furiously whipping something in a bowl, her cell phone pinched between her ear and her shoulder.

"We have to talk," he said.

Leah gestured that she needed a minute.

Jack leaned against a counter and crossed his arms, prepared to wait her out.

She gave him a few side glances as she whipped the hell out of whatever was in the bowl. "Uh-huh," she said into her phone. "Uh-huh. Uh-huh."

Something in her voice clued him in, and he pushed away from the counter, heading toward her.

With a squeak, she stopped whipping. "Uh-huh," she said, faster now, and in a higher octave. She held up a finger, indicating she wanted him to wait a minute.

But oh hell no was he going to wait another damn second. Instead, he reached for her phone.

"Hey," she hissed. "I'm on a very important call—"

He pulled it from her fingers and looked at the screen.
It was black.

He narrowed his eyes at her.

She winced and then jumped when the phone rang for
real, flashing "Grandma Elsie."

"I have to answer that," Leah said.

He held it above his head.

"Jack."

"Not until you explain your little stunt in there." In
case she wasn't clear on which "little stunt," he jabbed a
finger to the front of the bakery, where through the small
window between the kitchen and front room, he could see
his mom once again at the table waiting for him. She was
talking to Riley, who'd just showed up for work.

Probably telling Riley all about him and Leah being a
thing. *Jesus.*

Leah used his momentary distraction to push him back
to the counter and tried to crawl up his body for her
still-ringing phone. With those heels, she was plastered to
him, chest to chest, hips to hips, thighs to thighs, all their
parts lining up neatly—and damn if he didn't forget about
her phone.

Which is how she snatched it from him with ease.
"Hi, Grandma," she said breathlessly, shooting Jack a
reproachful look before turning her back to him. "You
okay?"

"No," Jack said, checking out her ass.

Behind her back, Leah waved her hand at him. "Shh!"

Still recovering from their full-body contact, he had to
let out a long breath as he realized that once again he'd
been the only one to feel anything.

And why the hell was he feeling anything at all?

Frustrated, he strode out to the front room and found his mom happily consuming a raspberry tart. "What the hell does it mean if I notice a woman's shoes?" he asked her.

She smiled sweetly.

"What's that? What does that smile mean?" he asked.

She refused to answer.

Leah spent the rest of the day baking like mad, an ear cocked to the door for Jack. She was torn between the terrible hope that he got a call from work—not a serious call, mind you, maybe just a cat up in a tree—and getting the inevitable awkward conversation between them over with. The problem was that she couldn't envision the conversation. No doubt he'd start with a *what the hell, Leah*, and she'd say…what? What could she possibly say? *I'm sorry I let my stupid, pathetic crush out of the bag*? No. Hell no. Maybe she could say *well, I thought pretend was better than nothing*. No, that was even more revealing.

Okay, so the real problem was that she had no excuse. None.

Yes, she'd wanted to ease Dee's mind, but they both knew there were far better ways.

Thankfully, Riley worked the front of the shop for her, serving their customers and allowing Leah to avoid having to face anyone. But eventually Riley had to leave to make the day's deliveries.

The moment she did, of course, was the moment the bell chimed. Leah came out from the kitchen just as Ben McDaniel walked in.

Ben was Jack's cousin, and when he wasn't in a third-world country designing and building water systems for war-torn lands with the U.S. Army Corps of Engineers, he and Jack shared a duplex a few blocks down, near the fire station.

Leah smiled at him, and knowing he wasn't one for small talk, she turned to pour him a coffee, black, and bagged up a bear claw.

His standard fare.

He paid, and then instead of leaving as he usually did, he leaned against the counter and drank his coffee, watching her over the lid. Deceptively chill and laid-back, he gave off an almost surfer-guy vibe, but in truth he was about as badass as they came.

"What?" she finally asked.

"You tell me what."

She lifted a shoulder. Look at her being all cool and casual. One had to be with Ben; he could spot a weakness a mile away. "I can't tell you if I won *Sweet Wars*."

He shook his head. Not that.

"I'm not talking about this morning," she said. At least not until she talked to Jack. Which she hoped to do…never.

Ben dug into his bear claw, looking as if he had all the time in the world, and for all she knew, he did. He'd just come back from being on loan to the Department of Defense for the past eight months in Iraq. Before that, it had been Haiti and the earthquake aftermath, and before that, Japan's tsunami, and so on.

But before any of those adventures, once upon a time, he'd actually worked in Seattle at a normal nine-to-five job—until his wife had died.

He finished his bear claw, balled up the paper, and

made a three-pointer in the trash can across the bakery with no visible effort. "Thanks," he said, and was gone.

Leah blew out a breath. Another bullet dodged, she thought and went back to work.

Since she'd been handling daily baking, she'd also taken on some responsibilities that were new to the bakery, such as a little catering. She created wedding cakes and baked for showers and reunions or whatever event came her way. The equipment—hello, ovens, looking at you—was killing her slowly, but she was still managing to enjoy it immensely. Two days ago, she'd created a dozen cream puffs for the B&B. The job had been incredibly stressful because the B&B was owned by three sisters, one of whom was a chef—a really great one.

Leah had angsted over those twelve stupid cream puffs like they were for the royal palace, spending hours making sure every fraction of an inch of each one was perfect. She had no idea if she'd succeeded until a few hours ago.

Tara had called from the B&B and said the cream puffs were so amazing she needed three dozen more for a baby shower, and could Leah rush the order for this afternoon?

Leah was currently rushing toward a heart attack.

Bent over the tray, she was obsessing over each little puff with one eye on the clock when Aubrey strode in.

The beautiful, cool blonde struck a pose in the center of the bakery as if she were mugging for the paparazzi, one leg out in front of the other so the slit on her skirt opened and flashed a trim thigh. She waited expectantly.

Leah looked up from her task. "Well hi there, Angelina Jolie."

"Not the leg," Aubrey said, annoyed. She wriggled her

foot, drawing Leah's gaze to the gorgeous leather boots. "I finally have better shoes than you. I won't be eating all month, but they're totally worth it. I need you to be jealous."

Leah laughed but bent back over her cream puffs. "I don't have time to be jealous. I don't have time to talk."

"Why?" Aubrey asked, giving up her pose. "You always have time to talk."

Leah swiped her brow, spreading a dab of frosting over her temple. "I've only got thirty minutes before I have to have these delivered. And if I keep talking, I'll mess them up."

"What are you smoking? They're perfect," Aubrey said, and actually reached out to take one.

Leah smacked her hand away. "Oh my God, don't touch!"

"Well, jeez. I just wanted one," Aubrey said, rubbing her hand. "And I take back what I said. You're not nice at all."

Leah sighed. "You can't have a cream puff. They're for a fancy gig at the B&B."

Aubrey rolled her eyes. "You do realize you're not on TV, right? This is Lucky Harbor, not Paris. Drop some dough in a vat of grease and slap them on a tray, and people will be happy."

"That's not true," Leah said. "And it does matter. Each order matters. They have to be perfect, or why would I bother at all?" Leah went still, then set her pastry bag aside and staggered back a step. "Oh my God."

"What?"

She stared at Aubrey in horror. "I've turned into my father. Quick. Shoot me."

"I would," Aubrey said, "but I'm not all that keen on prison. Maybe I should just call the people with the white straight-jackets to come get you."

"This isn't funny," Leah said. "I need sympathy."

"I don't do sympathy. Call Ali for that." Aubrey strode closer to the displays. "But while I'm here, I'll take two cannoli. They have lots of calories, right?"

"Yes."

"Good. They're for my sister. I like it when she's fatter than I am. And they're free today since you snapped at the customer and that's not allowed."

Leah bagged the cannoli and shoved her out the door just to get rid of her.

By the end of the day, Leah was frazzled and on edge. She'd finished her orders, but Jack hadn't called. His silence felt weighted and suspicious. She opened her back door and peeked out. No one. She stepped out and nearly jumped out of her skin when Ali came out of her door at the same time. "You scared the crap out of me."

"Did I?" Ali asked. "Who did you think I was?"

A big, built, pissed-off firefighter. "No one. Gotta go. Night—"

"Hold it right there," Ali said. Clearly she wasn't done working for the day because she was holding a vase and a sprig of baby's breath. "Explain about earlier."

"Well, the fuses blew, so—"

"You and Jack," Ali said. "Explain you and Jack."

"Listen, it's been a long day, and—"

"Oh no. You're not going anywhere. Not until you answer my question." She pointed the sprig at Leah. "You and Jack. Yes or no."

Leah sighed. "Yes. Okay? Yes." *Dammit.* "Sort of."

"Sort of," Ali repeated. "You take up with the hottest guy in Lucky Harbor and you don't tell me?"

"I thought Luke was the hottest guy in Lucky Harbor."

"The hottest guy's best friend then," Ali corrected. "And don't change the subject, missy."

Leah sighed again. "It's just pretend, Ali. I made it up."

Ali gaped at her, then let out a low laugh. "You made it up? You just decided you suddenly had to have him—which, hello, any woman with an ounce of warm blood in her body would understand—and then you figured you'd just say it out loud and it would be so? How does that even work? Because I'd like to have a million dollars—"

"This isn't a joke, Ali. I'm in big trouble here."

"No shit," Ali said on another laugh. "Jack's pretty laid-back but he's not a guy you can push around. He's not going to like being played with."

"I'm not trying to play with him. I'm just trying to make his mom happy."

"Oh. *Oh*..." Ali breathed. "I get it." Then she shook her head. "Except I don't."

Leah sighed. "You've seen Dee. The chemo and radiation are making her sick, really sick. She was feeling down, and I just wanted to..." She shrugged helplessly. "I don't know, make her feel better. She's so worried about Jack. She feels bad about some of the choices she's made over the years, choices that she thinks led to Jack not being big on relationships. She was *down*," she said again, guilt swamping her.

"Dee's been feeling down for a very long time," Ali said gently. "You know that."

This Leah already knew. She'd been there in those

years right after Jack's dad's death. She'd seen Dee slowly fall apart, and she'd watched Jack and Ben—teenagers at the time—have to hold it all together for her; the house, the bills, the memories, everything. Leah had done whatever she could but had still felt so helpless. "Maybe me and Jack being a thing will help."

Ali shook her head. "Jack would be the first one to do whatever he needed to do to make his mom happy. But pretending to be in a relationship? That doesn't sound like him at all."

Leah grimaced. "Yeah, well, that's because it wasn't his idea."

The amusement came back into Ali's gaze. "You sprung it on him?" She let the smile come. "Would've loved to see that."

"This isn't funny, Ali."

"Yeah, it is. You got Jack to actually agree to this *pretend* relationship?"

"Not exactly."

Ali stared at her and then laughed. She laughed so hard she nearly dropped her vase. Finally, she straightened and swiped at a few tears of mirth. "Oh God, this is good. Jack in a *pretend* relationship."

"A *secret*, pretend relationship," Leah reminded her.

"A *secret*, pretend relationship," Ali repeated. "The single women in town are going to go into mourning." She was still grinning. "Luke's going to love this."

"You can't tell him!" Leah said. "Everyone has to think it's real."

"Aren't you cute." Ali patted her on the arm as if she were a three-year-old. "Leah, it *is* real."

Leah gaped at her. "What? No. No, no, no. It's…not."

Mostly because she'd already had her chance and blown it.

Big-time.

Which actually put Jack on her ever-growing list of regrets.

Twice.

Ali just smiled and turned, heading back inside her shop.

"It's not," Leah called after her. "It's all for Dee."

Ali lifted her hand, waved, and shut the door.

"It is!"

"Whatever helps you sleep at night," Ali yelled back through the wood.

"Well, dammit." Leah whirled in the other direction and headed to her car. "It *is* pretend," she told her rearview mirror. "Completely."

Chapter 5

♥

Leah picked up her grandma for physical therapy, already mentally calculating the rest of the hours left in the day. She had to work on bookkeeping—her grandma had been extremely lax about that—and then there was the stack of payables about two feet taller than their receivables. But Leah was working hard on all of it and trying to increase business while she was at it, and it was starting to work.

"You're so sweet to do all this for me," Elsie said. "But honey, I could have taken the Senior Dial-A-Ride."

"I don't mind," Leah said as they parked at PT. "And I didn't want you to get stuck waiting."

"I have my lover," Elsie said and waved her ebook reader. "I can wait forever with my Kindle fully charged and ready to please me."

"A lover who can never leave you," Leah said with a laugh, turning off the engine. "Smart."

Her grandma's smile faded some. "Is that what you think of men? That they'll leave you?"

Since that was far too serious a conversation for the moment—and absolutely one she didn't want to have—Leah shook her head and reached over to hug her grandma. "You smell like roses."

Elsie huffed out a low laugh. "That's code for 'mind your own business, Grandma.'" Pulling back, she gently patted Leah's cheeks. "I'm happy to have you back, Leah. So happy."

"I'm happy to be back."

Her grandma's blue eyes held Leah's for a long beat. "It's been good for you, right?" she said. "Being here? Being happy here?"

And there it was. The elephant in the room.

Yes, Leah's childhood had not been happy here in Lucky Harbor. But her parents had retired to Palm Springs, thirteen hundred miles south. And after her dad's death, her mom had stayed down there. The distance worked for them both, more than it should. "Yes," she said. "I'm happy here."

"Your mom says you called the other day," Elsie said.

Leah made an obligatory call every other week, during which she and her mom had a shallow conversation. Yes, she was fine. Yes, she was still baking. No, she hadn't found a man to marry her... "I did," she said to her grandma. "She sounds happy."

Elsie's smile was just a little sad and a whole lot knowing. "I'm proud of you, honey."

"Yeah, well, you might want to change your mind about that when you find out that I ordered not one but *two* new ovens today."

"Leah!"

"I'm paying for them," she said quickly. They'd filled up her entire shiny new credit card, but she'd wanted to do it. "Grandma, it had to be done. You can't continue with the business you have without new ovens; you just can't. We're putting out too much product now. We needed to do this."

Elsie sighed. "But I don't want you to pay for them."

Leah ignored this to help Elsie out of the car, but Elsie grabbed her hand and squeezed it gently, waiting until Leah met her gaze. "I'm so very proud of you," she said fiercely. "You've been a godsend. A perfect godsend."

"Perfect?" Leah laughed softly. "I have faults, Grandma. Lots of them."

"Of course you do. Your biggest fault is that you care too much. And you work too hard. But the good news is that I really am starting to feel so much better. I'll pick up the slack again soon."

Leah nodded. That was a good thing. A *great* thing. She'd come home to help, and she'd done that. But it was time to move on soon. She needed to be gone before *Sweet Wars* got to the finals in three weeks.

Long gone.

"You're really doing better?" she asked Elsie. She couldn't—wouldn't—leave until she was sure.

"Oh yes. And you have your own life to get back to," Elsie said, then added with a sly hopefulness, "I'm guessing you have your own bakery to open?"

Everyone knew grand prize for *Sweet Wars* was $100,000 to open a pastry shop. "You know I can't tell you—"

"Phooey," Elsie said. "I hate contracts and rules."

Leah smiled, knowing damn well she'd inherited that trait. "I want you to just concentrate on enjoying your break," she said. "Are you? Are you okay with the way I'm running your bakery?"

"*Our* bakery, honey. And are you kidding? You've doubled business. I'll sure miss you."

Leah thought about staying and what that would cost her. Elsie, catching her hesitation, patted her hand. "No worries. I know there's more out there for you than being back here in Lucky Harbor. You were on the cover of *Martha*, for God's sake."

The nurse came out and called Elsie just as Leah's phone started vibrating. She pulled it out of her purse and looked at the screen.

Jack.

Her wits deserted her, and with a wince, she dropped the phone back in her purse, where it vibrated for another minute before finally falling into an irritated silence.

Jack wouldn't let her ignore him for long. She was thinking about that, and how she might explain herself to him, when Mr. Lyons came through the front door leaning on his cane.

"Hey, cutie," he said, signing in for his appointment. "Saw you on—"

"*Sweet Wars*," she finished for him. "I know. I can't tell you what happens, sorry." Three more shows. She had three weeks to figure her shit out. "Contractual obligations and all—"

"No, I mean I saw you on Facebook. You're dating Jack Harper. Good man, that Jack."

Leah stared at him. "What?"

"Yeah. Now, as far *Sweet Wars* goes, you're killing the

competition. I've got a twenty on you taking it, but I'd go up as high as fifty if you'd give me a little clue…"

"Don't you even think about giving him a clue," Elsie said, coming out from the back. "He'll use it to win against the other, less fortunate seniors."

"Ah, now that hurts." Mr. Lyons slapped a hand to his heart and dramatically staggered back a step. "The prettiest babe in town doubts me."

"Poker night, last week," she said. "You coaxed everyone into making it strip poker. Then you counted cards and won the pot, which was three hundred bucks."

"Okay, true." He winked at her. "Which you know firsthand since you were there."

"Grandma?" Leah asked, shocked.

Elsie waved her off and continued to glare at Mr. Lyons.

He simply flashed blinding white dentures. "How about I use some of my ill-gotten gain to wine and dine you? The diner's having a two-for-one special. My treat."

"I have plans."

"With that chain-smoking, stuffy, old, stick-up-his-ass Maxwell Fitzgerald?" Mr. Lyons asked.

"Why…" Elsie glanced at Leah. "Of course not. Don't be ridiculous." She wrapped her arm around Leah. "Good day."

"Elsie?"

Elsie turned back to Mr. Lyons.

"You know I'm just having fun, right? At our age, it's all we've got. Well, that and pumpkin pie night at the senior center. My offer of dinner stands," he added more seriously. "Even after the special's over."

Elsie looked surprised as Leah led her out the door.

They went home, and Leah made dinner. When Elsie had gone to bed, Leah took a long shower until she ran out of hot water. Afterward, she had a text from her self-proclaimed boyfriend.

Squinting her eyes to read it—because that always made things easier to take—she opened the text.

You can run, but you can't hide.

Chapter 6

♥

Jack's earliest memory was being four years old and proudly wearing his dad's firefighter hat to the dinner table. It'd been far too heavy for him, and he'd barely been able to see because it kept falling over his eyes, but his dad had laughed.

And Jack had loved the sound.

There'd never been a question of what he would grow up to be. He'd become a firefighter, like his dad.

Period.

His schedule at station #24 was busy but he didn't mind the odd hours, or the job, really. No, it wasn't jumping out of helicopters into massive wildlife fires—which he'd loved—but the work meant something.

And yet there was no denying he was restless as hell.

It was true that city firefighting could be exciting, but Lucky Harbor wasn't exactly "city." And if there wasn't enough of that excitement to suit his adrenaline-junkie soul, he told himself that at the ripe old age of thirty-two, he'd learn to deal with it.

He was still waiting for his brain to do just that.

He and Kevin ran to work, and he had to admit his knee was slowing him down some. He really thought he'd just rehab it himself, but after months of working on it, he wasn't so sure. And yet he'd been the surgery route before and knew what that would mean—an enforced down period. Since that didn't work for him, his immediate plan was to ignore it until he couldn't.

In the meantime, he did his best to fill his time with things that interested him. He'd become the county's hazmat specialist and had gotten additional certificates in fire management and arson investigation. His off-shift hours were filled with whichever adrenaline rushes he could find. Paddle boarding with Luke. Mountain climbing with Ben. Women.

He'd had a good run there too, he could admit. In fact, he was right smack in the middle of a good run. Or had been—until Leah's little bombshell.

It'd gotten out overnight that they were "dating," and he'd already fielded an unhappy call from Kayla, a waitress he'd had plans to see later in the week, telling him not to bother to call her back.

There'd been nothing but radio silence from Danica, a local flight nurse he'd casually seen a few times. It wasn't anything serious, nor would it be, but he hoped that meant she was on shift and not reading Facebook.

Facebook, the evil incarnate. Or maybe that was Lucille herself. Lucille was older than dirt, shorter than a yardstick, and Gossip Central. She'd posted the "news" of his and Leah's relationship and then pictures of them together throughout the years. This included one of Leah's middle school graduation, where his mom had made him wear a suit. Another of them at the pier with Leah clutching a life-sized teddy bear he'd won, with him posturing like a complete idiot.

Jack had been fielding calls and texts all damn day long—except from the one person he wanted to hear from, of course.

Leah, who was still avoiding him like the plague. She'd always been good at lying low when she wanted, and clearly that was her modus operandi at the moment. Unfortunately for him, she was going to get away with it now that he was on rotation for three straight days.

He and Kevin entered the station at seven in the morning to the sound of applause, which startled Kevin into barking like a maniac.

Jack set his hand on the dog's head and gave his shift crew a long look. "Never mind the assholes, Kevin."

Kevin quieted and sat, glaring at the crew for startling him.

No one looked apologetic. There was senior firefighter Ian O'Mallery, and Sam and Emily—both five-year veterans—one of whom was always partnered with their rookie Tim, also present. And then there were two paramedics, Cindy and Hunter.

All still grinning at Jack.

"Lieutenant's gotta girlfriend," Cindy sang. She'd made breakfast and was dishing out egg sandwiches.

Jack snatched one and scowled. "Don't believe everything you see on Facebook."

"How about everything we see with our own eyes?" Tim asked. "'Cause I saw you two at the pancake breakfast."

"Yeah?" Ian said, curious as a sixteen-year-old girl. "What did you see? Anything good?"

Tim shook his head. "I saw that I've got more game than our LT. *And* I'm pretty sure I have a shot at his girl too. She smiled at me. She's got a really hot smile."

"Which reminds me," Jack said. "You're heading to the senior center in fifteen minutes for their fire extinguisher training."

Everyone laughed but Tim, who scowled. "Hey, I'm tired of being the dickhead who gets all the grunt work."

"Then don't be the dickhead," Emily suggested and handed him her empty plate.

"Oh hell no," he said. "I'm not doing dishes again. Hey!" Tim called after her as she walked away.

"New guy always does dishes," she called back.

Their day started with a woman who'd run her car into her own mailbox and gotten trapped, and ended with rescuing a stoned-off-his-ass guy from up a tree—not that they ever figured out what he was doing in the tree.

The next morning, they were woken by a two-alarm fire, and everyone hit the trucks.

At the scene, Tim fought to the front to jump down first, but Ian grabbed him by the back of his shirt. "Remember this time, you're still on probation. Stay back. Observe."

"Come on," Tim said. "You all take turns being point. Let me do it for once."

"No."

The convenience store attached to the gas station was on fire. The building, as old as the rest of town, ignited.

Ian and Emily—with Tim allowed to shadow and assist—rescued two smoke-dazed victims from the store before it was fully engulfed—the clerk and a customer. But when everyone looked around, only Ian and Tim had come out. No Emily. Then they all heard the alarm bell on her gear going off. Her breathing apparatus was running out of air. She'd gone to a window to try to get out, but her air pack was stuck on the window seal. Jack got to her, yanking her out from the outside.

"Close call," Emily said when the flames were out, giving Jack a big thank-you hug from her perch on the back on the ambulance, where she was being treated for a few second-degree burns on her knees.

Too close. He was still sweating.

During the pickup, Jack made his usual walk around the site and found a vagrant in the back of the building, huddled between a smoking shrub and a concrete pillar, suffering from a minor head injury. They treated him at the scene, and then he was transported to the hospital.

Deputy Chief and Fire Marshal Ronald McVane was about a decade past retiring, but still sharp. He was on site taking pictures and making a post-incident analysis.

"Got a few cigarette butts in the lot," Jack told him. "Not surprising given that it's a convenience store. There's other material there, and what looks like it might have been a bucket of rags. Point of origin was there. The contents of the Dumpster went up like timber, catching the siding on the building."

"The vagrant?"

"Maybe," Jack said. "But he says he didn't start a fire. But he also swore that he saw Santa Claus smoking crack on the roof before the fire ignited." Jack shook his head. "Something about this whole setup seems too neat and smart."

"And the vagrant isn't either of those things," Ronald said and sighed. "Hell."

"This fire was set on purpose," Jack said.

"Hell," Ronald said again.

Back at the station, everyone was on decon duty, decontaminating their masks and regulators and refilling the air tanks. Most of them also used the opportunity to wash their gear, though some guys like Tim liked to leave it dirty to show how tough they were.

Tim was prowling the living room. "That fucking dog!"

The dog in question was sitting on the couch like he owned it, the tatters of a leather wallet scattered around him. There was a good reason he hadn't made it as a station dog the first time around. He didn't listen, he was the Destroyer of All Things Expensive, and he was smarter than all of them put together.

Tim snatched up the biggest piece of leather and thrust it under his nose. "You ate the cash and left the leather? You're killing me."

"Aw," Cindy said. "Don't yell at him."

"Did he eat *your* money?" Tim demanded.

"I don't have any," Cindy said. "Chill, dude."

"If you keep yelling at him," Jack said, "he's going to shit in your shoes later."

"He already did that!" Tim glared at Kevin. "Bad dog!"

Kevin's ears lowered, and he blinked as slow as an owl, looking a little confused.

Jack patted him on the head. "He has some separation anxiety that we're working on. We left him behind."

"Because it was a day call and too hot to keep him in the truck."

"Yeah," Jack said. "But he doesn't understand that."

"Then he should have eaten *your* wallet." Tim blew out a breath, calming down. "He has an eating disorder. He eats everything."

"It's called being a Great Dane."

Tim threw his hands in the air and plopped on the couch. "Just do something about him."

Jack turned to Kevin, who straightened hopefully, like maybe there was another wallet in his near future.

"Hear that, Kev?" Jack asked him. "I need to do something about you."

Sensing he wasn't going to be getting a doggie biscuit anytime soon, Kevin sighed, strode to his bed—right next to the couch—where he turned around three times and plopped down with a heavy "oomph."

Tim pointed at his own eyes and then at the dog. "Watching you," he said.

Kevin closed his eyes, set his head on his paws, and farted.

Jack went into his office. Writing up his report on the convenience store fire, he came upon something interesting. The building was in escrow. This always changed things. It was shocking how often a property owner became an arsonist, and he made a note for Ronald and their investigation.

Before bed, he checked his phone. Not a word from his pretend girlfriend. He fell asleep wondering if that was a good or bad thing.

The next day, the entire platoon once again ran ragged from start to finish. The first call came early. A drunk twenty-year-old idiot had set a fire at his parents' home, lighting a cigarette on the kitchen stovetop and leaving the flame on before falling asleep. The house had been built in the 1930s and had a balloon-frame construction, in which there was a gap between the inside and outside wall. They tried using a thermal imaging camera to find the hot spots, but that proved ineffective, forcing them to use a hook to pull out whole chunks of heavy plaster walls to check for flames.

The guy's elderly parents were pulled safely from the structure, but "Baby Al" was out cold. Until they tried to move him, and then he started yelling and pitching a fit. Jack and Ian went in and dragged the screaming guy out. Still drunk, he fought them tooth and nail, making it a real struggle to save the jackass's life. Jack took a punch to his left eye that pissed him off and ached like a bitch.

From there, they had a few medicals, a few regulars—people who called for attention—and a report of smoke at a house on the south side of town. The smoke was centralized in a bedroom that could have been on that TV show *Hoarders*. When they shoveled the furniture and debris clear, they found a myriad of wires: phone, clock, computer, and so on, all crisscrossed and frayed.

And also a giant vibrator. Like eighteen inches giant.

The entire platoon managed to remain professional until they were on the engine, and then as a collective whole they completely lost it, laughing all the way back to the station.

When the next episode of *Sweet Wars* aired, Leah hadn't planned on watching, but her grandma insisted, which was how she ended up staring at herself as she created a three-tiered lemon meringue tart as if her life were a DVD. She tried to remain distant from it, but though she was good at the distance thing with others, she'd never really mastered it for herself. So she took in her relaxed, smiling self whipping a meringue under the pressure of cameras, the other contestants, and the exceedingly tough, hard-assed celebrity judges.

Go her.

"I don't like the panel. They yell too much. But that host, he's a cutie."

Rafe Vogel was also the producer of *Sweet Wars*, and while he was most definitely "a cutie" on the outside, he more resembled a snake on the inside.

"And look at you," Grandma marveled. "I can't get over you," she said, as on screen Leah moved quickly and efficiently in spite of Rafe walking around stirring up angst and tension as he barked out the clock's countdown. "You're the doll of the season."

"No."

Elsie scoffed and reached over, picking up the current issue of *TV Guide*. Spread across the front of it was the entire cast, with Leah front and center.

Leah pointed to the woman next to her. "Suzie's good too," she said.

"Not as good as you." Elsie set the *TV Guide* down on the coffee table and clapped her hands in glee. "You won it. I know you did. So when do you leave? The prize was one hundred grand and your own bakery, right? In the place of your choosing? You going to give me a hint?"

"You know I can't tell you who won," Leah said automatically, thinking how in the hell was she going to do this? How was she going to get out of Lucky Harbor before everyone saw the finals? How could she just leave the bakery, Elsie, Ali...Jack.

"I'm just so proud of you, honey. I'll admit, you had me scared for a few years there. Switching colleges and career paths like other women switch hair color. I know your daddy didn't help, making you doubt yourself all the time. He wasn't a good man, Leah. Watching you suffer…" She shook her head. "I should have done more for you."

"No, Grandma," Leah said gently, putting her hand over Elsie's. "You did everything you could. You were always there for me."

"Always will be." She turned her hand over in Leah's and squeezed her fingers. "You've made something of yourself."

If only that were true…

Chapter 7

♥

Jack followed up his seventy-two hours on shift with a day of sleep for recovery. Then he and Kevin hit the park for Jack's weekly baseball game.

Kevin was an old hat at baseball. He had a routine. Tied to the dugout bench in the shade, he usually dozed through the first few innings, and then by the bottom of the fifth he'd be nosing through the guys' bags for snacks. If he played his cards correctly and gave the right player the puppy dog eyes, he might find a good lap to cuddle in.

No one had ever told him that he wasn't a lap dog.

Today when Jack arrived, Luke and Ben were already on the bench lacing up their cleats. The three of them went way back. Luke had spent summers in Lucky Harbor at his grandmother's house. Ben had lived with Jack and his mom when his family had detonated early on. After Jack Senior's death, Dee had raised both boys—and also Luke—as if they were brothers.

And they were brothers, in all the ways that counted,

which meant that they were a perpetual pain in each other's ass.

Ben looked up as Jack and Kevin walked toward them. He took in Jack's obviously careful gait—his knee was hurting like a sonofabitch—but didn't say a word.

Luke was much more blunt. "You look like shit," he said and held out a fist to Kevin.

Kevin lifted a paw and bumped Luke's hand. It was his one and only trick.

"I'm not the one with the flu," Jack said. "Sam's out, which leaves us without a backup pitcher."

"And…," Luke said.

"And what?"

"And you have something else to tell us," Luke said.

Jack looked at Ben, then back to Luke. "What else would there be?"

"I don't know, maybe the fact that you and Leah are getting hitched."

Jack, who'd just taken an unfortunate sip from his water bottle, choked.

Ben patted him on the back. Actually, it was more like a pounding that sent Jack forward a few steps.

"So, when's the big day?" Luke asked.

Jack swore, swiping a forearm over his chin to mop up the water he'd just spit out. "Ali tell you?"

Luke grinned. "You mean it's true?"

"No, it's not true. Jesus."

"There's a whole Pinterest thing on you two," Ben said, sitting on the bench. Kevin immediately leaped into Ben's lap. For years, Ben had been closed off, not wanting to be close to anyone. He was gone for months at a time, and when he came back, he rarely talked about the things he'd seen and done. Jack and Luke had long ago given up revealing their worry to Ben; it just pissed him off.

And no one wanted Ben pissed off.

But they did worry. A lot.

But Ben, who rarely let anyone touch him, simply wrapped his arms around the huge dog and kept talking. "Lucille's been pinning ideas for your wedding and inviting others to do the same."

Jack stared at him. "What the hell is Pinterest?" he demanded.

"Hell, I've been on the other side of the planet in a country without running water and even I know what Pinterest is," Ben said. "What the hell's going on with you and Leah?"

Jack blew out a breath. "Leah told my mom we were a thing."

"Ah." Ben nodded like this made perfect sense. Which was good. It should make perfect sense to someone.

"I'm fucked," Jack said.

"Yes," Ben said. "If you're very, very lucky."

Jack gave him a level-eyed gaze.

Ben shrugged. "She's smart, funny, and wears really hot shoes that make her legs look a mile long. You should've done her a long time ago."

"It's *Leah*," Jack said. What the hell was wrong with everyone? Ben had been there growing up. He knew what Leah had gone through; he'd heard the yelling every night. He knew Leah had sought comfort—platonic comfort—from Jack all through his high school years. He knew that they were just friends.

Of course, what he didn't know, *couldn't* know, was

how on so many of those nights that Leah had sobbed all over Jack, he'd done his best to give her what her parents wouldn't. "Love you, Leah," he'd whisper.

She'd clutch at him tighter. "Forever?"

"Forever," he'd promised, always. But that had been a damn long time ago. Before she'd walked away and not looked back. "It's not a real thing," he said now.

"Only because you're stupid," Ben said.

Luke started laughing and couldn't stop, so Jack shoved him and then sat down to exchange his running shoes for cleats. Since Luke was still cackling like a hen, he tugged his hat down lower over his eyes and stalked off toward the field.

He was first baseman, and since no one else could be bothered, he was also team captain.

And their best player. Usually.

But not today.

As he discovered the hard way, a bad mood apparently made his game shit. First he missed an easy fly ball and then a line drive. And then, to make his humiliation complete, he struck out.

Lucky Harbor enjoyed its baseball as much as he did, and the stands were full. He could see Danica on the top row. They'd talked about having drinks at her place sometime this week. He wondered if it was possible they were still on.

She waved at him.

He started to wave back, but then he saw his mom two rows below Danica. Sitting with...

Leah and her grandma.

His mom was beaming.

Jack couldn't be sure from this distance, but he thought

maybe Leah was squirming. She had good reason to squirm, since he was going to kill her later.

To make sure she knew, he pointed at her.

She slunk down a little and pretended not to see him.

From the dugout, Kevin whined. He loved Jack's mom, and he loved Leah. Basically Kevin loved the ladies, period. But not a single woman had ever enjoyed Kevin's way of greeting, which was a nose to the crotch.

Which is why he was tied up in the dugout.

At the top of the third inning, Luke, their catcher, called a time-out and jogged out to Jack. Ben strolled over from the pitcher's mound.

"What?" Jack said.

"You tell us what," Ben said.

"I suck today. So what? You two were both pussies last week. Maybe it's just my turn."

"You're not usually a pussy," Ben said. "You're usually more like your dad."

Solid. Steady as a rock. Never faltering, never taking a misstep.

Well, except for the one that had killed him.

"Get the hell off my plate," Jack said.

"Touchy," Luke noted.

"Needs a Midol," Ben said.

They played the rest of the game with a minimum of errors, but it was too late.

They got their ass handed to them.

Afterward, they hit the Love Shack, the local bar and grill. They were halfway through a pitcher of beer and sliders when Lucille walked by and snapped a picture of Jack.

"Hey," he said.

Lucille might be meddlesome, but she also sometimes kept Jack's mom company when she was in treatment and he was working. "What are you up to?"

"Who, me?" She smiled and slid her dentures around some. "Nothing at all. I just needed a picture for—"

"If you say Facebook…," he warned.

She smiled a little broader. "Ah, don't get all alpha on me. I just wanted to put up a pic of you and Leah side by side. Unfortunately, Leah's not nearly as accommodating as you." She thumbed through her photo album on her phone and then showed him a picture.

Leah, flipping off the camera.

In spite of himself, Jack laughed. But he wasn't laughing a half an hour later when he went to the bar for another pitcher for his table.

Danica was there, and he gestured for another drink for her, but she shook her head, her pretty blond hair flying.

"Hell no, I'm not having a drink with you," she snapped with surprising venom.

Huh. Not nearly as friendly as she'd been in the stands earlier at the game. Which meant… "You heard," he said flatly.

Her eyes were daggers. "That you're nearly engaged? Yeah, I heard, and B-T-dub? You're an asshole for humiliating me like this. Consider date number three off the table." She stood up. "Your loss, by the way, because I give *great* date number three." She started to walk away, but he caught her, a little surprised by her venom since things had been so casual between them. Still, he wanted to explain so there were no hurt feelings.

"It's not what you think, Danica," he started. "I—"

She tossed her drink in his face.

It was a fruity white wine.

Jack hated fruity white wine. He was still wiping it from his eyes when Danica snatched her purse and sashayed her very fine body right out of the bar.

Jack turned to the table where Luke and Ben were watching with great amusement. Ben offered him a silent toast with his beer.

Luke just grinned. "Man," he said to Jack, "she just went all cage-fighter on your ass."

At that, Ben actually let out a rare laugh.

And happy as Jack was to hear it, he could only shake his head.

That night, unable to sleep, Leah was in her grandma's kitchen working on her cream puff recipe, determined to figure out a way to produce them faster. She had the ingredients spread out before her when her grandma appeared in the doorway looking pleasantly round and comfortable in a big, fluffy robe that nearly swallowed her up.

"Oh," Elsie said, sounding surprised to find Leah up. "My goodness, honey. You're not still obsessing over making perfect cream puffs?"

"Just a little. I need to figure out how to make a larger batch and have them look as good as those from a smaller one. I can't seem to do it."

"But you're not on TV now. It's what's on the *inside*, not the outside, that matters."

"Are we still talking about cream puffs?"

Elsie smiled. "It's a lovely night. Why aren't you out?"

Leah laughed. "It's Lucky Harbor. Where would I go?"

"I don't know…the arcade, the Ferris wheel. Have a bonfire on the beach. Live a little!"

"I'm not sixteen, so the arcade is out," Leah said wryly. "And bonfires are illegal. It's high fire season right now."

"It's a sad state of affairs when a woman your age can't find fun."

"Baking *is* fun."

"Hmm."

From the depths of Elsie's purse on the table came the sound of her cell phone ringing. "I'll get it," Elsie said, and dove on it like a woman four decades younger, snatching the phone before Leah could get a look at the caller ID screen.

"*Hola*," Elsie sang sweetly, and then let out a big smile. "Why yes," she said, sounding very happy. "Yes, it's me." She glanced at Leah and lowered her voice. "Call me back in five? Great." She hung up with a sort of dreamy smile and then looked at Leah again. "You really should turn in, honey. It's late."

"I'm not tired yet."

"Oh, okay. Well, then *I'm* going to turn in."

"Who was that?" Leah asked.

"Hmm?"

"On the phone. Who was that?"

Elsie shook her head and pointed to her hearing aid. "Damn thing needs to be looked at, it's not working right." She turned away. "Night."

When she was gone, Leah just stared at the empty doorway for a long beat. Her grandma was keeping secrets.

But then again, so was Leah. She understood the need for privacy, more than most. And until she'd left Lucky Harbor, she'd never had any privacy at all, unless she'd been here, with Elsie. Difficult as it was, Leah would give her grandma the same consideration.

The night was quiet, and she moved about the house, cleaning up from dinner, straightening out some of her grandma's bills, switching money around to rob Peter and pay Paul, and checking email.

She had one from Rafe, offering her a "job opportunity that you can't possibly turn down for when you're done playing house in Mayberry." He went on to outline what they wanted from her, which was to have her host her own reality show, following a group of fledgling pastry chefs in their final semester of school.

Anxiety knotted in Leah's chest. Hadn't she needed exactly this, a reason to leave town soon, for when her grandma was all better?

She hit REPLY and typed up her requirements. She wanted producing credit, and she wanted out of Lucky Harbor *before* the finale of *Sweet Wars* aired.

She stared at the email for a long time before hitting SEND. Soon as she did, her phone beeped an incoming text from Aubrey.

Holy smokes, Batgirl. Tonight's bar incident is spreading faster than Lucille can work her phone. You do realize that you so owe Jack now, right? Like big owe. I expect details.

Leah blinked at her phone and then texted back. *WTH happened to Jack at the bar?* She stared at her phone, impatient for a reply that didn't come. Giving up on waiting, she searched for Aubrey's contact info and hit CALL. "What happened to Jack?" she asked when Aubrey answered.

Aubrey chuckled and then there came a low, male

voice in the background, murmuring something she couldn't quite catch.

"Who's that?" Leah asked.

"I'm just leaving the bar and apparently I need an escort," she said with careful disdain, sounding tipsy. "Even though it's just Lucky Harbor."

The low murmur came again, and Aubrey laughed, a little coldly. "I'm fine," she said, presumably to her escort. "Look, I have a stun gun, and I know how to use it. Fair warning, buddy."

"Aubrey, who is that with you?" Leah asked. "And you're not driving, right?"

"Nope. I'm going to call for a ride—"

"*I'm* driving you," the mystery male voice said, speaking low but perfectly clear, and Leah recognized it with relief.

Ben.

She relaxed, knowing Ben would take care of Aubrey whether she liked it or not. "What happened?"

"I had a real shit day," Aubrey said. "Do you have any idea the hoops you have to jump through to start up a business? The paperwork, the permits, the fees…I needed a drink bad. Okay, two. I needed *two* drinks, and I might have forgotten to eat dinner. And now Mr. Tall, Dark, and Mercenary here says I'm going to let him make sure I get home okay or else." She lowered her voice. "And I gotta be honest, that 'or else' is sort of making me curious—"

"I mean Jack," Leah said. "What happened to Jack?"

"Oh. Right. Well— Hey! You keep your hands to yourself, Mr. Mercenary, jeez!"

"You nearly broke your ankle," Leah heard Ben grate out. "Stop walking and talking at the same time."

"Fine," Aubrey said, and then came back to Leah. "Danica tossed her drink in Jack's face."

Leah gasped. "What? *Why?*"

"Apparently they were supposed to have date number three tonight, and according to Danica—who yelled this at Jack, by the way—everyone knows what happens on date number three. She said she wouldn't go on a date number three with a guy who was nearly, almost, maybe engaged. And that's when she threw the drink in his face."

"Oh my God. *No.*"

"Oh yes," Aubrey said, sounding greatly amused. There was also a male snort, as if Ben too found this very funny.

Leah did not. "Who told Danica that we were...nearly, almost engaged?"

"I don't know." There was a sort of murmured conversation, during which Leah assumed Aubrey was conferring with Ben. Then Aubrey was back. "Mr. Mercenary says maybe you should check the mirror."

"I didn't do it!" Leah said. "I didn't tell anyone." Except Dee, which she *still* felt like shit about. And Ali. And her grandma... Oh good God. "Okay, so maybe it was me, but I never said *engaged*! I said we were *dating*."

"Yes, but this is Lucky Harbor," Aubrey pointed out. "It's like playing telephone. I once thought I was dating the town clerk, and it turned out he didn't consider it 'dating' at all."

"That was not your fault," Leah said.

"But this might be your fault," Aubrey said.

Yeah. "This is bad. Very, very bad."

"No kidding, because now you've gotten Jack cut off of sex from every female within gossip distance," Aubrey said.

Leah thunked her forehead to the wall.

"Leah?" Grandma Elsie's voice came from the bedroom down the hall. "Is someone at the door, dear?"

"No, it's just me. Sorry to disturb you." She took a deep breath. "This isn't happening," she whispered. "Was he mad?"

"I think he was more shocked. I'm pretty sure he doesn't get rejected a lot."

"No," Leah agreed. Jack was usually the one doing the rejecting.

"So now you owe him."

Leah quivered at the thought but brushed that aside. "I'm not going to sleep with Jack. I was just trying to do him a damn favor."

"Oh, I doubt there will be sleeping involved," Aubrey said. "Danica was quite clear. She said she gives great date three. My guess is that it's at least oral. Maybe even the biggee."

"The biggee?"

"*Butt stuff*," Aubrey said in a dramatic stage whisper.

"Okay, that's it. Give Ben the phone."

There was a brief pause, then Ben came on. He didn't say a word, but she could sense his amusement.

"You'd better take good care of her," she warned him.

"Don't you think you should worry about your own problems?"

"I'm not kidding. You're driving her home, right? Just shove her inside her place, okay? Don't let her talk you inside. She's on a man embargo, but it's been a few months, and she's drunk..." Not to mention Leah had no idea how long it had been for Ben, and he was still trying to adjust to civilian life. He and Aubrey alone together was a disaster of massive proportions just waiting to happen. "She might temporarily forget about the man embargo and try to seduce you," Leah told him, "and then she'll hate you in the morning."

"So is it her virtue or mine you're worried about?" he asked.

"You're not taking me seriously."

"On the contrary, I'm taking you very seriously. But I'm a big boy, Leah."

She replayed back in her mind what she'd just said to him and realized that in man-speak, she'd just pretty much told him to go sleep with Aubrey. "Okay, you know what? Forget everything I just said."

He laughed softly. "You're cute when you backpedal. Haven't seen you do that in a while."

"Dammit! I'm coming down there right now. Wait for me. I'll take her home myself."

"I've got this, Leah."

"Ben—"

"Worry about yourself," he said and disconnected.

She agonized for a minute and then decided she couldn't live with herself if she didn't at least check on Aubrey, even if it meant seeing Jack. She drove to the bar, but though the place was still kicking, there was no sign of Aubrey or Ben.

But Aubrey's car was still in the lot.

Leah pulled out her phone and texted her.

You'd better be snoring and not having inappropriate rebound sex with Ben, who'd better not be having inappropriate stateside-again sex with you.

There was no response. *Crap.* But since she didn't have the moral high ground here, she tilted her head back and stared up at the moon. It was a gorgeous night. Warm. Quiet.

She didn't want to go back to her grandma's. She wasn't sure what to say to Jack, so going to him was out too. Plus there was that little matter in the back of her mind.

You owe him…

Rifling around in the back of her car, she came up with a bathing suit. Then, hiding beneath a towel, she changed.

A long, moonlight swim had always cleared her thoughts; hopefully tonight would be no different.

She bypassed the pier. It was illegal to jump off. Not that she had any problem with breaking a rule now and again, but it was low tide. She was restless, not suicidal.

She walked to the water, which was calm. A half moon cast a lovely, peaceful blue glow as she tried to swim off her regrets. Telling Dee that she and Jack were together. That it had gotten out to everyone in town. What had happened at the bar with Danica.

Leah had known Jack had been dating a couple of other women, and that hadn't stopped her. In fact, she hadn't even thought of them when she'd spouted off to Dee.

What did that say about her?

And now, thanks to Aubrey, she was also worried about owing him. At the thought of all that might entail, she got a full-body shiver. Deciding to attribute that to a chill, she kept swimming.

You're just a screwup, Leah. You'll never amount to shit.

She told her inner voice to shut up but couldn't help but wonder if, for the first time, Jack would turn his picker skills on her. Would he find a way to dump her as a friend, citing her inability to finish anything? No, that was nothing new. Her lack of morals, given the lie she'd told his mom? No, Jack lied too. His entire career was based on the lie that he'd wanted to be a firefighter like his dad, when she knew damn well he'd only done it out of obligation. Sure, he'd loved being a Hotshot, but she sensed his restlessness. He wasn't loving his job.

Damn. They were both so screwed up. She slowed a moment and glanced back to the shore, catching sight of a big, built, attitude-ridden shadow that changed the rhythm of her heart rate even more than swimming. She blew out a breath and kicked it into gear, going hard and fast so she'd be too winded to talk, much less think.

Maybe he'd get tired of waiting.

But Jack had the patience of Job, so it was far more likely she'd drown.

Unfortunately, he'd save her before that happened. He was good at saving her. Dammit. Trembling with exhaustion, she turned back, knowing she couldn't outwait him. She'd never been able to.

Chapter 8

♥

It wasn't all that difficult to find Leah, once Jack set his mind to it. Since the beginning of time, when she'd been troubled, she'd been drawn to two things.

Him.

And the ocean.

She hadn't come to him. That was new. There'd been a time when she'd have come to him no matter what was troubling her.

Except, of course, at the moment *he* was the source of her trouble, even though it was of her own making. The last time that had been the case, she'd left Lucky Harbor.

But he knew she couldn't leave now. She was here for her grandma, and though Leah had plenty of faults, her grandma meant too much to her. Unlike himself... He tried not to resent that, but there was no getting around the fact—he did resent it. He was pissed off that she had no idea what she'd meant to him back then.

Or now.

"Woof?"

The soft, snuffling question came from a sleepy Kevin in the shotgun position at his side. Reaching over, Jack ruffled Kevin's fur reassuringly, getting licked from chin to forehead for his efforts. Kevin wandered a little bit away and started sniffing. Knowing the signs, Jack grabbed a baggie from his truck and waited.

Kevin continued to sniff around each and every rock within a twenty-foot radius, and then repeated his efforts. Twice. Finally, he sat and yawned.

"Just do it already," Jack said, waving the bag. "Before the pretty girl comes out of the water."

Kevin tipped up his head and stargazed.

"Fine." Jack shoved the bag in his pocket, his eyes following the form swimming out past the waves. She'd always been a hell of a swimmer. He could see flashes of pale skin as she moved quickly and efficiently at a full-out pace.

Clearly, she was trying to outswim her demons.

His heart squeezed a little, making room for a few other emotions besides his temper. Empathy. Maybe even reluctant affection. He could've gotten into the water with her, but it was after midnight and Christ, he was tired.

Nothing good ever happens after midnight.

His mom had always said so, and in this case, he was willing to bet it was true. So he sat on the sand, positioned halfway between her car and the water, giving her no easy escape. And waited.

And brooded.

When Leah had first moved to Lucky Harbor, right next door to his childhood home, his life had been long summer days of riding bikes and body surfing, and longer summer nights lying in his bed listening to her father yell at her through the open windows.

You never finish a damn thing, Leah. Not one damn thing. And you never will... You're going to amount to nothing.

Jack had been missing his own father at the time, and his gut would coil into a knot as she'd been spoken to so cruelly and thoughtlessly. "What the hell is wrong with you?" her dad would yell at her. "Didn't you hear me? Are you deaf? Are you stupid? Maybe that's it, you're stupid. Is that it, Leah Marie? You're fucking stupid?"

Jack could still remember being flat on his back staring up at the ceiling, his hands fisted into tight balls, thinking that the wrong dad had died. It'd been the unforgiving, thoughtless wish of a grieving kid, but he'd never forgotten the fury coursing through him at what Leah endured.

Or how sick he felt for her every time she'd crawl out of her window and into his. She'd stand there bathed by the moon's glow, eyes filled with hurt, and he'd want to slay her dragons. He'd scoot over and make room for her, and she'd curl up on his bed, letting him hug her while she cried. And sometimes, much later, in the deep dark of the night after she'd finally fallen asleep, he'd cry too.

He shook all that off now. He didn't want to think of Leah as the skinny, mistreated, spitfire waif she'd once been. Nor did he want to think of her as his girlfriend, pretend or otherwise. He didn't want to think of her at all. He wanted to be in bed with Danica, losing himself in the softness of her lush body.

Instead he was here. Danicaless. And in spite of a very long shower, he still smelled like wine.

The wind kicked up, and the temperature dropped. Not long now, he thought. Leah was tough as hell when it came right down to it, but she'd never liked to be cold.

At his side, Kevin stirred, sniffing the air, glancing restlessly at Jack.

"Yeah, she'll come out soon," Jack assured him. And then they'd deal with this mess she'd made. He wasn't sure what he wanted more. To wrap his fingers around Leah's pretty neck, or...

And actually, it was the "or" troubling him now. Because he was having lots of odd and unexpected urges as it pertained to Leah, and he didn't know what to do about them. Once upon a time, she'd been the only highlight in his day, the only one to make him smile. She was still that person, but there was something new between them, and he wasn't sure if it was good. In fact, he was pretty sure he should be running like hell.

Finally she swam in, and then she was standing up in the water, and he nearly swallowed his tongue. It'd been a damn long time since he'd seen her in a bathing suit. Maybe since high school, when she'd been a head taller than all the other girls and skinny as hell.

She was still tall but she'd filled out in all the right places and then some. She wore a black bikini, nothing but a few straps low on her hips and two triangles over her breasts, and as a wave knocked her around a little, everything jiggled enticingly.

And suddenly he went from slightly chilled to very overheated. Good Christ, she was...beautiful. It should've assuaged his simmering temper just looking at her, but instead it stoked it, making him tense as hell.

Leah, on the other hand, was looking pretty carefree as she lifted her arms and shoved back her hair.

At the sight, his brain utterly clicked off.

She saw him then. He could tell because, from one blink of an eye to the next, she froze every single muscle. It'd have been fascinating to watch, except for the fact that she was freezing up over *him*. She'd never reacted this way before. He didn't like it. And besides, *he* was the wronged party here. *He* was the one who got to be pissy.

"You're still here," she said flatly.

Kevin, who clearly hadn't received the temper memo, bounded over to her, his paws going straight to her shoulders as he gave her the universal Kevin greeting—a lick from chin to forehead.

"You big oaf," she said, and then hugged him before pushing him off her.

Kevin sat happily at her feet, panting, looking up at her adoringly.

"Nice," she said. "But I don't have any doggie treats on me."

With a sigh, Kevin flopped all the way down.

Leah met Jack's gaze. "You scared me."

"You need to be more aware of your surroundings."

Dripping water everywhere, she crossed her arms over herself. "It's Lucky Harbor."

He rose to his feet. "Bad shit can happen anywhere."

She met his gaze for one brief beat and then looked away. "What are you doing here, Jack?"

"I figured as your 'almost fiancé,' I should see how you're doing."

She winced but didn't respond.

"What the hell is this all about, Leah?"

"You *know* what it's about," she said, hugging herself a little tighter.

She always got defensive when she screwed up, and since she'd screwed up a lot, she had a lot of practice.

"My mom has enough going on," he said. "She doesn't need to be lied to."

"Maybe not. But she does need to be happy to heal. And this made her happy. All week she's been glowing."

He knew it was true, and a stab of guilt hit him that he hadn't been able to make her happy without help.

Leah didn't say anything more, but she didn't have to. Yeah, she'd gotten them into this mess, but he knew damn well it'd been out of the goodness of her heart. Jack knew that she thought she owed him for all those years ago, when he'd done his best to protect her, the chivalry having been deeply ingrained by his dad.

But they were even.

In the dark, Leah shivered, and that chivalry made him feel torn between enjoying the sight of her cold and wanting to wrap her up in his arms. "Where's your towel?"

"In the car."

He pulled off his sweatshirt and tugged it over her head.

"I'll get it wet," she said.

"It'll dry."

"I'm—"

"Just wear the damn sweatshirt, Leah."

There was an awkward silence while they stared at each other as behind her the water pounded the shore.

"I realize that this is really hard for you," she finally said, pulling on his sweatshirt. "Having everyone think you like me *that* way. You'll just have to pretend."

He narrowed his eyes. Had that been sarcasm? Or...
Hurt?

"There was a time when I wouldn't have had to pretend anything," he said. "But you flaked out, remember?
You pretended, and then you left."

She grimaced, swallowed hard, and looked away. "We
were just kids."

Was that how it played in her head? Seriously? "Does
it make you feel better?" he asked quietly. "To downplay
what we were to each other?"

She closed her eyes. "We were friends, Jack. Friends
who'd made a quick, knee-jerk, stupid decision to become naked friends and sleep together."

"Yeah. And then one of the friends didn't show," he
said, much more mildly than he felt.

"It was a bad idea. I was leaving."

"Which you forgot to mention."

She dropped her head back and stared up at the sky. "I
couldn't stay, Jack."

He took in her expression, filled with memories, and
nodded. "I know. But you should have told me you were
going."

"You had another girl in your bed by the following
weekend."

Had he? Hell, probably. But she wouldn't have meant
anything to him. Not like Leah had. His chest tightened
at the memory of the hole she'd left in his life. He didn't
want to go through that again. "I missed you."

She said nothing, and he shook his head. Fuck it. He
started to walk away, and then she spoke.

"Brandi Metcalf."

He stopped. "What?"

"Brandi Metcalf was the one in your bed by the next weekend." She turned her head and glared at him. "Pretty, blond Brandi with the perfect boobs." She emphasized this by cupping her hands out in front of her own breasts. "So don't even try to tell me you missed me."

He shook his head. Apparently he wasn't the only pissed-off one tonight. "How about the women I'm dating now?" he asked. "What am I supposed to tell them?"

She hunched her shoulders a little bit, clearly getting irritated on top of defensive. "You're the one who taught me how to dump someone, back in high school. You said"—she affected a lower voice, presumably imitating him—"just look him in the eyes, Leah, with your own gaze all carefully dialed in to sad and regretful. And then you say, 'I'm sorry, I just really need to work on myself right now.'" She went back to her own voice and gave him an eye roll. "You said that no one could argue with that."

Had he said that? Jesus. "I was an asshole, Leah."

She gave him a look that said he was *still* an asshole. So he proved it. "And who says I'm dumping anyone?"

She faltered for the first time, taking a minute to choose her words. "I guess I thought that for the sake of your mom, you'd do yourself in the shower like all the rest of us sex-deprived people." At that, she started to stride past him, but he caught her arm.

"Okay," he said. "Let's have it."

"Let's have what?"

"Well, I know why I'm pissed. Why the hell are you pissed?"

"It's not like it's going to be a walk in the park for me either," she said, giving him a little shot to the chest. "Pretending to like you."

"Me?" he asked, flabbergasted. "What the hell is there not to like about me?"

The sound she made assured him that she had volumes on the subject. "Don't get me started."

"I want to know," he said.

"Fine. You watch that stupid ice fishing show like it's a religion, you're a horrible backseat driver, you drink out of the milk carton—and FYI, so does Ben—you don't put the cap on your toothpaste, or put the lid down on the toilet, and you shush me when you're watching sports."

He stared at her. "That's quite a list of shortcomings," he eventually said. "Is that all?"

"No." She shoved her wet hair from her face, though she managed to keep her regal stance, nose firmly in the air at nose-bleed height. "I held back because I didn't want to be overly rude."

He laughed softly. "Don't hold back, Leah. Let's hear all of it."

"Well, your truck has more sporting goods than a store, you never say you're sorry, and your girlfriends look like supermodels. I mean, what is that? There's nothing wrong with real boobs, you know!"

He took it all in and had to admit that he couldn't say she was wrong, about any of it. "And yet you call *me* The Picker."

She ignored this. "*And* your mom told me that you need knee surgery again. You're just too stubborn to get it done. So you can add ornery to the list."

He blew out a slow breath. "It's not ice fishing," he said. "It's crabbing. And sometimes I *lose* the cap on the toothpaste, or Kevin eats it. And I don't need knee surgery; I'm fine."

Leah snorted. "You're always fine. Your knee could be falling off and you'd say you were *fine*."

"I fail to see the problem."

She snorted again, and he was starting to feel greatly insulted. "You're not exactly a walk in the park, Leah."

"No?"

"No. You're flighty, you live for your every whim, you downplay any real emotion you feel."

She hugged herself tight. "Good thing this is all pretend then, isn't it," she said softly.

"Yeah."

She was freezing. And hauntingly gorgeous, so damn gorgeous standing there wet and silvery by the moon's glow, like a goddess. It's *Leah*, he had to keep reminding himself. Leah, who'd once beaten him in a marshmallow-eating contest, only to puke all over him. Leah, whose dark-green eyes had a way of telling the world to bite her. Leah, who'd run off on him and left him heartbroken. He took a step into her—for what exactly, he had no idea—and she poked a finger into his chest.

"God," she said. "You're so..." Words apparently failed her, but she let out a sound that managed to perfectly convey how annoying he was.

"Ditto," he said, and then grabbed the finger drilling a hole between his pecs and tugged her hard enough that she lost her balance and fell against him.

He wrapped an arm around her waist, entangling a hand in her wet hair.

She went still as stone and stared into his eyes. And then lowered her gaze to his mouth.

Yeah, they were in sync there. Suddenly he couldn't breathe. Hers caught audibly in her throat, a good sign, he decided. Maybe she wouldn't knee him in the balls. Testing the waters, he grazed her jawline with his teeth.

She shivered.

Then he slid his mouth to the very corner of hers and was rewarded by the clutch of her hands on his shirt. Having her hold on to him like this, like he was her only anchor, sent a bolt of lust straight through him. "Leah," he murmured, hearing the surprise in his own voice, feeling the heat course through him as he finally—God, finally—covered her mouth with his.

Her lips parted for him eagerly, and he groaned, drowning in the erotic collision of her hot tongue and chilled, wet body.

Serious trouble. He was in serious trouble.

Because he had a taste of her now, a damn good taste, and it was better than he could have imagined, making him want the rest of her. With his fingers still in her hair, he pulled her in tighter, slanting his mouth across hers for more. She moved with him, into him, making the connection all the sweeter.

No. Sweet wasn't the right word.

Hot. She was so hot she was turning him inside out. And then she made another of those soft, surrendering sighs deep in her throat, the sound slaying him. She still had a death grip on his shirt and had managed to catch a few chest hairs while she was at it. He didn't care. Sliding a hand beneath his sweatshirt, he cupped her ass over her wet bikini bottoms, rocking into her.

She had to feel what this was doing to him. And given that she was breathing like she was running out of air, and still holding onto him tightly enough to bruise, she also had to know where this was going.

Kevin "woofed" softly, an I'm-tired-of-being-ignored woof. Jack waved at him to shut it and then kissed Leah some more, sinking deeper into her taste, her softness, her scent, all while wondering how the hell she could drive him crazy and make him ache at the same time. It was a feat that totally wrecked his equilibrium. Maybe it was just the kiss. Because holy shit, the kiss. He still had a handful of her sweet ass and he squeezed, wanting more. But they were outside and the night's temp was quickly dropping. She was wet, trembling with the chill, and there was absolutely nowhere to go with this. Not here, not now. He'd had no business kissing her like he had an endgame, and knowing it, he regretfully pulled back.

She blinked as if waking up from a dream. "What—" She cleared her throat. "What was that?"

"Insanity. It's going around."

She rolled her eyes but staggered a step as if her equilibrium was off too, giving him some grim satisfaction.

Kevin whined again, and Jack gave him the evil eye. Kevin sighed and sat.

Leah touched her lips as if to hold in the taste of him. "I'm sorry," she finally said.

"For?"

"Putting you in the position of having to pretend to like me."

Ah, hell. He drew a deep breath. Pretending wasn't his strong suit, and he could have said so. He could have also said that he liked her for real. But he wasn't going to. He'd been there, done that, bought the T-shirt, and he wasn't interested in a repeat performance. In fact, if he was going to pretend anything, it was going to be about *not* liking her. "Leah—" He broke off when Kevin nudged him in the gut and whined again. "What?" Jack asked him. "What's the matter?"

Kevin hunched and unloaded a mountain of poop. "Oh, for—" Before Jack could finish that sentence, Kevin shifted over a few feet and hunched again.

"Holy cow." Leah covered her nose. "What the hell are you feeding him?"

"Everything." Jack went to his truck for a shovel. He'd just tossed the bag into one of the trash receptacles when Kevin hunched again.

"Are you kidding me?" Jack demanded.

Kevin panted happily. Clearly feeling fifty pounds lighter, the dog pawed at the sand with his back legs, head proudly lifted as he then pranced toward the truck as if he were king.

Leah was still standing there looking shell-shocked.

"I know," Jack said. "It's bad. Breathe through your mouth. It helps."

She did just that, pulling his sweatshirt up over her mouth so all he could see was her eyes. It didn't matter. He had the taste of her on his tongue, the feel of her body still in his palms. He wanted to drag her up against him and plunder. Talk about bad ideas. "It's late," he said.

"Is that what you would have told your date tonight when she invited you in at the end of the night? That it was late?"

No. He'd have had her naked before midnight.

Naked and happy.

But this was Leah…and he tried really hard to not think about Leah naked.

Or naked and happy…

Except lately, he seemed to be doing nothing but.

Ever since she'd sprung this whole relationship thing on him, he'd thought of little else, and it was slowly driving him over the edge.

But he could get over that.

Or at least he could try.

Except now there was also this, *her*, in a little, itty-bitty, black bikini and his sweatshirt coming down to her mid-thighs, looking like his greatest fantasy come to life, and he didn't think he could handle any pretense at all. "Leah—"

"No," she said, shaking her head, backing away. "You know what? Let's not discuss this like rational human beings. Clearly we can't do that."

And in his sweatshirt and an air of righteousness, she headed to her car.

Chapter 9

♥

Leah yanked open her driver's door, but before she could slide in, Jack caught up with her, caging her in with one hand on the roof and one on the opened door. "Hold up," he said.

She turned to face him. "Move, Jack."

"I don't think so." His voice was calm as always, but there was an undercurrent now, the slightest tension. Which, coming from Jack, was tantamount to being wildly upset.

She didn't care.

All she knew was that he'd just kissed her, *really* kissed her. And it'd been so amazing that she'd lost herself in him, in a big way. He'd taken her in his strong, warm arms, and in that moment nothing else had existed. Not her fears, her screwups, her uncertainty, nothing.

How did he do that? Take her so far out of herself?

Even more shocking was watching him take care of his mom, Kevin, everyone around him, including her. The thought temporarily had all her bones melting and her good parts waking up and doing a boogie dance of happiness because she'd actually—gasp—*felt* something.

But Jack didn't want to feel anything for her. He didn't even want to pretend.

Her gut clenched because this was her fault. She'd wanted things to be different this time. The people here in Lucky Harbor, unlike her stupid school and show, mattered. Her grandma mattered. Her friends mattered. *Jack* mattered.

Picturing failing any of them, her chest tightened into a ball of anxiety and blocked her air passage.

"Leah." Still holding on to her, Jack pulled the hood of the sweatshirt up over her wet hair, then dipped down to look into her eyes. "It's not a rejection."

She braced herself to hold his gaze, but her throat was tight because it sure as hell felt like one. Which was only fitting, since she'd done the same to him. It'd been a long time, but sometimes it felt like yesterday.

It'd been her high school graduation, and there'd been alcohol involved. The party had turned a little crazy, and she'd gotten herself in over her head.

Jack had been her white knight, taking her home, sneaking her into bed before her dad could catch sight of her.

Leah had jokingly pulled Jack down over the top of her and said he should give her what she'd been looking for. He'd looked into her eyes, and with all his nineteen-year-old cockiness, told her if she'd been sober he'd be happy to show her exactly what she'd been looking for, and that he would ruin her for all other men while he was at it.

In the way of stupidly intoxicated seventeen-year-old

girls, she'd brazenly told him that she'd be sober tomorrow, and she expected him to make good on that promise.

The next night had come, but she'd been too afraid to go through with it because what if she blew it? What if she didn't have enough experience to interest him? What if she didn't turn him on?

But most important, he'd dumped every girl he'd ever been with. Did she want to be that girl, the one who lost him over one night?

So she'd choked. Panicked.

Run.

He'd never given her any indication of minding either way, so she'd figured no harm, no foul. She'd done the right thing because their friendship had been the most valuable thing in her life.

And she hadn't been willing to risk it.

Even as young and foolish as she'd been, she'd known that much. She'd much rather be in his life as his friend than in his past as an ex.

Now she'd risked all that with her lie to Dee.

"It's not a rejection," he repeated. "It's a time-out. We're just going to our own corners to think." He paused. "Do you understand?"

"Yes, I understand. I understand I'm such a bad idea that you need to think."

"No. We're a bad idea."

In her mind there was no difference, and she tried to slip into her car, but again he held on, pressing her into the door, cupping her face, and tilting it to his. At his touch, her body softened. Ached. She had to close her eyes against the unexpected onslaught of emotions.

"Leah. Look at me. Please."

It was the "please" that did it, softly but authoritatively uttered. Incapable of not responding, she did as he asked and met his gaze.

He ran a hand over his face and rolled his shoulders in an apparent attempt to assuage his weariness. It was such an unconsciously sexy move that it was hard to concentrate on the matter at hand. Which was that she was mad. And maybe hurt.

"You're one of the most important people in my life," he said. "I can't pretend things with you. I tried that already."

And she'd hurt him. She honestly hadn't realized that she even could, and she still wasn't quite sure that she believed it now. Jack Harper wasn't one to pine over anyone. "I'm sorry I got you into this," she said with real regret. "So sorry. But I think now we should try to see it through." She couldn't have said why she needed to so badly. "For your mom, Jack."

He was looking at her, into her, but she was good at building walls of self-preservation. Good at not letting people in. In the old days, she'd never been able to pull that off with him, had never wanted to, but in the years since, she'd learned new skills.

"We need rules for this," he said.

It took a moment for the words to sink in, and then the relief made her weak. "So we're going to do it?"

"With rules."

This didn't surprise her. The big, built alpha loved his control, and he loved rules. Hell, his entire world was run by rules. Not for him, of course, but for everyone else. "Let me guess," she said with a hint of amusement. "You don't want me to wear green toenail polish?"

He shuddered. "Hell no. But we have things to work out, Leah."

"Like?"

"Like the fact that this isn't real."

She absorbed the unexpected pang of the words. "Of course not."

"So no hurt feelings."

"No hurt feelings," she said softly. "How do you want to do this in public?"

"There's only public," he said. "Otherwise we're just... us."

"Okay," she managed, wondering why she was feeling raked over the coals. "So...in public. PDA. Are we going to agree on a level? Minimal? Moderate?"

He scowled. "PDA?"

"Public display of affection."

"I know what it is. I just don't know why we have to figure that out right now."

"Moderate," she decided. "Maybe hold hands, greet each other with a kiss, that sort of thing?"

He let out a barely there sigh, like this was paining him, and she started to get a little insulted. "How about the Fireman's Picnic?" she asked. "Do I get to be your date for that or do you already have a blond bimbo planned?"

"The picnic's not for another month," he said with the horror of men everywhere when faced with a decision more than five minutes out. "Just how long do you plan to play at this?"

"It's for your mom," she reminded him.

"How long, Leah?"

She stared up into his dark-caramel eyes. "I don't know."

He held her against her car, making her lose her train of thought. "You really think we can pull this off?"

She wouldn't have to pull off anything, not that she'd admit that. "Hey, I once took method acting for an entire semester. Piece of cake. And it's not like you're hard on the eyes. Dating the hottest firefighter isn't going to be a hardship."

He stared at her for a long beat, giving very little away. "You think I'm hot."

"You have a mirror, right?" She paused, giving him a chance to say that maybe she wasn't hard on the eyes either, but he didn't, and she decided to get out while she was ahead. Squeezing from between him and her car, she slid behind the wheel. She had to give him a little push to shut the door so she could drive off. Glancing back in her rearview mirror, she found him watching her go, a pensive expression on his face. He was confused.

She touched her still-swollen lips and thought, join my club.

She was two blocks away when her cell phone rang.

Jack.

"Hello?" she answered, breathless.

"I think you're hot too," he said. "Actually, you're a knockout, Leah."

She had to pull over and draw in some air. "I'm sorry," she said. "Can you repeat that?"

"You're a fucking knockout."

"Thanks," she whispered, but he'd already disconnected.

Jack pocketed his phone and looked at Kevin. "So a show of paws. Am I the biggest idiot on the planet, or the smartest?"

Kevin yawned.

"Yeah, you're right. Idiot." His only excuse was that she'd made him dizzy as hell, kicking him a little off balance and a lot off his toes.

He loaded Kevin into the truck and slid behind the wheel. Kevin climbed into the back, but halfway home he claimed the front passenger seat again, leaning in to lick Jack's jaw.

"Why do you smell like beef jerky?" Jack craned his neck and looked in the back. Yep, Kevin had gotten into and eaten his way through the emergency kit.

Again.

But at least Jack wasn't thinking about kissing Leah. Much.

He pulled into the duplex that he and Ben had bought together five years ago now. It was a two-story Victorian and freshly painted thanks to Ben's recent handiwork.

Ben's side of the house was dark, so Jack let himself and Kevin inside, not bothering with any lights since his immediate plan involved some serious shut-eye. He went for just that, but instead he ended up with hot, restless, erotic dreams involving Leah, both in and out of her black bikini.

Leah let herself into her grandma's dark house and ran right into a soft body.

"Oh," Elsie said, startled. "You're still up?"

Leah turned on the light. "Are you okay? Why aren't you sleeping?"

"Oh, you know." Elsie let out a little laugh. "My old bones creak and wake me up." But Elsie didn't look old. She looked…guilty. "Okay, so I was out. I…had a meeting."

"At midnight?"

"Is it that late?" Elsie asked. "Huh."

"Who did you meet?"

"Max Fitzgerald."

Elsie was on the Historical Society board with Max. She'd complained about him for years and years, calling him a liver-spotted, tight-lipped, tighter-assed renovation nazi.

The name fit. "Why did you have such a late meeting? You forget to pay your dues or something?"

Elsie grimaced and pulled her coat tighter around herself, but it didn't miss Leah's attention that Elsie was wearing her good "going out" shoes. Leah, once the master sneaker, felt her eyes narrow. "Grandma, what's going on?"

"Okay, but just remember, this all started out with me trying to surprise you," Elsie said.

"Me?"

"Yes. You've been working so hard and without a single word of complaint."

"Grandma," Leah said, both touched and irritated, "I love being here with you. I have nothing to complain about."

"But you've taken over so beautifully, and the place is such a mess. I know it is, Leah; don't even try to deny it. I just wanted to see what kind of renovations we could make. Cheaply, of course. Something to help you."

"I'm good with how things are," Leah said. "Other than wanting new ovens." She meant this, one hundred percent. In fact, the truth was that she actually loved the bakery's slightly antiquated setup. It made her work hard, made her think, made her concentrate. She liked having little brain power left over for anything else.

Like what the hell she was going to do in two weeks when the *Sweet Wars* finals aired and the gig was up? Or why she was happier here, back in the place that had once upon a time been the bane of her existence, than she'd been anywhere else.

Although she suspected this was because of a certain big, bad, gorgeous firefighter who, thanks to her own doing, was now her pretend boyfriend.

And a hell of a kisser.

"Well, you're a doll for putting up with everything," Elsie said. "Anyway, I wanted to see what I could do and ran the thought by Max first."

"Oh, Grandma," Leah said softly. "You give him way too much power."

"And he said I was absolutely welcome to make any renovations."

"Yes, because you have every right to," Leah pointed out. "Grandma—"

"And so I was just having a drink to thank him, and he…invited me to the firefighter's ball next month," she ended in a rush.

Leah opened her mouth again, but Elsie cut in before she could speak. "No. Don't say whatever it is that you're going to say. I was wrong about him. Okay, yes, he can be a fuddy-duddy, but he's also very conscientious about our town's history and takes his job seriously. And actually, he's a very nice man. I'm sorry if I let you think otherwise, especially because I know you don't think all that highly of the male race in general. And maybe that's my fault too, for not correcting your notion that they're all temperamental horse's patoots. That was just your daddy, honey."

"Well, I know that."

Elsie smiled a little sadly. "Do you? Because you're quick to judge a man, and even quicker to cut one out of your life."

This threw Leah off her game a little. "Of course I know it," she said. "I like men, Grandma." She'd been on her own a long time. Twelve years, actually, since the day she'd driven out of town at age eighteen and not looked back. She'd had relationships. Granted, nothing that had lasted, but as she'd told Dee, it only took one...

But did she really believe that? "I've had boyfriends."

"Had? Past tense?" Her grandma's eyes were sharp. "Don't you have a boyfriend right now?"

Well, she'd walked right into that one, hadn't she? "You mean Jack."

"Do you have more than one?" Elsie asked with a laugh.

Jack woke up before his alarm thanks to a sensation of being crushed. Sitting up, he turned on the light.

At some point in the night, Kevin had climbed onto the bed with him. The dog lay on his back, all four legs straight up in the air as if he were roadkill, snoring loudly enough to rattle the windows.

He had nearly the entire bed.

"Hey," Jack said and nudged him.

Kevin stopped snoring but didn't move a single muscle.

"I know you're awake."

Kevin slit open one eye.

Jack pointed to the floor.

With a sigh, Kevin heaved himself up and stepped off

the bed. He sent Jack one soulful look over his shoulder before heading out of the room. Two seconds later Jack could hear the sound of Kevin slurping water out of his bowl, and no doubt drooling everywhere while he was at it.

Jack rolled out of bed as well, showered, and then hit the road. He'd hired a day nurse for his mom, both to keep her company and to make sure she was getting everything she needed, especially when Jack was on shift and couldn't help her himself.

But when he stopped by his childhood home on the way to the station, Dee was already up and dressed and sitting at her kitchen table.

Kevin bounded into the room and would've taken a flying leap at her, but Jack grabbed his collar just in time.

"Gak," Kevin said, eyes bulging, tongue hanging out.

Ben stood behind the stove cooking a big spread of bacon, eggs, and french toast. "I thought you were home, still in bed," Jack said.

"You thought wrong."

Kevin, desperate to get at Dee, whined.

"Sit," Jack told him.

Kevin barked. His bark was loud enough to pierce eardrums, and everyone in the room winced.

"Not bark," Jack said. "*Sit.*"

Kevin offered a paw.

Jesus. "Kevin. *Sit.*"

Kevin turned in three circles and plopped down to the floor, which shook like an earthquake under the one-hundred-and-fifty-plus pounds.

Dee laughed. "Such a sweet boy."

Kevin smiled at her.

"Sweet, my ass," Jack muttered.

Ben began loading a mountain of food onto a plate, which he then brought to Dee.

Dee, who always ate less than a bird whenever Jack had tried to feed her, beamed at Ben. "Thanks, sweetheart." She gestured to Kevin, who all but scrambled his circuits trying to get up at the speed of light. Like a cat on linoleum, his paws fought for purchase as he raced to her side.

"Now you be a very good boy," Dee said to him, patting him on the head, which was level with hers. "Be a very good boy and sit for me. Can you do that, Kevin? Can you sit for me?"

Kevin sent her an adoring smile and sat.

Jack shook his head. "Fucker."

"Such a good boy," Dee cooed. "So much better than my potty-mouthed son."

"He's not a good boy," Jack told her. "He's a menace to society."

Kevin sent Jack a glare of reproach.

"What are you doing here?" Jack asked Ben.

"It was your turn to stock the fridge."

By "fridge," Ben meant Jack's fridge, as Ben didn't use his own. "Yeah? So?"

"So you bought beer, cookie dough, and peanut butter and jelly."

"Oh, Jack," Dee admonished.

"Hey," he said in his defense, "I got the basic necessities."

Ben shook his head. "No wonder you're single," he said in the tone that they both knew would rile Dee up, which in turn would effectively get Jack in trouble. Ben's favorite thing to do.

"He's not single," Dee corrected. "He's got Leah."

"Right," Ben said dryly. "Almost forgot."

Jack gave him a look. This didn't appear to bother Ben in the slightest. "So where's Carrie?"

"I don't need a nurse this week," Dee said. "I didn't want to waste your money, so she took on another patient."

"Mom, forget the money. I want you taken care of when I'm working."

Dee pointed at Ben.

Ben saluted her with his spatula.

Jack slid a look to Ben. He knew his cousin felt he owed Dee his life—multiple times over—for taking him in and keeping him on the straight and narrow.

Not that she'd always managed to keep Ben on the straight and narrow, but he'd turned out okay. If you counted being a little off your rocker okay...

"I'm fine," Dee said again. "Or I would be if I wasn't worried about you."

"Me?" Jack asked. "What about me? I'm fine too."

Ben, flipping a piece of french toast, gave a snort that made Jack feel twelve again and defensive as hell. "What?"

"Nothing. It's just that you're awfully cranky for someone who's fine," Ben said lightly.

"I'm not cranky."

Ben shrugged.

Dee's smile faded a little bit. "Are you cranky?" she asked Jack. "Why would you be cranky? I saw Leah yesterday afternoon, and she said things were great. You didn't mess things up with her since then, did you?"

Of course he had; thank you very much. Jack sighed and looked to Ben.

Ben just raised a brow, the asshole. "It's six in the morning," Jack said as evenly as he could. "How much could I have messed anything up?"

Concern filled Dee's gaze. "Oh, Jack," she murmured. "Was it your phone?"

"What?"

"You know," she said, waving a hand. "Your phone. I read in *Cosmo* that if a woman looks in her man's phone and he has anyone in his contacts with only a first initial, that means it's a..." She lowered her voice to a whisper. "Booty call. Grounds for a breakup. As is having eight contacts with the name Brandy, because chances are that they're exotic dancers you've met on business trips."

Ben pointed at a stunned Jack with a spatula. "No matter how much your girl presses you about your Brandys, deny everything until death."

Dee waved an irritated hand in Ben's direction. "You're not taking me seriously."

"Mom, I didn't mess anything up."

"Then where is she?"

"Leah?"

"No, the Tooth Fairy," Dee said, making Ben grin again. "Where is Leah, Jack?"

Probably concocting some new way to make his life a living hell, he thought darkly. Oh wait, *she'd already done that*. Ever since the kiss on the beach—kisses plural, as in many, many amazing kisses—he'd done nothing but think of her plastered up against him, or better yet, beneath him, soft and wet, sighing his name in pleasure...

And yet there was his mom, looking at him with those eagle eyes of hers, the ones that could always tell when he'd messed something up, so he ruthlessly clamped

down on the fantasy and shrugged. "It's six a.m.," he repeated.

"So she's baking?"

Right. She'd be baking. He nodded.

Dee relaxed and went back to eating. She had color in
her cheeks and looked happy. Jack would like to say that
he'd put that happy look on her face, but he hadn't. Ben
had, with his food.

And Leah, with her lie.

Ben was making another plate, loading it full for himself, and Jack snatched it.

Ben muttered "fucker" beneath his breath, which Dee
either didn't catch or ignored. "You going to be around
today?" he asked Ben.

"I don't need a babysitter, Jack," Dee said.

Jack didn't take his eyes off Ben.

Ben nodded.

"She's got an appointment day after tomorrow at ten,"
Jack said.

"I can drive myself," Dee said.

Ben nodded again affably. "But you'll let me take
you."

"I'm fine—"

"Of course you are," Ben said smoothly. "But this isn't
for you. It's for your idiot son. We don't want him worrying like a little girl while he's on the job."

Dee relaxed. "Of course not. But you have a life too,
Benjamin."

Ben lifted a shoulder. "I'm…in flux."

Ben didn't talk much about his job. Being a civil engineer sounded innocuous but it wasn't the way Ben
did it. His last job, where he'd gone into Iraq for the

DOJ to design and build water systems for some of the war-torn towns, had obviously gotten to him, big time. Usually when he was in Lucky Harbor he went back to his woodworking, and actually he was a hell of a furniture maker when he wanted to be. But he hadn't picked up so much as a single tool since he'd been back.

So yeah, he was in flux. He *lived* in flux.

Luckily, he never spent much of his income so he had some flexibility. Others in Lucky Harbor hadn't been so lucky. The economic downturn had been hard on many of the businesses, and there were a lot of properties in trouble and on the market.

But things were starting to turn around. A few new businesses were coming in, and some of the properties were being built up and renovated, when the historical society loosened their bulldog grip on the regulations and permits.

There'd been some noise from the biggest developer sniffing around, a Mr. Rinaldi out of L.A., who was snatching up as many of the available properties as possible. He had three or four in escrow at the moment, including Elsie's bakery. He'd promised the current residents that nothing would change, but the rumor was that he planned on getting a whole strip of buildings on commercial row and running the town.

There were mixed feelings about this. Any commerce was good. It brought in money and kept people employed. But Lucky Harbor residents were used to being a tight-knit community, and there were fears that this was going to change.

Jack didn't care about that, but he did care about the bakery, so he hoped Mr. Rinaldi's word was good.

"What's that, honey?" Dee asked.

"I didn't say anything," Jack said.

"Yeah, you did," Ben said. "You mumbled something about the bakery."

Dee smiled. "He's got his girlfriend on his mind."

Jack put his empty plate in the sink, kissed his mom, and left, ignoring Ben's knowing smirk.

Chapter 10

♥

Leah's breath caught as Jack's body pressed into hers. His hands stroked up her sides and then his thumbs were brushing over her nipples. Moaning, she arched closer as he kissed her long and deep, grinding his lower body into hers. He was hard, so deliciously hard, and she ached for him. Tangling her hands in his hair, she kissed him deeper until he groaned her name.

Oh, how she liked the sound of her name on his lips.

Then his clever fingers found their way into her panties, and he let out another groan before breaking the kiss and nipping at her ear. "Jesus, Leah. You've got to remove your hand."

What?

She opened her eyes and realized that Jack was standing over her, where she'd fallen asleep at her grandma's desk. He was fully dressed and breathing heavily, making her realize that her right hand was cupping the bulge behind his zipper. She snatched it away as if she'd been burned, and he stepped back, leaning against the file cabinet.

It took her a shockingly long moment to catch her breath, but even then, she could still feel the bulge of him in her palm. The *big* bulge of him… "What are you doing?" she demanded.

"You were moaning and flushed and sweaty. I came close to check on you, and you molested me."

She groaned in embarrassment and covered her face while he laughed softly. In spite of the tension in every line of his body, he flashed a smile. "Busy, huh?"

There was a lull at the bakery every day around ten in the morning. Since Leah was usually up by 4:00 a.m. to bake and then serving customers by 6:00, that lull came with the urge to nap.

Usually she combated this with copious amounts of caffeine and something from her day's wares that had lots of sugar, but today she'd been stuck in the teeny-tiny office facing a stack of her grandma's bills. A little overwhelmed, she'd set her head down and clearly fallen asleep. "Yes," she said. "I am very busy." She bit her lip. "And sorry, about—" She gestured to his crotch. "Though it's your fault for not knocking. Why are you here?"

"Donuts."

"Donuts." She huffed to her feet, pushed past him, and headed out front. "You interrupted the best sex I've had all year for donuts."

"That's sad."

"Exactly why I needed the end of that dream!"

In tune to his soft laugh, she loaded him up a box of donuts and shoved him out the door.

* * *

From the bakery, Jack headed to work. His amusement had shifted into a solid, churning need centered right at his groin, which hadn't yet gotten the message that he wasn't getting any, despite how Leah's fingers had felt cupping him. Thinking about how she'd looked in the throes of her sex dream made him hard all over again. He'd told her she'd been moaning and hot and sweaty. What he hadn't told her was that she'd whispered a name.

His.

He blew out a breath and forced that from his mind—as well as the image of taking her on that desk, her long, gorgeous legs wrapped around him—so he didn't walk into the station with a boner.

Station #24 sat at the end of commercial row, between the pier and downtown. Once upon a time, the two-story brick building had housed the town's saloon and theater, but it'd long ago been converted to a firehouse.

There were three large garage doors out front, opened to reveal a fire engine, a ladder truck, an ambulance, and the county OES Hazardous Materials response vehicle. Beyond the garage, there was a utility-sized kitchen and a big open living room. Upstairs was a large sleeping area that looked like a frat dorm meets Three Little Bears, except it was the Six Little Bears with rows of twin beds.

Over the years, they'd added a pool table, an X-Box, a flat-screen TV, and some huge, comfy couches. Home away from home or, as they all spent more time here together than they did with their various loved ones, just *home*.

Half the staff were great cooks, and the other half knew how to order in with equally great skill. Eat Me,

the local café, served the station on command, as did the
Love Shack, the bar and grill down the street.

The station was staffed on a full-time basis with a ro-
tating staff. They shared the site with Washington State
Fire—where, by no coincidence, Jack had gotten his start
in the first place as a rural firefighter, aka a Hotshot.

As head of shift, Jack usually arrived before anyone
else, but today Tim was already there, head buried in a
laptop. "Hey," the rookie said, barely looking up. "The
B rotation caught a fire yesterday at the auto-parts store.
Lucky bastards."

Jack had already heard from Ronald since the fire was
of suspicious origin, but he looked over Tim's shoulder at
the pictures of the scene on the laptop.

"Burned hot," Tim said. "Real hot. Bad luck for Lenny
Shapiro."

Shapiro owned the auto shop. "Maybe it wasn't luck at
all."

"You think it was arson?" Tim asked, surprised. "Nah,
man, those rags shoved in that bucket…stupid place for
them. Real stupid. Lenny should have known better." He
shut his laptop. "You watch, on our rotation we'll get
all medical calls. Or a false alarm. We never get the fun
ones."

Jack went to his office and brought up the fire pictures
on his computer. As Tim had noted, there'd been oily rags
left in a bucket near a stack of boxes, and they'd ignited.
But this was now the second fire in two weeks where oily
rags were discovered in a bucket.

Jack went over everything he had on the fire and
moved on to the paperwork required of him as the LT,
while his unit worked their daily chores, pulling the

equipment out onto the long driveway to be washed, stocked, and inventoried.

Jack had deposited the proceeds from the Firemen's Breakfast the week before, but he still had to make the statements for the beneficiaries. The breakfast itself had been made possible through the generous donations from the local businesses such as the B&B, the café, the art gallery, and many more, and they each would get a statement and an individual thank you. The FD had set a new record this year for number of meals served, and the profit would guarantee that the seniors would be getting three square meals for the rest of the year without cutting into the town's general budget.

He was just finishing up when they got their first call of the day from the library. As Tim had groused, it was a medical call, but then again, at least fifty percent of their calls were. A teenager—there with his entire class—had found the staff ladder irresistible. He'd climbed up twelve feet before his belt had gotten caught on the shelving unit, leaving him hanging upside down over the rest of his delighted class.

Jack was going to guess that it would be college before the kid lived it down.

After that, in quick succession they were called to a traffic collision and then a near drowning in the harbor. Later, they took the engine and truck to the elementary school for their annual Firefighters at School Day. By the end of that visit, every single kid between the ages of five and ten wanted to be a firefighter when they grew up.

Jack had once been one of those kids. He could still remember the day his dad had brought an engine to school. Jack had already known every inch of the truck and gear—hell, he'd been playing with it all since before he could walk—but he'd still been as enthralled as his friends. He'd remained enthralled until the day his dad died on the job. But by then, Jack's fate had been sealed. Because how did the son of a devoted legend do anything other than follow in his father's footsteps?

After the kids had gone back to class, Jack began reloading all the supplies and gear. He heard the *click-click-clicking* of a pair of heels, and his pulse jumped once as he thought *Leah*, but it wasn't her. It was one of the teachers, coming around the back of his truck, seeking him out.

Rachel Moore was a pretty brunette he'd met at the gym. They'd been flirting back and forth for a few weeks now, and the last time they'd run into each other during a workout, she'd suggested maybe having a drink sometime.

"Heard about what happened at the Love Shack," she said, carefully neutral.

Since this statement could cover a lot of ground, and he wasn't sure if she was on a fishing expedition or simply making conversation, he made a noncommittal sound.

"People are saying you're…engaged."

Yep. Fishing expedition.

"Is it true?" she asked.

Jack looked into Rachel's pretty green eyes and suppressed a sigh. A deal was a deal, and though Rachel wasn't—as Leah had so delicately put it—a blond bimbo, Jack had agreed to the insanity. Sort of. "I'm not engaged," he said. "But—"

"No, stop. I understand." Her smile was a little forced now. "But you should have told me, Jack. When we were at the gym, we flirted. Or so I thought." She shook her head. "I didn't realize it was just flirting. My mistake." With that, she turned on her heel and took her very hot self back inside the school.

Jack blew out a breath and headed around to the front of the truck, where Tim was waiting with a wide grin. "Hey, at least she didn't toss her drink in your face."

Jack narrowed his eyes, and Tim sighed. "Let me guess. The senior center again, right?"

Back at the station, they were in the middle of carrying hoses up and down the five flights of stairs on the training tower in the yard when the alarm went off.

They were sent to the senior center with reports of smoke pouring out of the kitchen. Knowing the seniors of Lucky Harbor, this could mean anything. Last year, Mrs. Burland had been making soup for herself when she'd had a heart attack. No one had known she was down until her soup had evaporated and the pan had caught fire. Mrs. Burland had lived. The kitchen, not so much.

Tim was in his seat, leaning forward, as excited as if he'd hit the lottery. "Please be a fire," he said. "Please oh please be a fire."

Ian slid him an annoyed look. "Remember, Rookie, follow our lead."

"Let me take point this time," Tim said. "Please?"

"No point," Ian said. "LT's point."

But this time when they got there, the only person in the kitchen was Lucille, wearing a neon-green velour track suit and bright-white athletic shoes.

"Jesus," Tim muttered, holding up a hand to block his eyes. "She's brighter than the sun."

Lucille gave him a Vanna White smile. "Hiya!" Then she snapped his picture.

"You reported a fire," Jack said. "Where is it?"

Concentrating on her phone now, messing with the camera setting, Lucille was distracted. "I realize this is going to sound so wrong, but…" She looked at them. "Could you all take off your shirts?"

Ian laughed.

But Jack wasn't finding the humor. "Put the phone down, Lucille."

"Aw. Please? Just one shirtless pic? You can't even imagine the online traffic boost we get from shirtless pics."

"The fire, Lucille," Jack said. "Where's the fire?"

"Oh. *That.*" She blew out a sigh. "It's all that fuddy-duddy Mrs. Burland's doing."

"She have another medical emergency?"

"Does being a pain in the behind count?"

Jack resisted pointing out that *she* was the pain in the behind. "Is there a fire or not?"

"My goodness, you're in an awful hurry today. I tell you, storytelling is a lost art nowadays. A real shame too, because—"

"Lucille."

"Fine!" She sniffed in irritation. "I wanted to make everyone my cheesy toast special. Except a little piece of bread got caught in the toaster and a tiny little flame popped up, and Mrs. B called you."

Jack turned to the toaster. No smoke. No flames.

"I tried to tell her she was overreacting," Lucille said. "That she at least needed to pass out or something to make it worth her while."

"Don't you mean *our* while?" Tim asked.

"No." She smiled at the rookie. "Because if she passed out, she'd have had a shot at CPR from one of you hotties."

For the first time ever, Tim looked relieved to *not* be point.

Chapter 11

At the end of the week, Leah stopped by the station with a box of fresh pastries. The big doors were wide open to the bright sun, and the trucks were out in the driveway, being washed by the platoon of Station #24.

Cindy and Hunter were on top of the ambulance. Ian and Sam were head deep in the open compartment. Tim was untangling some hoses. And Jack was on top of the fire truck, wearing his navy-blue firefighter BDUs and reflector sunglasses.

No shirt.

Leah tripped over her own feet but managed to catch herself.

"Aw," Tim said, getting to her first, quickly relieving her of the pastry box. "You're the best girlfriend ever."

Jack had straightened on the fire truck and was looking right at her. She could tell because her nipples got perky.

Tim leaned into her. "Hey, when you're done playing with the old guy, you let me know."

"Why?"

Tim grinned. "So I can show you what a young guy can do."

Leah laughed and waved at Jack.

He didn't smile or wave back, but he did hop down agilely. By the time he ambled over to her, he had to push his way through the crew. Leaning in, he looked into the empty pastry box.

"Two kinds of people here, LT," Tim said with mock sympathy. "The quick"—he flashed a grin—"and the hungry."

Jack slid Tim a look that might have had a smarter guy messing his pants. Pretty sure she was saving Tim's life, Leah pulled a white bag from her purse and handed it to Jack.

"What's this?" he asked as if she were handing him a spitting cobra.

"Look for yourself."

He opened the bag and peered inside, his expression not changing one iota.

"What is it?" Tim wanted to know. "You leave your tighty-whities at her place?"

Jack turned his head in Tim's direction. Leah couldn't see what Jack's expression was exactly, but Tim heaved out a sigh and headed back to the hoses.

"So," she said when they were alone. "Hi."

"What are you doing here?" he asked quietly.

"Pretend dating you," she said, watching him take a second look into the bag at the two cream cheese croissants she'd packed. "How am I doing at the pretend-girlfriend thing so far?"

"My girlfriends all greet me with sex," he said.

She laughed and his mouth twitched, and she knew she had him. The relief that hit her made her knees wobble. Or maybe that was just Jack and all that bronze skin stretching across the tough, sinewy muscles in his arms and chest that tapered to a set of abs that had her mouth watering.

"Don't do this," he said, and her smile faded. "Don't make it a spectacle."

"Is that what you think I'm doing?"

"I don't know what the hell you're doing, which is my point."

And oh, how he hated not knowing every little last thing. "Maybe I just wanted to bring you a treat," she said. "You telling me I don't remember your favorite?"

"I'm telling you that you no longer know me. And my mom isn't even here, so there's no point to this now."

"Fine." She reached for the bag to take it back, damn him, but he was much quicker than she, lifting it out of her range.

She wasn't a small girl. Never had been. From the fifth grade, she'd been taller than most of the boys in her life. But not Jack. Jack had a way of making her feel petite.

Feminine.

Sexy.

Damn him anyway.

He shoved his hand into the bag, pulled out a croissant, and took a large bite. Then he closed his eyes and groaned.

"Good?"

"Shh. I need a moment."

She found herself fascinated by his Adam's apple as he swallowed.

"Oh yeah," he said, voice thick and husky. Hypnotic. "This is the stuff. Save me the rest of these, whatever you have at the bakery. I want them all."

"Let me see if I have this right," she said. "No to the playing-the-girlfriend thing unless your mom's watching—" She broke off when he licked some sugar off his thumb, the sound of the suction making her quiver just a little bit. "But," she managed with what she hoped sounded like utter disinterest, "you want me to save you the rest of the cream cheese croissants."

He tilted his head down enough to eye her over his dark lenses. "Problem?"

She sent him a smile that had far more vinegar than honey. "Not even a little bit."

When the next episode of *Sweet Wars* aired, Jack and the rest of the platoon watched it in the station living room. Ben had come by with popcorn and a chew toy for Kevin. "Dee's good," he said to Jack before he could ask. "Made her soup and toast for dinner, which she ate. Lucille's with her. They've got *Magic Mike* on DVD for after *Sweet Wars*." Ben shuddered. "I vacated the premises."

Tonight's challenge was baklava, and Jack immediately relaxed. Granted, baklava was an incredibly difficult dessert to make because of the many layers of phyllo dough required, which he only knew because Leah said so whenever she made it. But the good news was that she did often make it for the bakery, and in his humble opinion, it was the best on the planet.

"She's got this one in the bag," Ben said, tossing Kevin a piece of popcorn, which he caught in midair with a snap of his huge jaws. "She tell you how she did?"

Jack turned up the volume. "Shh."

"He doesn't like to talk about her," Tim told Ben. "He's touchy as hell."

Jack turned up the volume even more. The camera loved her. Leah looked amazing as she made the challenge look effortless, even when Rafe got in her space and started questioning everything she was doing.

"Amazing," Ben said. "She's amazing." He nudged Jack. "Way too good for you."

"This is what I'm saying," Tim said, tossing up his hands and looking around for affirmation. "I totally have a shot at her, right?"

Jack, never taking his eyes from Leah on the screen, reached casually for more popcorn. "Take a shot and I'll end you."

Ian and Emily snickered.

Tim scowled. "I'm pretty sure you can't threaten me," he said. "It's sorta illegal. Tell him, Ben."

Ben slid him a look that was even more deadly serious than Jack's had been.

Tim pulled his hand back from the popcorn bowl and sank farther into his seat. "Whatever. I could totally have a shot. If I wanted one."

Jack was pretty damn sure that wasn't true. Actually, if he had to go off of Leah's behavior, there wasn't a guy in Lucky Harbor who had a shot.

Except maybe him.

At least until he'd blown that by being an ass. Not that he was sorry. Because he didn't want it to be real.

And maybe if he kept telling himself that, he'd believe it.

* * *

That night, Jack was sleeping like shit, wondering how the hell it was that Leah was permeating his dreams and pissing him off even there when a storm hit. The lightning flashed first, lighting up the large station bedroom like day.

Kevin leaped off his pallet and onto Jack's bed, landing right on Jack's stomach, knocking the air out of him as the dog buried his face in the crook of Jack's neck and whined like a baby.

Across the room, Sam sat straight up in bed with a "what the fuck—" just as the ensuing thunder boomed, rattling the windows and shaking the building on its axis.

"Holy shit," Tim said from his bed. "You think we'll get a good call out of this?"

He hadn't even finished the sentence when another bolt hit, followed by an immediate crack of thunder that nearly burst their eardrums.

"Yeah," Tim said, excited. "We'll get something good."

Kevin whined again and pressed tighter to Jack. Jack hugged the big oaf close and managed to sit up. Because Tim was right. Unless the storm planned on bringing moisture with it, those lightning strikes were dangerous as hell, and they were going to get action.

At the next bolt, Kevin whimpered and tried to climb Jack like a tree. Jack held the big baby tight and thought of Leah. She'd always hated thunder and lightning. During the craziest of storms, he always thought about her. Did she still get scared? Standing up with Kevin still in his arms, Jack transferred him to Tim's bed.

"Jesus," Tim complained but let the dog crawl under the covers. "Your paws are cold."

Jack strode to the window and shoved it open. The temp hadn't dropped much, but the wind had kicked up into high gear. Tumbling dark clouds churned up the sky like dark-gray wool blankets in a dryer, but not a single drop of rain fell.

"Precip?" Sam asked.

"No."

"Damn," Ian muttered.

"Yeah." Jack pulled out his cell phone and stared down at it as indecision warred with the need to know she was okay. Fuck it, he thought, and slid his thumb across the screen to access a blank text.

You okay?

Just as he hit SEND, another window-rattling bolt hit, and then, not all that surprisingly, the fire alarm sounded. A two-alarm, meaning two companies would be responding. Not good.

"Why are the fires always at three in the morning?" Ian wanted to know.

"Karma." Jack pulled on his clothes and shoved his feet into his boots. "For every time you've woken us up with those stupid late-night booty-texts you get."

"You're just jealous now that you're wearing a ball and chain," Ian said. "And how's that working out for you, by the way? 'Cause you're grumpy as hell, so I know you're not getting any. I thought that was the whole idea of an almost-fiancé."

"If you're tired of Leah, I'll take her off your hands," Tim offered.

Jack ignored this and got out of the room first. Tim,

knowing the last one out had to do the paperwork, swore, shoved Kevin off of him, and scrambled after Jack. They suited up, boarded the vehicles, and while heading to the scene, put on their air packs.

Each firefighter was assigned a very specific job, but that job shifted with each rotation. So sometimes Jack was the ladder, sometimes the engine. Sometimes he drove, sometimes he was tails. Everyone had their favorite position. Ian preferred driving. Emily liked the ladder. Some guys were just better at some jobs. Jack was good on the medicals with teenagers or old people, so he usually got that job instead of, say, Tim, who didn't have the experience needed and often came off as an impatient asshole.

On the way, they all dove into the bag of candy that Ian pulled out of his pocket, laughing at Tim when he dropped his and Kevin inhaled it before anyone could stop him.

"Candy's bad for him," Jack said. "Don't let him have any more."

Tim turned to Kevin. "You hear that? Candy's bad for you. Give it back."

Kevin licked his chops and wagged his tail for more.

The joking halted on a dime when they got to the fire.

Just outside of town was an older residential section. Hardworking, lower-middle-class families lived here, in a row of apartment buildings close together and in need of repair. In this particular complex, there were three floors of units, most likely full of sleeping families.

And flames were shooting out the roof.

The other station had responded and arrived at the same time. So did Ronald. As deputy chief and fire marshal and the highest ranking official there, normally he'd be incident commander, but he passed this off to Jack, who did a quick walk around of the perimeter while the ladder was positioned to open up the roof and let out the hot gases accumulating in the upper floor of the building.

Until that happened, the danger could only escalate.

Jack relayed by radio that they had fire out two windows of the first floor on the south side, extending up into the second floor and the attic. A third alarm was struck, and the coordinated attack began.

"Holy shit," Tim breathed, sounding awed as he stood still at Jack's side staring up at the flames. "Holy shit. Let's go! We'll head into the—"

Jack caught him up by the back of his gear. Firefighters were taught from day one to never enter a structure alone, but it was usually the first thing an excited rookie forgot. "You know you're on exterior with Emily." At LHFD, they practiced what was known as the two-in, two-out rule. Anytime someone entered a hazardous environment, there was an equal number of personnel available outside the hazard area to rescue those who entered in case they got into trouble.

Emily and a pissed-off-looking Tim moved into position on the exterior. Sam joined the ladder team and headed to the roof. Jack and Ian would clear the interior and make sure everyone was out.

Forcing the rear door, they hit the stairs, standing at the top floor, doing a sweep, banging on doors, getting people out. Panic and fear always made people clumsy and difficult to maneuver. Jack and Ian moved fast and efficiently together, searching each apartment, working in sync with the other platoons by radio.

By the time they'd finished the floor, the smoke was so thick they were working blind, even with their self-contained breathing apparatus.

When they finished they started again on the secondary search, even if everyone was confirmed out, because sometimes people forgot that Johnny had a friend sleeping over, or that Uncle Joe didn't work tonight, and so on.

They were on the stairs to the second floor when they heard it, the sound of the team on the roof. They used a pike pole to push down on the ceiling below, letting smoke and gases escape from above the fire. It was always a gamble working on a roof that may or may not be able to handle the weight of the guys, the gear, and all the equipment, and tonight the weather wasn't helping.

But from one moment to the next, the heat and smoke lifted, and everyone in the interior took a breath of relief. They worked to finish clearing the building, most people happy for the help. Of course, Jack and Ian came across the one cantankerous old guy who wasn't. Neither was his snarling poodle. The man was waving a baseball bat, yelling about his "constitutional right to remain put."

"You also have the constitutional right to die here," Jack said. "But do you really want to?"

The guy lowered his baseball bat. "Bum leg," he admitted. "'Nam. Me and Killer here are just guarding our valuables."

"What do you have that's worth more than you and Killer?"

The old man scratched his head. "Well, when you put it like that…"

In the end, Jack carried him and Killer out, the six-pound poodle snarling and yipping in his ear the entire time, and Jack decided a one-hundred-and-fifty-pound pesky Great Dane with an eating disorder wasn't so bad after all.

Then the radio crackled, and out came the words that struck terror in all their hearts.

"Northeast corner of roof collapsed. Firefighter down."

Ian whirled to face Jack, eyes wide. "Fuck!"

Jack ordered Tim and Emily to enter and finish evacuating, and he and Ian fought the flames back up to the third floor, smoke curling around them, thick and unforgiving.

At the top, they met Tim hitting the stairs, carrying Sam. "Got to him," he said.

"You were told to stay on evacuation," Jack said.

"Firefighter down," Tim said simply.

Jack held his temper because now wasn't the time or place, but not following directions was a good way to get someone hurt, or worse.

And Tim knew it.

Sam had fallen through the roof, landing perilously close to an air vent. If Tim hadn't gotten to him, he might have fallen another twenty feet to his certain death. He was bruised and bloody from a few fairly deep gashes, but mercifully nothing seemed broken.

Half an hour later, the flames were out and so was everyone who'd been inside.

They'd gotten lucky. Three hours from start to finish, and other than Sam, there'd been no injuries.

The building wasn't as lucky. The firefighters had all done their best not to destroy more than was necessary but they'd opened up the place to ventilate it, breaking windows and tearing down sheetrock to do so. Checking for hot spots was always messy, but it was just too dangerous not to do it. If they'd left any embers smoldering, the fire could renew itself hours and hours later.

So when it was all said and done, the roof was completely gone, the building had lost three units on the top floor, and there was extensive smoke and water damage.

Back at the fire truck, tensions were high among the crew. No one had liked what Tim had done, but neither could anyone argue with the results.

Ian shoved Tim out of the way. "Move."

"Jeez," Tim said, staggering. "Take a Midol."

"Shut up."

"What the hell is your problem, man?"

"You. You're my problem," Ian said.

Tim looked confused.

"You didn't follow procedures, and you ignored a command," Jack said.

Tim didn't look concerned. "I saved a guy's life. One of our guys. You're all pissed off because I got there first. What are you going to do, give me the shit jobs? Dishes? Send me to the senior center?" He laughed and shook his head. "Oh, wait. I already do all that. You're just jealous because I got to be the hero today."

"A hero wouldn't call himself a hero," Ian said.

"You guys are all assholes. Jealous assholes." He climbed into the truck. "Where's my candy?"

Kevin uncurled his big body from his sleeping spot in the driver's seat and blinked at them. "Woof."

Tim searched high and low, and swore. "Goddamn dog. Did you eat my candy?"

Kevin hunched over and yakked on Tim's boot, a slimy mess that was all that was left of Tim's candy.

Chapter 12

By the time they debriefed, got back to the station, and deconned the masks and regulators and refilled the air tanks, dawn had broken and Jack was off shift. After a night like they'd just had, sleep would be impossible, no matter how tired he was. He had adrenaline coursing through him and needed...

Something. A hard run, a fast bike ride...

Sex.

Too bad he had a pretend almost fiancé who'd gotten all his options cut off in that department. He and Kevin stepped outside the station to head to Jack's truck, both man and dog stopping short at the sight of a woman leaning on it. Long, toned legs were shown off to perfection in low-riding jeans and leather boots, and the snug tank with an unbuttoned cropped sweater over it wasn't so bad on her curves either. She wore a baseball cap, but there was no mistaking that auburn hair falling to her shoulders, lit to a fiery gold by the rising sun.

Leah.

When had she gotten so damn beautiful?

She did her fair share of staring right back, which had his heart executing a funny little beat in his chest. Yeah, he thought, still keyed up.

Kevin recovered first with a joyous bark and rushed her. Leah wrapped her arms around the dog and gave him a big, warm hug that gave Jack a twinge.

Jealous of a damn dog...

Leah loved Kevin up, murmuring into his fur. "You big knucklehead. Scaring me like that. When the call went out that a firefighter was down, I..." She shut up and squeezed the dog tighter as Jack went still.

"You have a scanner?" he asked.

She lifted her head, and for the first time he got a good look at her. Eyes shadowed, face tense. "Grandma does," she said.

"No casualties."

"That part didn't get transmitted," she told him.

How many nights had his mom looked just like that, waiting on his dad to come home? Too many.

And then had come the night that his dad hadn't come home at all.

"Stop with the scanner," he said gruffly and tossed his bag into the back. He didn't want to ever see her waiting and anxious because of him. "Just turn the fucker off."

"Right." She let loose of Kevin, eyes flashing. "I'll just turn the fucker off. And my damn head and heart too. How's that, Jack? Is that how you do it?"

Well, hell. He was way too tired for this. "Leah—"

"Never mind. I get it."

"Do you?"

"Yeah. You don't want a relationship, pretend or otherwise. You never have."

He didn't bother to point out that he'd told her so, multiple times. "My life doesn't lend itself to one," he said instead.

"I wonder, Jack, if you've said that so often that you actually believe it." She shook her head. "Your staff at the station, all the other rotations...more than half of them are married. Have families even."

He was absolutely not doing this here, now.

Ever.

"Jack," she said, still sounding furious. "You could have the same thing. You don't have to cut yourself off like you do."

Did she think he didn't realize that other people managed the job and a life? Of course he knew it. Just as he knew, after watching his mom struggle all these years, that he personally wasn't capable of it. "I don't want anyone to care for me that way. I don't want to ruin anyone's life like—"

"Like your dad ruined your mom's?" Leah asked after a terrible beat of painful silence. "Oh, Jack." She rubbed her forehead and softened her voice. "You're not responsible for what happened to him, or her. And as for controlling anyone's feelings, that's the most asinine thing I've ever heard. You can't. You can't control my feelings any more than you can control how I breathe." She studied him for a beat, and then shook her head, looking as frustrated as he had. "And talking to you is like talking to a brick wall," she said, picking up a big purse at her feet. From inside, she came up with a smaller white bag that smelled like heaven. "Breakfast," she told him. "Don't ask me why, because honestly I don't know."

"Leah," he said when she'd whirled off. Jesus. "Leah, wait."

She stopped but kept her back to him.

"Thanks," he said to her stiff spine. "For the food." He paused. "And for...caring."

"Thanks right back at you," she said in what might have been a slightly grudging tone.

"For?" he asked, confused.

"For being too stubborn to get hurt."

This tugged a low laugh out of him, and she turned to face him, still in a temper given the light in her eyes. "Your knee okay?"

No, actually, it wasn't. It ached like a son of a bitch, but he'd live. "I'm good," he said.

She gave him an eye roll accompanied by a sound that spoke volumes on what she thought of his definition of "good." "You're such an idiot."

"In more ways than one," he agreed.

"Yeah?" She sounded greatly interested in hearing more of his idiocy. "What's more idiotic than turning down no-strings sex?"

He went still. "You never said no-strings sex."

"You should learn to read between the lines, Jack," she chided softly. "And you call yourself a ladies' man."

He laughed. "Oh, trust me. I'm well aware how little I know about the ladies."

He could admit that he'd had more than his fair share of meaningless attachments. But what she didn't seem to get was that nothing about her was meaningless to him.

"So what do you want to do?" she asked.

"About?"

"I know you're not going to sleep. You're going to go do something to let down all that adrenaline coursing through you. What's it going to be?"

The list of possibilities clicked through his head, each involving a different version on the same theme, her naked—except for those boots—and beneath him.

Or over him.

Or however he could get her.

In fact, he actually got hard standing there having it all flash through his head.

But this was Leah, he reminded himself for what felt like the thousandth time. Leah, who had always been fickle with her heart and its wants. If he let himself fall for her again, losing her this time would kill him. Which meant that he was going to go for Door Number Two—his motorcycle and the narrow and windy and isolated roads outside of town.

It would work.

It would have to.

"Jack?"

"A fast bike ride," he said.

She nodded and got into her car.

Well, that was that, he thought, and he and Kevin got into his truck. But as they pulled out of the lot, Jack realized Leah was following him.

Apparently, she was coming with.

And for the life of him, he couldn't have said whether he was relieved or terrified.

Leah pulled in behind Jack at his place, not at all sure what she thought she was doing. The whole "firefighter down" thing had rattled her much more than she'd thought, to the point that she'd needed to see him. Needed to be with him every bit as much as he needed to burn off his excess adrenaline.

She let out a breath and decided not to think beyond the fact that he was okay, and that she was grateful for the few mornings that Riley opened for her.

She got out of the car. It was going to be a lovely day, already nice and warm. The leaves were changing, slowly turning from green to every shade of gold, brown, and red under the sun and just starting to fall.

Someone had painted Jack's and Ben's duplex. Probably Ben, since she doubted that Jack had any spare time right now between his work and caring for Dee.

Leah was still pretty steamed at him, although she didn't examine why too closely as she got out of her car.

He was standing at the top of his driveway looking at her. Without a word, he let Kevin inside the house.

He was in jeans that were faded at all the stress points, and he had some *most* excellent stress points. His T-shirt said LHFD on the pecs and was stretched tautly across his broad shoulders. His hands were loose at his sides, his face carefully blank, but everything about him gave off a warning: *bad 'tude alpha alert.*

She didn't care.

Nor did she know what she thought she was doing.

Okay, that was a lie. She knew. She watched him walk toward her, clearly favoring his knee, which had her taking a deep breath. "You need to get off that leg," she said. "What did you do, jump out of a window? Carry someone? Run the stairs?"

"All of the above."

She knew this should reach right inside her heart and squeeze hard, and it did. Which was a good part of why she got even madder. Since he was now close enough, she poked a finger into his chest, hard. "You've paid your dues, Jack. You paid them a long time ago now."

"What are you talking about?" He grabbed her finger and pushed it away. "And ouch."

"Do you think the only way you can match your dad's legend is to die like he did?" Letting her fears finally escape, the ones that had been choking her ever since hearing those two terrifying words "firefighter down," she let him have it. "You have some sort of stupid martyr complex. You won't be happy until you die like your dad, is that it? You're not Superman, you know."

"Jesus, I know that."

"Do you? Do you really? Because we both know that the uniform comes with an expectation. Especially as the son of a hero."

He shrugged, like, *what am I supposed to do*, and she let out a sigh. "You don't have to follow the exact same path to honor his memory. You know that."

"I know that you don't know what you're talking about," he said.

"Don't I? You're always doing your duty, what's expected. In fact, you've never done anything unexpected in your life—"

He proved her wrong by cutting her off with a hard kiss.

And she learned something else—apparently a brain couldn't hold onto anger when unexpectedly pummeled by sheer lust, because she let out a gasp of desire and flung her arms around his neck. Letting out a low, very male sound of satisfaction, he took the kiss deeper, rougher, stroking his tongue to hers. Leah welcomed him with a shocking eagerness that she'd have to hate herself for later because she had no room in her brain for anything but the erotic, sensual feel of him against her. In fact, the heat of him burned through her clothing. She didn't know who was moving—maybe it was both of them—but she found herself grinding against him, and then he thrust a muscled thigh between hers and she greedily rode it. She might have drowned in him then, but from behind them a door opened.

Tearing herself from Jack, Leah's breath came out in ragged pants as she whirled to the duplex.

Ben stood on his stoop in nothing but navy-blue boxers, looking big, bad, and rumpled. "What the hell?"

"Go back inside," Jack told him.

"And miss the show?"

"We're just…working something out."

Clearly in no hurry, Ben leaned against the doorjamb. "That kind of 'working something out' could get you arrested for indecent exposure."

Jack gave him a look that would have had Leah needing to check her pants, but not Ben.

"Fine," Ben said. "But you have a bedroom. You might want to think about using it before pictures of you two jumping each other's bones ends up on Facebook."

The door shut behind him, and Leah let out a shuddering breath. There was a hum of something coursing through her veins, a combination of things. Fear, which had been present ever since she'd heard the "firefighter down" go out on the scanner. Aching regret, for starting this whole mess in the first place. And lingering anger, which she suspected was really misplaced worry.

And something more.

Need.

For him.

Whatever Jack wanted to believe, she knew him. Maybe she knew him better than just about anyone else, in spite of all the years they'd spent apart.

He was unhappy. Oh, the stubborn ass would never admit it. Hell, he'd deny it, and this sparked her temper all over again because he was standing there stoic and edgy, the adrenaline still pouring off him in waves.

It made her want to hug him, which was just about as smart as wanting to hug a caged leopard. But that was Leah. Drawn to things that were bad for her. And Jack was bad for her, always had been. Not to her physical well-being, of course. Nothing as simple as that.

Nope, he was lethal to something else—her heart.

Shaking his head, muttering something about needing to be alone now, Jack headed to his garage. Inside was his lovingly restored Indian motorcycle. Shoving on his helmet, he straddled the beast.

And Leah's heart hitched. After his father had died, there'd been a period of time when Jack had gone feral. Wild. She'd always known when he'd been about to go off and do something stupid because there'd been a certain energy to him, the kind he had now. And oh, how that wild side of him appealed to her. Back then, she'd always begged and pleaded to be a part of that trouble.

He'd never let her, not once.

Looking back, she knew why. He'd been protecting her, in the only way he knew how. And he was still doing it. That's what the other night had been about, his "rules" about no hurt feelings.

In light of that, she had no explanation for the kiss he'd just laid on her, absolutely none. This was probably because her brain hadn't kicked back on yet. God knew her body was still trembling in hopeful anticipation.

The thing was, though, she no longer needed protection. She handled herself. And she could handle him too. She wanted to, especially because he had that look in his eyes, the one he got when he was especially tired or angry. It made him seem especially rough around the edges and wary, as if maybe he knew he couldn't count on his normally sharp senses to keep him functioning. She'd never say so, but she liked him best this way because it proved he wasn't a superhero at all, but just a man.

Either the fire had gotten to him more than he'd let on or he was worried about his mom. Maybe both. Hell, maybe it was her too. Clearly, he'd intended to get out, go a little crazy, blow off steam. But this time, she wasn't going to be sent home. Stepping close, she put a hand on his arm. "Take me with you."

"Hell no."

Refusing to be left behind, she simply stepped close and got on the bike behind him. She felt him exhale deeply, but before he could make her get off, she slid her arms around his waist and pressed her face to his back.

And that was absolutely the undoing of the last of her anger because even though he'd showered, he still smelled faintly like smoke, and the reminder of what he did every single day only made her want him all the more.

"Leah." Gruff. Pissed. His muscles flexed beneath her cheek but she held on, her palms flat against his abs. A wordless response rumbled in his chest—most likely an oath—and then he was reaching up and pulling off his helmet, which he handed back to her.

"No," she said. "I'm not taking your helmet—"

"Wear it or get off."

She knew how to pick her battles so she took off her baseball cap, grabbed the helmet, and pulled it down over her head.

"Hold on," he said.

And then the bike leaped to life beneath his very capable hands. So she did as he'd ordered.

She held on...

Chapter 13

♥

In five minutes, Leah and Jack were out on the highway, going fast enough to make her heart pound as they leaned into the S-turns.

Or maybe that was from being plastered up against his back, her legs spread by his hips, every inch of her in contact with his body.

And his body. Holy cow. How had she never been affected by how tough and built he was? Combined with the rumble of the horsepower beneath her, his body had her in a state that only got more and more pronounced the higher they climbed.

There was a cliff on their right now, where far below the Pacific Ocean pitched and rolled, fog lingering in long, silver fingers on the frothy water. The Olympic Mountains stood on their left, tall, majestic, rugged, and wearing their pretty fall colors.

Ahead of them, the road wound its narrow way upward, and Jack steered into the sharp curves. A sign warned them to keep a lookout for unexpected animal crossings. Out here, that could mean deer, bears, anything really. But nothing crossed their path at all, and Leah could feel some of the tension slowly leave Jack.

Half an hour later, the sun was much higher in the sky, and they were up near Beaut Point. A fitting place, as Jack had been the first person to ever bring her here.

She'd been in eighth grade, and the day had sucked. In the girls' locker room after PE, she'd realized someone had hidden her clothes. Standing there in nothing but her undies, the five mean girls who always made her life a living hell had surrounded her. She'd been tall even back then and had developed breasts early, which she'd hated, just two more ways in which she'd been different from everyone else. She could still feel the heat of embarrassment and shame standing there nearly naked as one of the girls had shoved her.

Leah'd gone down on her ass. Before she could scramble back up again, there'd been the sound of the door slamming open, and the girls had scattered.

And then a shirt had been tossed over her.

When she'd looked up, Jack had stood there, shirtless, scowling at her. "I've told you," he'd said. "Just hit one, any one of them, *hard*. One time is all you need."

The next time the girls had surrounded her in the locker room, she'd done just that.

And had gotten suspended for a week.

But the punishment from her father had been far worse. He'd yelled and screamed at her until her ears had been ringing. She'd dared to interrupt the tirade, attempting to tell him that this wasn't her fault, and he'd slapped her.

Later that next night when she'd crawled out of her bedroom window and into Jack's, he'd been waiting for her. They'd sneaked into his garage and "borrowed" his mom's car. They'd come here and then had climbed down to the mouth of the caves and sat watching the stars swirl in the sky far above.

It still ranked as the best night of her teenage years.

Now Jack stopped the bike so they were overlooking the ocean far below. He turned off the engine, and they sat there a moment, still. Not speaking.

Hell, Leah was hardly breathing.

Still locked around Jack like white on rice, she didn't want to break the spell. Right now, right here in this moment, she wasn't worried about her grandma. About money. About the bakery. About her future and what the hell she was going to screw up next. She wasn't worried about anything, in fact. She felt…safe. And maybe content.

Although maybe "content" wasn't quite right, since her entire body was humming with a sort of anticipation and heat that spoke of the very opposite of content.

She was aroused.

Not sure exactly what Jack was feeling, she started to get off the bike, but he took one of his hands from the handlebars and gently squeezed her fingers, where they were resting low on his abs. "We have a rule in place," he said.

Right. No one gets hurt because this wasn't real. "Then why did you kiss me like that? Like you wanted me so badly you couldn't help yourself?"

He didn't answer for a long moment. "I don't want to ruin our friendship," he said.

"We've managed to not ruin anything so far." She pulled off the helmet and set it behind her. "And we've done some pretty stupid stuff."

"Not yet, we haven't."

Her arms went around him again, flattening her hands on his abs, which clenched. Lightly, she let her fingers drift up and down. "I know you, Jack," she murmured. "I know what you need right now."

He let out a long breath when her hands drifted up high on his chest, and then low again, just to the loose waistband of his low-riding jeans.

"Aren't you even the slightest bit curious?" she wondered. "To see what it'd be like between us?"

He made a very male sound, one that told her he'd given it more than a passing thought.

"It'd make our lie to your mom half true," she said.

"*Our* lie?" he asked so dryly that she laughed.

"You know what I mean."

He caught her wandering fingers in his and brought their joined hands up to his mouth, brushing his lips against her knuckles. "I have another rule."

She dropped her head to his back and laughed again. "Mr. Control. Fine. What's this new rule?"

"No promises."

Her heart caught. Once, a long time ago, she'd made him that promise, and she'd broken it. She'd never let herself believe that it had really mattered to him, but she could admit that he had reason to doubt her. "I'm good with no promises."

"Yes," he said. "You are."

Ouch. "I have a rule too," she said evenly, pulling her hands back and sliding off the bike.

He cocked his head, waiting.

"If there are no promises, at least keep your...options from your mom."

"Options?"

"Yeah. I'm not going to go to all this trouble only to have the whole thing messed up by one of your blond bimbos."

She'd expected him to smile. He didn't. "Who?" he said instead. "Who are your options?"

She shivered at his commanding tone. Sexy, in a cave-man sort of way. "Maybe I have several."

He just leveled her with a narrow-eyed, steely stare and waited her out.

"Fine," she said, caving like a cheap suitcase. "I don't have any. Happy now?"

"I'm something, but happy isn't it." He studied her a moment longer, and she returned the favor. The exhaustion was shadowing his eyes. There was a rough, two-day growth on his square jaw and strain in those broad shoulders.

Drawn to him like a moth to the flame, she held out her hand to him. Without hesitation, he put his in hers, letting her pull him off the bike.

They climbed down to the caves and sat there, completely alone, watching the morning sun shimmer on the water three hundred feet below as it crashed into the rocky shore.

"Yes," he finally said, startling her.

"Yes what?"

Turning his head from the water, he looked at her, his eyes filled with enough heat to blow her hair back. "Oh," she breathed, and her nipples hardened. "You mean..."

Suddenly her mouth was dry, and all she could do was swallow hard. "Here?"

"You change your mind already? After all the convincing arguments and fact citing?"

No. Hell no, she hadn't changed her mind. This had been her idea, after all. Except...dammit. Some of that same old panic she'd felt that night long ago flooded her now.

Because this wasn't just any guy.

It was Jack, and expectations were at a lifetime high, at least for her. What if she didn't do it for him? What if she wasn't everything he needed? What if she screwed this up? "What if it doesn't work?" she whispered.

"What if what doesn't work?"

Not willing to let him see her fears, she went on the offensive. "Um...what if we don't turn each other on?"

He blinked, and she realized he was truly flummoxed by this question. Not getting turned on had never occurred to him. If this wasn't so deadly serious, she'd have laughed because he was such a guy.

"You get naked first," she decided.

"Why?"

Her heart was pounding, and her palms were slick with nerves, but she gave him a cool smile. "Well, what if you're ugly beneath all those clothes? I might have no choice but to rethink my options."

He narrowed his eyes again. "New rule."

"Oh my God. Now? You want to talk about your rules now? I don't want to discuss your other women right now, if you don't mind."

"No others," he said. "Not for me, and not for you. No options, period."

Her heart was at stroke level now. "So…an exclusive pretend relationship."

"That's right," he said, eyes surprisingly serious. "Tell me we have a deal, Leah."

This wasn't exactly a hardship for her, not that she was going to say so. "Deal."

He paused. "That felt too easy."

She smiled, trying to look innocent. Because he was getting off topic. And besides, they both knew he wasn't ugly beneath his clothes. He was perfect. Not wanting to lose control of this situation, she rose to her feet and pulled off her sweater.

He watched her, not moving a single, big muscle.

"Well?" she said.

"Well what?"

"Are you turned on?"

"Leah, I've been turned on since I kissed you over a week ago on the beach. But—"

"No. No more buts," she said quickly and kicked off the boots she'd gotten in Amsterdam, trying to look sexy while doing it.

Problem was, he still wasn't looking impressed, so she pulled off her tank top and then hesitated. She hadn't dressed for seduction, hadn't realized…and she was wearing a plain cotton, black sports bra that covered her more than a bathing suit would.

Worse, Jack didn't appear overcome with lust.

"Now you," she said desperately. "You have to lose something."

"But you're not finished." He leaned back on his elbows, all long, sprawled-out grace. The caged leopard at rest…

Good Lord. "Fine." She shoved off her jeans. Dammit.

To go with her sports bra, her panties were laundry day panties, faded yellow, and worse, they had "Thursday" printed across the butt.

It was Sunday.

Jack grinned.

"This isn't supposed to be funny." Mad, she bent over, reaching for her tank top, determined to get dressed again and somehow find her dignity while she was at it.

Somehow.

But Jack, moving silent and fast as a wild cat would have, stepped up behind her.

"Forget it, Jack—"

"Shh." With his big body snug at her back, his hands went to her hips, holding her in place.

She froze, thinking he'd heard or seen someone—but he didn't move. "What are you doing?" she hissed.

"I like this position."

Straightening up, she tried to push free, but he held her still, his hands sliding up from her hips to her breasts, his quick, clever thumbs rasping over her nipples. "And this one," he said low and husky. "I really like this position too."

He was hard—she could feel him pressing into her— and that went a long way toward soothing her bruised ego. Turning in the circle of his arms, she faced him so her breasts smashed into his chest.

"And this one," he murmured, his hands sliding down to cup and squeeze her ass.

The rest of her embarrassment and anger dissolved, and she felt a reluctant smile curve her mouth. "I'm getting the idea you like all the positions."

"Every single one," he assured her.

Chapter 14

♥

Around them, the day went on. Insects buzzed. The sun warmed. The wind, what there was of it, stayed outside the cave rustling only the very tips of the two-hundred-foot-tall pines surrounding them. The sounds were as familiar to Leah as her own breathing and brought comfort.

The man in front of her had always brought comfort too. But now, in this moment, he brought something entirely different.

Holding her gaze, Jack stroked a strand of hair off her forehead. "Still with me?"

"Yes," she said with far more confidence than she really felt.

Seeing right through her, he smiled. "We're going to do this, Leah," he said calmly. "We're going to take one for the team."

Oh God. *Yes.* It was what she wanted, desperately. But...had she coerced him into it? Into wanting her?

Of course she had.

If only she wasn't standing there in her plain cotton underwear. The *least* she could've done was arm herself with something really silky and lacy. No, wait. Armor. Yeah, armor would have been perfect. Something to protect her heart—

"I want you, Leah."

Some of her doubt must have still been visible because he cupped her jaw and met her gaze. "I want you," he repeated softly, his fingers sliding into her hair.

The words and his voice melted her. It was just that simple for him, she realized, as he stared her down, letting her see the hunger in his gaze. It'd been a long time since he'd looked at her like that. She'd have liked to savor it, but she couldn't resist the promise in every line of his body.

"You want me too," he said. "Bad."

She held the eye contact, trying to outlast him, but she was losing the battle and he knew it. His slow smile said so.

Yeah. She wanted him.

Bad.

He was looking at her with the absolute confidence he always seemed to carry. It might have been infuriating if she had room for anything but the need. The desperate need. But… "Here?" She looked around them. "Now?" The cave was secluded, and the area around it completely deserted. Their only company was the sun slanting through the trees, dappling the forest floor with dotted patches of shade. There were a few bees and other various insects, and hopefully no bears, but…

"Here," Jack said. "Now." He backed her to a huge, ancient wall of rock, trapping her there with a hand on either side of her face. "This was your idea," he reminded her. "And, as it turns out, a really good one." Showing none of his earlier resistance and certainly no mercy, he pressed into her, caressing her body with big, sure hands. "You're wet," he murmured with a hint of naughty accusation as his hand moved between her thighs.

"It's from when I was thinking about my options," she said.

He slid her a look as he let a finger stroke over her slowly. Purposefully. "Is that right?"

"A-absolutely."

"So it's not for me at all, is that what you're saying?" One of his long, callused fingers played with the edge of her panties, and she couldn't breathe for the need.

"N-nope," she managed.

"Liar." Then he laughed softly. Cocky. The bastard. His hand continued its wonderful torture, and she strained closer for more.

He'd never touched her like this before, never, and yet her body quivered as if it were recognizing a long-lost lover's touch. And far before it seemed possible, he had her writhing against him, breathing unevenly and desperate. "How," she managed, unable to get the rest out. *How did he know how to drive her crazy?*

He trailed his mouth along her jawline to her ear. "You're good at hiding," he murmured, his voice low and serious, no trace of teasing in it now as he lightly ran the pad of his finger just beneath her panties.

So close to where she needed him.

And yet so far...

"But your eyes," he went on. "They don't hide a thing, not from me. Neither does your body."

Had anyone ever known her so well? It was both a terror that he did, and a relief. She could let go, forget, forget everything but this. Her hands fisted in his hair and pulled until his mouth was a breath from hers. "Now," she said, hearing the desperation in her voice. "You said *now*." She pushed his shirt up his chest. It was a glorious chest, and her mouth watered with the need to lick him from sternum to his low-riding jeans waistband.

He took over before she could, tugging his shirt off over his head in that one smooth motion that guys always make look so easy, and her breath caught. He was all smooth, hard muscle, in perfect proportion.

He tossed the shirt behind him and reached for her. She pulled him in, a little clumsy and a lot eager, kissing him with all the pent-up frustration that the uncertainty and anxiety of being back in Lucky Harbor had brought. She opened for him, pressing closer, harder, kissing him with everything she had.

He let her be the aggressor a moment, stroking her back, her hips, teasing her by slowly stroking his fingers lightly down her ribs and stomach, the rough pads of his fingers drawing goose bumps to her skin. Grasping her bra, she began to tug it over her head, but he took control then too, pushing her hands away to do the job himself.

She watched his eyes as he tossed her bra the same way he'd tossed his shirt, watched as he stroked her bare breasts with one hand, the other sliding beneath her panties. She moaned at the contact, which made him let out a very male sound of pleasure.

Then he dropped to his knees in front of her and dragged her panties down her legs, leaving her completely exposed to his hot gaze.

"Jack," she murmured.

He scraped his teeth gently across her hip bones before moving lower. "Too late to run," he said, and stroked his fingers over her until she trembled. Then he leaned in and put his mouth on her.

Her fingers tangled in his silky hair as he took her, not with the same untamed ferocity that she'd kissed him with, but a doggedly patient precision that told her how much her pleasure meant to him. He found her rhythm with shocking ease and settled in, and suddenly the game was no longer a game at all, but something much more personal.

And satisfying.

When she came and her legs collapsed, he caught her.

"Now you," she managed. "Take off your pants." Without waiting for him, she tried to do it herself.

"Easy," he murmured, his large hands brushing hers aside to free himself.

Her breath caught again. She couldn't help it; he was so perfectly, beautifully made. "I don't have a condom," she breathed, disappointment a physical ache.

He pulled one from his wallet and she nearly whimpered in relief. Spreading his shirt on the ground, he lowered her onto it, following her down, moving over her, running hot, open-mouthed kisses over her body until she could have instantly combusted. "Jack."

He slid nine inches of perfection inside of her, and she did combust then, crying out, rocking into him as she came again. "Oh my God," she managed. "Did you feel that?"

"Leah, you're all I feel."

Undone by him, wanting to drive him as crazy as he'd

driven her, she lifted her hips so he could sink in even deeper.

He groaned. "Do that again."

When she did, he dropped his head back, throat and shoulders corded tight, pleasure etched in every line of his face. "Oh fuck, yeah." With surprising gentleness, he fisted his hand in her hair and tugged so she was looking directly into his eyes, which had gone dark with passion.

Her body throbbed, and unbelievably, the heat started to build within her again. "Jack."

He answered by thrusting into her hard and lowering his mouth to hers. "Right here."

Her nails dug into his skin as he moved; she couldn't help it. And staring into his eyes, she let him drive her right over the edge. Again. This time she wasn't alone; they came together with shuddering impact. It was the single most erotic, intimate moment they'd ever shared.

She came back to herself slowly, realizing she was plastered all over him. The sun was shining into the cave as Jack pulled her in closer, nuzzling at her temple, apparently perfectly content to lay with her in the morning sun.

He didn't move or speak. But after a while she was afraid she might be coming off as too clingy, so she tried to separate herself, but he tightened his grip.

"Not yet," he murmured.

Leah dropped her head to his shoulder and tried not to put too much into the fact that having sex with Jack had been better than every other experience of her life.

Combined.

Jack spent the rest of the day with Ronald going over the open fire reports.

Actually, that wasn't true. He spent the day lost in fantasies involving a naked Leah on a mountaintop...

But in between replaying that over and over in his head, he managed to do some work. In the afternoon, the station got a call saying a woman was reporting that she had a garter snake in her house, and they needed to come get it out. Jack, as the head of station, told dispatch to tell her that unless it was an emergency, they didn't remove snakes from homes. He referred her to animal control. He hung up and met Ronald's wide grin. "What?"

"You turned away a damsel in distress."

"Animal control handles snakes."

Ronald just kept grinning.

"It's their job."

"Uh-huh," Ronald said, sounding hugely amused. "Or...you hate snakes."

Jack rolled his shoulders because he would swear he could feel a snake crawling over him right now. It'd been twenty-something years since it'd happened but it still made him shudder. "Me hating snakes has nothing to do with it."

"I remember your dad telling me a story about a garden snake that got into your bedroom. It crawled through your bedroom window and dropped into your bed. You woke up with it on you. After that, you slept in your parents' bed for a month."

"I was seven."

Ronald just cracked up.

Two minutes later, another call came in, direct to Ronald's line, which he answered on speaker.

It was the mayor. "Listen, I need you to do me a favor. My neighbor is calling me at the office. She's got this snake in her house, and I can't get away to go help her out."

Ronald was still grinning widely when he looked at Jack as he answered. "She called you about a snake?"

The mayor blew out a breath. "Listen, she's new. She's hot. And I'd like to date her. I can't get away from the office, and animal control put her on hold. Can you go get the fucking snake or not?"

"I'll send someone to save your future sex life," Ronald said, and disconnected. He tossed Jack his keys. "Go get 'em, Tiger."

Jack grabbed Ian, the only other guy he knew of who was also terrified of snakes. Misery loves company and all that... They dressed in their bunker gear, with Ian bitching the whole way that Jack owed him big.

The woman looked shocked to see them in full gear but led them down the hallway to her bedroom.

Jack stood in the doorway, sweating like a whore in church. Ian pushed him into the room, where they began their search. Ian went to the closet. Jack swallowed hard and dropped to his knees to look beneath the bed.

And hell. There it was. A two-foot-long, harmless garter snake that was taking years off Jack's life just looking at him. Jack jerked back and fell to his ass.

Ian stared at the bed like it was a bomb. "It's under there?"

Jack could only nod.

Ian gulped, appearing frozen in place.

The woman's voice came from down the hall. "Did you find it?"

"Yes, ma'am," Ian said, his voice sounding like Mickey Mouse. He grimaced and cleared his throat.

Jack found his legs and went out to the engine, where he grabbed a pike pole. He shoved it at Ian, who shook his head adamantly. "You're head of shift," he said.

Jack considered using the pike pole on Ian's head, but there'd be a lot of paperwork afterward, so he resisted. And then, holding his breath, he went back to his knees and peered beneath the bed.

The snake was looking right at him with those obsidian eyes. Slowly Jack reached in there with the pike pole and snagged the motherfucker. Shaking like a leaf, he walked it outside.

The snake slithered off into the bushes and vanished.

And Jack had to lock his knees and gulp in air. Christ. He needed a new job.

Ian came out of the house, looking fully restored back to his good humor as he clapped his hand on Jack's shoulder. "We did good," he said.

Jack slid him a look. "We?"

"Hey, I had your back, man. If you'd dropped him, I'd have snatched him up for you."

"If I'd dropped him, you'd have shit your pants."

Ian grinned. "Well, now we'll never know."

At the station, Jack went back to the reports. He had the convenience store fire and auto shop fire reports side by side. Ronald wasn't convinced either was arson, but Jack couldn't get past the feeling that both points of origin had been buckets of rags, accidentally ignited. It just all felt far too pat, too convenient, and Jack didn't believe in coincidences.

Nor could he buy the vagrant's story of a Santa on crack theory, though that seemed more solid than the vagrant himself setting the fires since he'd been at the homeless shelter on the night of the auto shop fire.

And then Jack discovered something they hadn't known—the auto-parts store had been in escrow too. To a Mr. Rinaldi, the same man in escrow to buy the convenience store. Jack ran a search on him. The guy had a squeaky-clean record and a well-documented history of cleaning up and turning around downtrodden areas.

It didn't make sense. Not a lick of it made any sense at all.

That night, Leah made dinner for her grandma and was so distracted she burned the chicken and undercooked the rice.

Elsie, always a good sport, still ate everything with her usual gusto.

"Sorry," Leah said. "I can't believe I failed dinner so badly."

"I can." Elsie smiled. "Your mind is somewhere else."

This was very true, but she didn't want to go there. "I need to head into Seattle this week. I want to hit up that new restaurant supply warehouse. I need to borrow a truck."

"Ask Jack," Elsie said slyly. "I'm sure he'd take you wherever you wanted to go."

He'd taken her to heaven just that morning, not that she'd tell him so. His ego didn't need the boost.

"So what did you do today?" Elsie asked. "It's rare for you to take a day off. You left early and were gone until past noon."

Jack. She'd done Jack.

With effort, Leah pushed the tactile memory of his big,

warm, strong body wrapped around hers out of her head. "Nothing much."

"Really? You didn't see anyone exciting?"

"In Lucky Harbor?" She forced a laugh. "Who would that be?"

"Jack."

Leah's pulse skipped a beat. "Why would you think that I was with Jack?"

"Other than the two of you are dating?" Elsie asked, sounding amused. "Because someone saw you with him."

Leah dropped her fork and rice splattered everywhere as her heart kicked into gear. "Saw us? Where?"

"On Highway 219, on his bike."

"Oh." Feeling foolish, she relaxed. On the highway. On his bike. Good. That was really good. No one had caught them, exhibition-style, at the caves.

"That Jack," Elsie said. "He sure grew up nice, didn't he?"

Leah flashed to how he'd felt moving over her, his broad shoulders blocking out the sun, his voice a whisper against her ear, the fierce look in his eyes as he slowly, purposely took control and drove her right out of her ever-loving mind... "Yes," she said a little weakly. "He grew up real nice."

"And he's so responsible. He runs that entire station, and he uses his position to give back to the community. Last month, he came over and taught all us seniors how to do CPR. Of course that was right after Edward had his heart scare, which turned out to be a bad case of gas. But Jack made sure each and every one of us could revive someone if need be. So sweet."

"Sweet," Leah agreed. He did have his moments...

"And the town sure is talking about you two. Everyone's all aflutter that yet another of our eligible bachelors has been taken off the market."

Leah swallowed wrong and choked.

Elsie brought her a glass of water and smiled. "And you've made Dee so happy."

Leah caught her breath and sobered as guilt stabbed through her. "Yes."

Elsie's eyes were knowing as she squeezed Leah's hands. "You're sweet too," she said quietly.

Leah opened her mouth and then shut it again, not sure what to say. That she'd lied about being in a relationship with Jack? Or that she wasn't all that sorry to be pretending…?

Neither was something she wanted to discuss.

Elsie poured them each a second glass of wine, then lifted her glass to Leah. "To whatever Jack did to distract you so."

"Grandma."

"What? I'm old, not dead. And I haven't seen you look so dreamy-eyed since…well, ever."

"I'm not…dreamy-eyed."

Though she'd gone to the store for condoms…

"Honey," Elsie said slowly. "About the bakery."

"What about it?"

"I'm not sure how long I'm going to keep it going after you leave."

Leah set down her fork so she didn't drop it again. The bakery had been her grandma's first love for…well, for as long as she could remember. It wasn't just a shop, it was her grandma's identity. Warm apple pies and fresh sourdough bread and chocolate chip cookies. Hopes and dreams. Comfort. Leah couldn't even remember a time when Elsie hadn't smelled like vanilla or cinnamon. Oh God, she thought, her gut tight. Maybe her grandma was sick? "What do you mean? Are you okay?"

Elsie smiled. "Don't look at me like that. I'm fine. I'm more than fine. I'm actually...enjoying the time off. I'm old, honey."

"No—"

"I am. And I'm tired. And watching how hard you're working to keep my business going is making me more tired. You understand, don't you?"

"Of course," she said. "Maybe I could stay and help—"

"No. No way." Her grandma adamantly shook her head. "You're destined for bigger things, Leah. Way bigger things. *Sweet Wars* will be over soon enough."

Leah couldn't stop thinking about that as she helped her grandma to bed. How had the season of *Sweet Wars* gone so fast? She'd planned to be gone before the finals aired, and yet she was still here. More unsettling, how could she go? And when she did, what would it be like to come back to Lucky Harbor the next time and have there be no Grandma Elsie's bakery?

She couldn't imagine.

She watched some old movies on the couch. She must have drifted off because a sound startled her awake.

Elsie stood by the front door in bright-white tennis shoes, her favorite dress, and her purse clutched to her chest. "Oh," she said in surprise when Leah sat up. "Oh, honey. You startled me."

"Grandma? What are you doing?"

Elsie smiled. "Well, I thought I'd just go get us a paper."

Leah looked at the clock. "It's the middle of the night."

"Coffee. We need coffee for the morning."

Leah blinked the last of the sleep from her eyes and stood up. "I'll get it."

"Oh no, I can do it. I don't want you to have to get dressed, or—"

"Or know that you were sneaking out?" Leah asked.

Elsie grimaced. "What clued you in?"

"Well, you're about as clandestine as a bull in a china shop."

There'd been a few crazy teenage years when Leah had done her fair share of sneaking out. Her dad had always kept an extremely tight leash on her, so tight that she'd lived in perpetual danger of strangulation. It'd been painful. Beyond painful. She'd had to do all her homework immediately after school, then show it to him. And if she'd gotten anything wrong, he'd rip it up and she'd have to start over. "You can't get anything right," he'd snap. "Do it again. Do it perfect or don't bother at all." After homework, she had to put in three hours minimum at his dental office, helping with the filing and housekeeping, or whatever was needed.

That had been the worst part.

Spending time with him. She'd never been able to do anything right, and her self-esteem had suffered. This had all been made worse by the fact that she'd not really fit in at school either. She'd never been the girlie-girl, or the athlete, or particularly social, and then there'd been her ruthless 9:00 p.m. curfew, no exceptions.

So she'd sneaked out.

A lot.

She'd sneak out to walk the beach alone. Or go to

Jack's. But if the water was rough and Jack was out somewhere with Ben raising trouble, she'd gone to her grandma's.

Elsie had always seemed to expect her. She'd greet Leah with a warm hug and then they'd go into the kitchen and bake something. Elsie always let Leah take the lead there, allowing her come up with whatever concoction she wanted, no matter how crazy it sounded.

It'd soothed Leah's aching heart and fueled her creative soul. There'd been no recriminations, no judging, and blessedly, no yelling. Elsie had never questioned her need to run away, had never so much as hinted at the worry she surely must have felt knowing that Leah had walked two miles in the dark to get to her.

And now it was Leah's turn to swallow *her* urge to ask the questions, to express the worry, and there was a lot of both. What the hell was her grandma planning to do out there in the middle of the night? "What if your knee gives out?" Leah asked her. "What if you get tired?"

"Well goodness, honey, I'm not that old."

"Of course not," Leah said. "But it's not safe."

"I've got my smartphone and a backup battery, along with my tablet and a can of hairspray. If anyone comes at me, all I have to do is swing my purse at them and I'll knock the perp right on his ass." She demonstrated by giving her purse a broad swing and knocked the lamp off the foyer table. "See?" she asked.

Leah picked up the lamp and righted it. Elsie was the most calm, rational, logical person in her life. In fact, Leah had counted on that calm, rational logic more times than she could count.

But this didn't seem calm or rational. Could it be the

start of dementia? Alzheimer's? Is that why Elsie had mentioned giving up the bakery? Leah's heart clutched at the thought of losing the most important person in the world to her. "Where do you really need to go? I'll take you."

Elsie sighed. "I really thought you'd be sleeping."

This was not an answer and didn't assuage Leah's worry in the slightest. "Okay, what's going on?"

"I didn't want to tell you, but I...have a date."

Leah just stared at her. Years ago, her grandma had been married for only a short time before her husband had died of lung cancer, leaving Elsie pregnant and alone. She'd never remarried. Nor, as far as Leah knew—and despite Elsie's claims to having had a "wild streak"—had she appeared to ever date. "A date," she repeated.

Elsie smiled. "I know. Hard to believe, right?"

"No," Leah said, shaking her head. "You're fun, and sweet, and smart. And pretty."

Elsie laughed now, the sound light and musical. She was pleased. "Oh, aren't you the one. And the same goes. Leah…" Her smile was warm. Caring. And utterly without judgment. "I'm fine. My life is exactly what I want it to be. Can you believe that?"

"Well…sure."

"Can you say the same about *your* life?"

Leah opened her mouth and then closed it.

Elsie gently patted Leah's cheeks. "Don't *ever* wait around for your life. Go get what you want. Because believe me, no one's going to give it to you. You should know that by now." She moved to the door. "Don't wait up, honey."

And then she was gone.

Leah watched out the front window as Elsie got into her car and drove off.

"What the hell just happened?" she asked the quiet living room. But she already knew. Her grandma had proven that she had better social life than Leah did.

Chapter 15

♥

It's your day off," Ronald said the next day when Jack walked into his office. "What the hell are you doing here?"

"You get anything back from forensics on the convenience store or auto shop fires?"

Ronald studied Jack for a long beat. "Not yet. Why?"

"I've been thinking."

"Uh-huh. With head number two, I hear. You've caught yourself a girl."

Jack didn't bother to sigh. "Whatever you've heard, it's greatly exaggerated."

"Well, that's a damn shame," Ronald said. "I was hoping it was true." He paused. "Your daddy wouldn't have wanted you to be the job, Jack. And you are. You're working full-time firefighting and taking up the slack for me."

"About the forensics—"

"Saw your baseball game, you know." Ronald leaned

back, hands behind his head, sighing with pleasure as he put his feet up. "You sucked ass."

"I had an off week. Listen, about the—"

"You couldn't hit worth shit. And you lost that fly ball. I've never seen you choke like that before."

Jack leaned forward and thunked his head on Ronald's desk.

Ronald laughed. "Son, go home. Go take that girl of yours out. Have some fun."

Fun. If fun was having Leah beneath him, panting out his name in that breathy way she had of making him feel superhuman, then yeah. He could use some more fun. He lifted his head. "In the report for the convenience store, we recorded that footprint in the mud along the west wall. Men's size thirteen. Sneaker."

"Yes. The one the vagrant claimed was his."

Jack opened his mouth, but Ronald cut in. "I know, he was barefoot when we found him, but he admitted that he'd been wearing sneakers earlier, remember? He'd gotten hot and kicked them off."

"We never located the shoes," Jack said, knowing if they matched that print to the actual footwear the vagrant had been wearing, he was as good as sunk in court. But it wasn't the right direction. Jack could feel it. "You were working on the tread to name the brand. Did you get that?"

Ronald frowned. "Not yet. I had it sent out. That could take a few weeks. We don't have it on urgent, since we're not sure we have arson here."

"A size thirteen isn't a standard size," Jack mused.

"No."

"And the vagrant's foot is size ten."

Ronald was already shaking his head. "You know as well as I do that he doesn't have his own shoes. He wears whatever he took out of someone's trash or what someone gave him. He claimed to not remember where he'd left the shoes."

"Did you ask him if they were too big for him?"

Annoyance crossed Ronald's face. "Before or after he said he saw Santa on the roof smoking crack, Jack? We both know those shoes weren't his. The question is, was there an arsonist and was the print his?"

"The print showed heavy tread loss," Jack said. "Especially on the outside of the shoe."

"Yeah? So our guy is a runner. So what?"

"So that's also an unusual wear. It's a guy who doesn't roll his ankles inward enough, tending to stride on the ground with the outside edge of his feet. Walking or running on the outside of the foot like that puts a lot of pressure on the legs. Possibly causing shin splints or stress fractures."

"So we're looking for a big-footed runner with a shin splint or stress fracture. Perfect. That narrows it down."

"It's a start." Jack moved to the door, then looked back. "We didn't find any prints at the auto shop fire."

"Not size thirteen, no. And nothing to lead to a perp. Just the bucket of rags."

Jack stood up. "I'm going back to the convenience store site. Check the grounds with a fine-toothed comb."

"You're off duty."

"I have the time."

Ronald took off his glasses and swiped at them with the hem of his shirt. "How's your mom?"

"Better. A lot better," Jack said.

"I asked her out. She tell you that?"

Jack sat back down. "No."

"She said she wasn't ready," Ronald said.

"It's been twenty years."

"Maybe you could put in a good word for me," Ronald said. "Tell her I have a lot more time these days because there's some big, fancy hotshot on my heels, trying to take over my job."

Jack rolled his eyes and strode out the door.

A few nights later, Jack watched the next episode of *Sweet Wars*. The challenge was to create a tart. Jack found himself soaking up the sight of Leah working on a rum sponge tart, once again working calmly and efficiently while everyone else was 'running around like chickens with their heads cut off.

"How's she doing?" Ben asked, letting himself in and plopping onto the couch next to Kevin, who immediately crawled into his lap.

"You're looking right at her," Jack said.

"I mean here. In Lucky Harbor." Ben had brought another bag of popcorn and smelled like a movie theater. "With her boyfriend."

"You know it's not real. And if you plan to feed that shit to Kevin, you walk him. The last time you gave him popcorn, it required three doggie bags."

Ben tossed Kevin a kernel just to be an asshole. "Not real, huh? I guess that's why you bought condoms."

Jack slid him a look.

"Your receipt's right here, man." Ben nudged the piece of paper on the coffee table with his foot. "A twelve pack, which is either a really impressive one-night stand, or you're thinking long term." He cocked his head and squinted to read that far. "Yep, twelve extra-large condoms *For Her Pleasure*. Aw, that's real considerate."

Jack rolled his eyes and went back to the show.

"So which is it?" Ben asked.

"What?"

"An impressive one-night stand or long term?"

"Shut up."

"Long term," Ben decided. "Quite a commitment, a twelve pack…"

Jack snatched the popcorn and shoved some into his mouth, his gaze on Leah. Which did he want? Hell, all he knew for sure was that he craved her. She was easy on the eyes. And easy to hang out with. She was smart and funny and kind, and he never got tired of being with her.

This thought brought him up a little since it was entirely different from any thought he'd ever had about a woman. But it was true. When he wasn't with Leah, he thought about being with her again. And when something cracked him up or made him think, or *anything* really, he wanted to tell her about it.

Like now. On screen, she was talking, smiling, and kicking ass. No one on the cast came even close to her easy talent. And he wanted to tell her so.

"See that?" Ben asked, pointing to the screen. "That host guy—the one who dated that hot chick from *Big Brother* last year—he's into Leah big time. You notice?"

Jack watched as Rafe Vogel kept finding excuses to end up at Leah's station, twice bumping up against her.

Leah didn't seem to mind all that much, smiling up at him, laughing into the camera while everyone around her was sniping and yelling at each other as the clock counted down.

"You think Leah's two-timing her fake boyfriend?" Ben asked casually.

Jack slid him a look. "Why are you here?"

Ben grinned and grabbed back the popcorn. "You have the bigger TV."

The next morning, Jack got up at the crack of dawn and nudged Kevin. "Let's go."

Kevin did his imitation of a dead dog.

"We're running to the station, dude. Gotta work off all the shit we ate last night."

Kevin squeezed his eyes shut tighter, and Jack shook his head. "If you stay here, I'm going to let the little girls next door dress you up like their pony again."

Kevin opened a single eye and assessed Jack for his level of seriousness. With a loud sigh, he lumbered out the door with Jack.

Kevin wasn't a great running partner. In fact, he was a downright horrible running partner, trotting along at best, stopping to smell every flower, rock, and imaginary foe between home and work. Halfway, he was nearly unmanned by a cat that popped out of the bushes and snarled at him. Kevin, always a lover, not a fighter, tried licking the cat's face, which earned him a bitch-slap. Bewildered and hurt, he ducked behind Jack, where he stayed until they got to the station.

There, Jack grabbed the first hot shower of the day. The first guy to shower always made out because the building's plumbing was cranky. If you didn't get the first shower, you weren't guaranteed hot water. They were a family at the station, and they did as family did—they bugged the shit out of each other. Normally, it was acceptable for the first one up to use as much of the hot water as possible, just because. But today Jack hurried, dressed, and then grabbed the keys to the supervisory unit, heading out the door only to bump into Tim, who'd clearly just come in from his own run. In shorts and a damp T-shirt, he reached for keys as well. "Hey," he said with a nod to Jack. "Going for donuts."

They typically took turns going to the bakery every morning, grabbing a box of whatever Leah had fresh, and bringing it back for the other guys. And it was definitely Tim's turn.

But Jack didn't want Tim to go to the bakery. *Jack* wanted to go to the bakery. He'd told Leah that nothing would change between them, but that'd been before they'd had the hottest sex of his life up on a mountaintop.

Now he wasn't so sure that *everything* hadn't changed. Because now he knew how she kissed, how she tasted...the sexy little sounds she made when she came. "I'm going to get the donuts," he said.

"It's my turn," Tim said.

"No, it's not."

"Yeah, don't you remember? Sam went last time and—"

"I got it," Jack said.

Tim stared at him, then let out a slow smile. "Right. Because you and Leah are a thing. You see the show last night? Her and that Rafe guy? Some serious chemistry there."

"The show was filmed six months ago."

"So they're not together?"

Jack headed to the door. "Let it go."

"I don't know, man. Maybe you've been dumped and you don't even know it."

"Tim?"

"Let me guess. The senior center?" But Tim was cracking his ass up as Jack slammed the door and stalked to the truck. An idiot. He was a fucking idiot.

And he didn't mean Tim.

Chapter 16

♥

Jack tied Kevin's leash to the bench in front of the bakery. "Stay."

Kevin immediately hopped up onto the bench like he owned the thing.

"Down," Jack said.

Kevin indeed went down. He laid down, across the entire bench.

Since there was no one else around, Jack shook his head and walked into the bakery. The bell above the door tinkled, and the usual delicious scents assaulted his nose. Vanilla, sugar, cinnamon, and a hundred others that made his mouth water and his brain go straight to Leah.

And his other body parts as well.

Like Pavlov's dog, he thought, with a shake of his head.

There were people seated at the tables, and a few more at the counter still eyeing their selections, among them Lucille and Mrs. Burland. Mrs. B had been Jack's second-grade teacher, and he still twitched whenever she gazed at him with those hawklike eyes that saw everything.

Leah came out from the back carrying a huge tray. She was wearing two tank tops layered over each other, a short denim skirt, and high-heeled ankle boots that had a bunch of cutouts in them and were so damn sexy it made it difficult to put a thought together. Her arms were tanned and toned, carrying her burden with ease as she bent and began reloading the shelves of her glass-front display.

She served a couple of customers before glancing his way. Lucille and Mrs. B were down at the other end of the counter, and Jack scrambled for something clever to say but the only thing he could think of wasn't clever at all.

He wanted to ask about the "fuck me" shoes.

Instead, he kept his mouth shut. Or he tried. He blamed his caffeine-deprived brain. "Nice shoes."

He heard Lucille chuckle, but when he glanced at her, she was busy looking at donuts.

"What's this new thing you have about my shoes?" Leah asked.

"I don't know." But he wanted to see her in those boots and nothing else. He leaned over the counter and caught a whiff of whatever she'd washed her hair with. Something with coconut, which made him hungry and not for food. "You smell good too."

"You're in a bakery," she said dryly. "Everything smells good."

He was a little stymied by her tone, but before he could ask her about it, someone tapped him on the arm. Turning, he looked down at all four feet of Mrs. Burland.

"Hey, you hoodlum, no cuts."

There'd been a time when her voice had struck terror

in his heart. And he supposed that if she was still judging his character on his "little hoodlum" eight-year-old self, the one who'd painted her desk chair with superglue and let the hamsters free in the ventilation system, then she had good reason to call him a hoodlum.

"He's not a hoodlum," Lucille said.

"Really?" Mrs. B asked snidely. "I take it he didn't rearrange your Christmas reindeer lawn ornaments every year so they were…copulating."

Lucille fought a grin and lost. "No, he didn't."

Jack sighed, gestured Mrs. B ahead of him, and waited while she curtly snapped her order at Leah.

"And make sure the cannoli is vanilla," Mrs. Burland told her. "You don't make good chocolate cannoli."

"Yes she does," Jack said.

Mrs. Burland turned an eagle eye on him. "She's already yours, Harper. No one likes a kiss-ass."

"I'm not *his*," Leah said. "I'm my own woman." She thrust a bag of baklava at Mrs. Burland. "It's made with phyllo dough, which is much lower in fat than the cannoli."

"I want cannoli. I am paying you for the cannoli." Mrs. Burland waved a few bills.

Leah pushed them away. "And Dr. Scott paid me to give you something low-cholesterol instead."

Mrs. Burland snatched the baklava and huffed off.

Leah turned to Lucille, who smiled. "Jack can go first," she said.

Leah gave Lucille a look. "So you can eavesdrop?"

Lucille grinned. "Well, of course. But also the good men don't wait around. You don't know that yet because you're still a spring chicken."

"You're not worried about him waiting around for me," Leah said. "You want your daily dose of gossip."

Lucille had the good grace to look slightly guilty. "People like to know what's going on, that's all."

"What's going on," Leah said, "is that you're both holding up my line."

Both Lucille and Jack turned and looked behind them. There was no one else in line.

Lucille looked up at Jack. "Seriously," she said. "You can go first."

"Seriously," he said. "No thank you."

"Because you and Leah have to talk?" Lucille asked hopefully.

"If I say yes, will you get the hell out?"

"Jack," Leah said admonishingly.

Lucille didn't seem bothered in the slightest. She pointed to a coffee éclair. "Anyone ever mention that those look like a one of them toys you can buy at the dirty stores? What are they called, dildos?"

Jack laughed, but Leah looked horrified. "Lucille!"

"Hey, this is the modern ages, honey," Lucille said. "Women don't have to hide the fact that they buy devices for themselves. After all, that's what a nightstand drawer is for, right?"

Jack didn't want to know what Lucille kept in her nightstand drawer, but the thought of looking in Leah's was giving him a whole bunch of fantasies.

Leah packed up a bag and thrust it at her.

Lucille just grinned. "You're my favorite," she said to Jack.

"Favorite?" Jack asked.

"Yeah, you've got some competition, you know." At

Jack's expression, she laughed. "So you *don't* know…"

Jack looked at Leah. "That host guy?"

Leah blinked. "Who?"

"I noticed that too," Lucille said. "The whole town noticed. What?" she said at Jack's long look. "We gather to watch it at the bar. Anyway, that's not what I'm talking about."

"Lucille," Leah said, "I think your phone is ringing."

"Oh, I don't have my phone on me." She looked at Jack. "And you. You have no one to blame but yourself. You haven't put a ring on it, so she's got some real good options."

"Lucille," Leah said again, more tightly. "How much do you like my pastries?"

"More than George Clooney's sexy tushie."

"Then you'll stop talking now," Leah said.

"Honey, a man should know what he's up against." With that, she patted Jack's arm and left.

Jack met Leah's gaze.

"I'm sorry," she said.

"No worries. I can't think past wondering what's in your nightstand drawer anyway."

"You're bad."

"So bad I'm torn between begging you to let me watch you use whatever you have in there or offering my services to replace it."

She went pink as Lucille poked her head back into the bakery. "Oh, and don't forget about the Facebook poll, Jack. You might want to round yourself up some votes. Tim's out in front right now, with Ben right behind him."

Jack looked at Leah, but she was suddenly very busy wiping down counters. "A poll," he said.

"Honestly, don't you ever go online?" Lucille shook her head. "You young people." She vanished again.

Without a word, Leah began loading up a box for the fire station. She closed the box and handed it over. "I added a few old-fashioned glazed donuts for Tim. I was out of them the other day, and he had to help me change some fuses and said I owe him."

"Tim's on your list of options?"

"Not *my* list," Leah said. "Facebook."

"And Ben's on it too."

"Apparently."

"And I'm…third."

"Actually, I think you're fifth," she said. "Someone put Rafe on there."

"Rafe."

Leah shrugged.

Jack wasn't actually worried that she was involved in something with Rafe. Six months was a long time, and long-distance relationships weren't Leah's strong suit. Plus, one of the very best things about her was how loyal she was, to her very core. If she'd had something going on with anyone else, she wouldn't have slept with him. Logically, Jack knew this. But he wasn't feeling all that logical at the moment. "Where would *you* put me on the list?" he asked softly.

"Does it matter?" She met his gaze, her own suddenly hooded. "No promises, remember? And this is just pretend."

Well, hell. He'd walked right into that one. Reaching over the counter, Jack settled a hand on her wrist.

Quicker than he, she pulled free. Then she vanished into the kitchen.

He looked around. No one was paying them any mind at all. Outside on the bench, he could see Kevin, sitting in Mr. Lyons's lap now. Since Mr. Lyons had his bony arm wrapped around the huge dog, Jack assumed they were both amenable to the arrangement, so he hopped over the counter and followed Leah into the back.

She was hauling a fifty-pound bag of flour to her work station, arms straining. He reached for it, and she gave him a don't-you-dare look. Ignoring that, he took the bag and carried it for her, setting it down where she pointed.

"Leah," he said to the back of her head as she worked at getting the bag open. "We need to talk."

"So talk." She was struggling, dammit, and he reached around her to help just as the bag opened and flour poofed out in a big white cloud.

She went still, then slowly turned and faced him, face and hair and chest covered in flour. "Look what you did."

"Me? I was trying to help you."

"Then why aren't *you* white?"

They both looked down at his firefighter uniform. Navy-blue BDUs, navy-blue T-shirt with the firefighter logo on his left pec. Radio on his hip. Not a speck of flour on him. He solved that by hauling her up against him and wrapping his arms tightly around her. He felt her freeze for a beat, then her arms came around him with a soft sigh of acquiescence that made him instantly hard. Lowering his head, he took a nibble of her neck, absorbing her quiver as she rocked against him. "And good enough to eat," he murmured.

She laughed, the sound music to his ears even as she pushed him away. "Now look at you," she said.

He had a full imprint of her down his front, including two round white spots on his chest where her breasts had been, and then there was the patch of flour right over his crotch, where hers had pressed nice and snug like it belonged there. He grinned, his first of the morning.

"You're a nut," she said with a shake of her head and a helpless half smile. "And everyone's going to think we went at it in here."

"So?"

Her smile faded. "So we already did that."

He let his smile fade too, let her see how serious he was. "You said that wouldn't change anything, Leah."

"It hasn't."

He caught her as she tried to move away and reeled her back in. "Then why are you changing right before my eyes?"

Her gaze slid over his features, landing at his mouth, where she lingered for a beat too long.

"Leah. Talk to me."

There was a flare of heat in her eyes before she dropped her head to his chest. "It's my body. It's not listening to my brain."

He knew what her body was saying because it was plastered to his, soft and warm and pliant. "And your brain's saying…?"

"That we are *not* going to do it again. It was wrong and awful and…wrong."

This was news to him. "Awful," he said carefully, trying to reconcile the word with the woman who'd had at least three orgasms in that cave on the mountaintop. In fact, he'd gone to sleep every night since remembering exactly how it'd felt to hear her breathily pant, "Oh, please, Jack, oh yes, Jack, omigod, *yes!*" He took a deep breath. "Awful," he repeated stupidly.

She lifted her head from his chest and took in his expression. Whatever she saw had her eyes darkening, and she bit her lower lip. "You think you can prove my brain wrong?"

"Oh yeah."

She paused, glancing around as if to make sure no one was listening. "How long do you have before you're missed at the station?" she whispered.

Not much shocked him, but this did.

"There's our bathroom," she said. "It's small, but—"

"We're not doing it in the bathroom."

"You're right," she said, nodding, turning away. "The storage closet. There's even some props in there—"

He tugged her back and wrapped his hand in her ponytail, tipping up her face so he could look into her eyes, all the possibilities playing havoc with his common sense. "Much as it kills me, not the closet either. At least not until we get a few things straightened out."

"More rules?"

"Yes."

She sighed. "Great. I'm so not good at rules."

No kidding. "You'll be good at mine."

"What's that supposed to mean?" she asked, and then her eyes widened. "Oh my God. You're not one of *those* guys, are you? Like a...dom?"

He just stared at her. "What?"

"Someone who ties up their sub and...dominates them."

"I know what a dom is," he said slowly. "I meant *what the hell?*"

"It's very popular right now," she said. "And okay, maybe I've always had a little teeny-tiny fantasy about being tied up. Just to try it. And a light spanking might be all right, but if you think I'm going to call you sir and bend to your every whim, *you're* going first."

On his hip, his radio went off, but he just stared at Leah. He'd completely lost all coherent, cognizant thought.

"Jack?" she said. "Earth to Jack."

He blinked.

"I think you're being called." She actually looked pretty relieved as she pointed to his radio. "Right? Isn't that you? I think you've got to go."

She was right, his radio was squawking, and he considered retiring from the job right there on the spot so he didn't have to leave.

As if reading his mind, she shook her head and let out a low laugh. "Go."

He pointed at her. "We're coming back to this."

The bakery phone rang and she turned toward it, but he caught her hand and pulled her back around. "I'm serious, Leah. We are going to finish this."

She gnawed on her lower lip some more. "I—"

"Do *not* forget where we were."

"Um—"

"Never mind," he said. "I'll remember enough for the both of us."

Chapter 17

♥

Leah was just closing up the bakery that night when Ali came in the back door. "Need cookies," she said.

Leah was used to people coming into the bakery all stressed out and desperate for a sugar fix. Without breaking stride, she opened a bag and began stuffing some cookies into it. She was halfway through that task when the back door opened again, and in came Aubrey.

Aubrey pointed at the white bag. "Whatever she's having, double it."

Leah flipped the OPEN sign to the CLOSED side, shut off the lights in the front room, and pulled out a couple of chairs. She poured three serious mugs of milk and dumped all the day's leftovers onto a tray.

Finally, she sat, getting off her feet for the first time since five that morning. She shoved a blueberry tart into her mouth, drank down half the mug of milk, and leaned back with a sigh. "Okay. Who's going first?"

"I'm fine," Ali said, stuffing in a cookie. She was wearing jeans and a tank top. She had dried clay on her jeans and a few flower petals in her hair, and what looked like some paint on her chest. Her hair was piled on top of her head, with a lot of it escaping in wild, frizzy tendrils, but she did indeed look fine. And happy. "I was just hungry," she said, mouth full.

"I'm fine too," Aubrey said. "If you count 'fine' going through that dusty old bookstore, where the newest book I have in inventory was printed back in 1959 and is a list of rules for a woman's place in society—which include the grocery store and laundromat. The shelves are rusty and everything's claustrophobic in there. It's a mess."

Both Leah and Ali looked Aubrey over. She was in white jeans and a red tee, and there wasn't a speck of dust on her. "It must have been awful," Leah said dryly.

"It was. I'm tossing everything."

"So you taking on the project then?" Leah asked.

Aubrey shrugged. "The shop needs me. And it also needs new bookshelves and new furniture, including big, fat, comfy couches where people sit and talk about books and knit and drink tea."

"Tea?" Leah asked.

"Tea," Aubrey said. "People who read like tea. I'll sell coffee too, damned good coffee." She paused. "Not that I want to put you out of business with my own awesomeness," she said to Leah.

"I'm not worried," Leah said.

Aubrey nodded. "I'm going to sell ebooks too, though that's going to require some serious updating of the building's electrical, and then some fancy Internet setup."

Both Ali and Leah laughed.

"What?" Aubrey said with a scowl.

"In this building you can't run the toaster and flip on a light in the bathroom at the same time without blowing fuses," Leah said. "Have you talked to your uncle?"

"He's not willing to put a penny into the building because it's in escrow," Aubrey said. "But the new owner promised upgrades. So fingers crossed this thing goes through. It'll mean good things for all of us."

"Well, except for Leah," Ali said. "She's going to be leaving soon."

Leah looked at her. "Tired of me already?"

"You going to tell us that you didn't win *Sweet Wars*? That you aren't only an episode away from starting up your own pastry shop with a hundred grand in your pocket?"

Leah got very busy rearranging the pastries on the tray in front of them. "I signed a contract," she started. "I can't talk about—"

"Fine," Ali said agreeably. "Let's talk about Jack instead."

Leah slid her a wary look. "What about him?"

"How's it going?"

Leah squirmed a little bit and glanced at Aubrey, who was looking eager to hear her response. "Fine."

"Fine?" Aubrey asked. "You're dating the hottest firefighter in town, and it's going 'fine'? What's the matter with you?"

"I don't really want to discuss it."

Ali snorted and Aubrey divided a look between the two of them. "What am I missing?"

"Nothing," Leah said quickly.

Aubrey looked to Ali, who lifted her hands. "Not my tale to tell."

Leah sighed. "You're a big help."

"I want to hear the tale!" Aubrey said. "What is it? Does he wear women's underwear? Snore? Oh! Does he have a small d—"

"Oh my God," Leah said, and stood up.

"Hey, aren't you at least going to answer any of the questions before you storm out of your own place?" Aubrey asked.

Leah turned back. "No, no, and most definitely no." She picked up the tray of pastries and hugged it close as both Ali and Aubrey hooted with laughter. "You're both cut off."

"Aw, don't go away mad," Ali said, laughing.

"I don't care if you go," Aubrey said. "But leave the pastries."

Leah moved back to the table. "I have a question."

"No answers until you put down the tray," Aubrey said.

Leah set the tray down and bit her lip.

"Spill it," Aubrey said, mouth already full as she gave her a go-ahead gesture with her hand.

"Okay." Leah took a deep breath. "Have either of you ever secretly started to like someone, and then you sort of blow it, and I don't know, say, vanish for a while? Like for years. And then you come back, and it turns out you still feel something for him, but now he's over you and also a little wary. So you then blow it again by making it so you're together but it's pretend. Only you don't want it to be pretend…"

They were both staring at her, goggle-eyed.

"You know what?" Leah said. "Never mind." She started to turn, but Aubrey caught her and pointed to a chair. "Sit," she said.

"I'm such an idiot," Leah said, and sat.

"Yes." Aubrey patted her hand. "But the good news is that I know all about being an idiot."

"Me too," Ali said, raising her hand. "I'm quite the experienced idiot."

Leah's phone vibrated. Her grandma. "Hey," she answered. "I'll be out of here in just a few—"

"Are you listening to the kitchen scanner?"

Leah glanced at it. She'd turned it off as Jack had asked. "No."

"Town Hall's on fire."

Leah hurried down the street, Ali and Aubrey at her side. It was only a two-block walk, but they heard the sirens and saw the ominous plume of smoke the minute they'd stepped outside the bakery.

It was dark outside now, but commercial row was well lit. And if it hadn't been, the flashing strobes and the glare of headlights made it easy to see the scene.

The entire block was cordoned off, and yellow police tape stretched everywhere, holding the crowd back. Police officers were standing guard. Fire trucks and emergency vehicles were angled between police cars, lights flashing.

The spectators were multiplying, spilling onto the street and clogging up the sidewalk. Leah moved as close as she could and stood there in shock. Ali found Luke and came back to Aubrey and Leah with news. "It started as a car fire in the back lot," she said. "Possibly set purposely. The car exploded and the building caught."

"Oh my God," Aubrey said. Up until six weeks ago, she'd worked inside the building as an admin to the town clerk. "Did everyone get out?"

"Yes."

"Except for the firefighters," Dee said from right behind them, looking pale and shaken. "They're still inside, including Jack." She reached for Leah's hand and gave her a smile that didn't quite meet her eyes. "But it's okay. It's going to be okay."

She was talking to herself, and knowing it, Leah pulled her in for a hug. "Of course it's going to be okay. Hell, this is your crazy son's idea of fun."

Dee let out a watery laugh and hugged Leah so tight it hurt to breathe. "Oh, Leah, you're so good for him, you know that?"

Again she felt that now-familiar stab of guilt.

Dee held on to her. "You're just so much stronger than I could ever hope to be."

If only that were true.

Chapter 18

Several hours later, the fire had been put out. There was still a police presence, but the crowd had dwindled.

Jack was supervising the cleanup and going through the scene with Ronald. Town Hall had been saved, though there was some fairly extensive damage to the second floor and the roof, both of which had caught when the car exploded.

They'd found a few cigarette butts in the alley, which had an excellent view of the back of the Town Hall building. And beneath the burned wreckage of the car, the same incendiary device that they'd found at the auto parts store—a bucket of oily rags.

This was no vagrant.

It was 2:00 a.m. before Jack got back to the station. By the time dawn arrived and he dragged his tired ass—and Kevin's—home, he was gritty-eyed and exhausted. Far too exhausted to be surprised when he found his mom and Ben waiting for him.

They dragged him out to breakfast, and then they went with Dee to her doctor's appointment, where they got good news from the results of her last tests.

The treatment was working.

It was nearly noon by the time Jack got home, with bed firmly on his mind.

Leah was sitting on the top step of his porch in a sundress, another of her cropped sweaters, and strappy, high-heeled sandals that had a bow around her ankle. Kevin bounded over to her like he hadn't seen her in years. She gave him a full body rub that had the dog sinking to the ground in boneless ecstasy, rolling onto his back, with his legs straight up in the air, tongue lolling.

Leah smiled and shook her head at his antics. "You boys are all the same," she said. "You just want to show off your junk." She pulled a doggie biscuit from her purse, and Kevin wriggled like a beached whale trying to right himself in a hurry.

"Sit," she said firmly.

"He doesn't sit," Jack said.

Kevin sat.

"Good boy! Oh, what a *very* good boy," Leah said in that high, silly voice that all women used with dogs and gave Kevin another big, warm hug.

Kevin glanced back at Jack, who would have sworn the dog was grinning at him. "Careful," he said. "Or I'll let you adopt him."

"No thank you," she said. "I don't have big enough baggies."

Jack moved to the top step and sat next to her. He told himself it was because she always smelled so good and he wanted to get the scent of the fire out of his nostrils.

And also because his legs were so tired he didn't think he could keep standing up. "So."

She pulled her bottom lip into her mouth. "So…"

"Where were we?"

She flushed. "I don't remember."

"Seriously," he said. "How is it that your nose isn't a foot long by now?"

She smiled and handed him a small white bag. "Happy birthday."

He should have known she would remember. She always remembered. "What is it?" he asked cautiously. And with good reason. One year, she'd gotten him a gift certificate for a spa treatment that had turned out to be for a male Brazilian wax. He'd never cashed that one in… Another year, she'd left him a pair of really huge women's underpants on his truck antenna out in front of the station along with a "love note" from a secret admirer. That one had taken a while to live down.

"Open it," she said, sounding far too innocent.

"Do I need insurance first?"

"Maybe it's just what you wanted," she said.

What he wanted was her in his bed wearing nothing but those sexy shoes. He started to open the bag, and Kevin moved in close, licking his chops hopefully.

"You already got yours," Jack told him.

Kevin whined.

"I'll tell you what," Jack told him. "If you sit, maybe I'll share."

Kevin offered a paw.

"No, I said sit."

Kevin barked.

Leah laughed, the sound going a long way toward reviving Jack. Shaking his head, he opened the bag. Cream cheese croissants. "I like the lack of public humiliation with this one," he said as he pulled the first one from the bag.

She smiled. "I figured it was time to grow up just a little bit. Aren't you going to go inside to eat?" she asked.

"Nope." He downed the croissant in two bites and pulled out number two. "Can't wait that long." He swallowed. "You made these when the cast from *Sweet Wars* guested on the *Today Show*."

"Yes."

"And you fed one to that host guy, whatever his name is."

They both knew damn well that he knew Rafe's name. Leah didn't respond, just pulled something else from her big bag. A thermos.

Milk, which as it turned out was gloriously, icy cold. He washed down the croissant, filling his stomach with something more than adrenaline and acid. "God, you're good."

"That's what they tell me." She waited until he'd taken a big, long gulp. "As for Rafe." She paused until he looked at her. "I did sleep with him," she said quietly.

The milk went down the wrong pipe, and he choked. When he could breathe again, he swiped his face with his forearm. "I didn't want to know that."

"Yes you did. But it was only once. I didn't like him enough to repeat the experience."

Their gazes met again and held as he wondered if she liked *him* enough to repeat *their* experience. In his pocket, his phone vibrated. He ignored it. "Go on," he said.

"There's nothing else to tell." Standing up, she moved to the porch railing and leaned on it, staring out into the bright morning. "He got pissed off and made a big stink about how if I didn't sleep with him again, I was going to blow the chance of a lifetime."

Jack narrowed his eyes. "He threatened you?"

"He was just blowing off steam after getting rejected. I could have handled it better." She shrugged. "He wasn't my type. We weren't a thing. You'll see that in the finals, where he ignores me completely."

Feeling a whole lot better, he looked at her and realized she wasn't feeling better at all. She was tense. "You okay?"

She let out a low, mirthless laugh that told him she wasn't, and why.

It hit him then, like a bucket of ice water. She'd been watching the fire last night with everyone else in town. Watching and worrying. He remembered those years his mom had made herself sick with the strain and stress and fear of waiting. Just the thought of having a woman do that for him had always been enough to keep himself from letting anyone get too close. Lots of other people managed to do the job and have families, and it all seemed to work out. But after watching his mom fall apart when his dad had died, Jack had known he'd never be one of them.

He set the bag and the thermos down and stood up. Turning her to face him, he stepped into her, his boots on the outside of her pretty shoes, his hands gliding up her arms to her face, which he tilted to his. "I'm really good at what I do, Leah."

"Yes," she agreed. "I know."

"I'm not my dad."

"I know that too."

"I'm trying to honor his memory," Jack said. "Trying to live up to what he believed in, but trust me, I have no intention of being a hero. Not like he turned out to be."

She set her hands on his biceps and looked into his eyes. "There was a time that wasn't true," she reminded him. "When you were wild and reckless."

"I'm past that," he assured her. "*Long* past. And knowing what my mom went through, how she suffered, it's made it easy to say no to any sort of deep relationship."

"To *any* relationship."

He lifted a shoulder. "Fine. Yeah. I stay away from them."

"Except for one," she said, and drew in a deep breath. "Me."

This was true. His relationship with her had stood the test of time—although not without its share of bumps and bruises along the way.

"Because we've been friends," he said. "Not lovers."

She arched a brow.

"Until recently," he allowed.

She took in his expression. "Let me guess," she said quietly. "We're going back into negotiations on our rules." She pulled out her phone. "Go ahead," she said. "I'll take notes."

"This isn't funny."

"Well, give the man an A."

Irritation bubbled at the base of his skull. His very tired skull. "Tell me this, Leah. Where do you see this charade going? Or ending?"

Something flashed across her face that he couldn't quite interpret. Maybe guilt.

"I don't know," she admitted. "I didn't think that far.

It's not like this was premeditated," she said, voice heavy with regret. "I only meant to make your mom happy—"

"I know." And he did know. "It's worked. She's eating. Getting up and out." He shook his head in marvel. "She's happy. But…"

"You're not," she said softly. "Happy."

"You want to know what I think?"

"Probably not."

"I think you're using this opportunity to avoid whatever the hell you're running from this time."

She stared at him for one stunned beat before pushing at him. "I've got to go."

"Shit," he muttered, catching her, pulling her around, and pinning her to the railing. "I'm right, aren't I? You ran from whatever happened. Was it Rafe?"

"No." In his arms, she squirmed. Her hair tickled his nose, caught on the stubble of his jaw. It smelled good. She felt good too, and like always when it came to being with her, she both aroused and frustrated the shit out of him. "So are your plans to run from me, Leah? Because that's next, right? And how are you going to explain that?"

She sighed and dropped her forehead to his chest. "I don't have plans to go anywhere, Jack. Does that make you feel any better?"

When he didn't respond, she lifted her head and let out a mirthless laugh. "I see that makes you feel worse," she said. "Since it means you're stuck with me. Aren't we a pair? Look, I really do need to go. Apparently I can only pretend to like you in small doses."

Ignoring the fact that they were visible to anyone coming down the street, he pressed into her again, plastering himself to her from chest to thigh.

An electric charge zinged between them, heating the air. She didn't move, not a single muscle.

He couldn't say the same since he went instantly hard.

"Jack," she whispered, gaze on his mouth. "Don't. We're too bad at this."

"So let's go back to something we're good at," he said, and kissed her, long and hard and wet. It wasn't enough. Fisting his hands in her hair, he held on to her and plundered. With a moan that soothed his soul, she wound her arms around his neck. "Damn you," she murmured against his mouth. "*Damn you.*"

With a growl, he backed her into his front door, unlocking it, pulling her inside.

They staggered like drunks into his living room, still kissing while attempting to strip each other.

Kevin, thinking they were playing, was jumping up and down on his back legs like Scooby-Doo, trying to get in on the fun.

"Sit," Jack told him.

Kevin barked. *Jesus.* "Kevin, bark."

Kevin sat.

Leah was shaking with laughter when Jack once again took her mouth with his. The urgency hadn't abated. She got his shirt unbuttoned and off one arm. He kicked off one boot while ripping off her sweater. She tripped over the boot, and they both went down onto his couch.

She landed on top, forcing the air out of his lungs with her bony elbow. Hell, she very nearly unmanned him completely with an ill-placed knee. None of it mattered as he continued to kiss her like she was better than air.

And in that moment, she was.

Chapter 19

♥

Leah sat up to take in the glorious sight of Jack sprawled beneath her on the couch. He wasn't like any other man she'd ever been with. Even when he was in a hurry, he never let anything rush him.

She'd watched him at the fire. Calm, level-headed, never losing his cool.

Now he lay still with deceptive languor, deceptive because she could feel him, thick and hard between her legs as she straddled him. Weaving her fingers in his, she slowly slid his arms up, resting them above his head on the back of the couch. Holding him like that, she rocked against him.

He groaned, simmering heat radiating from his big body. "Leah, kiss me."

Oh yes, she'd kiss him, but first she let go of his hands to shove his shirt up. "Mmm," she said, and stared down at what she'd exposed. Warm skin and ridged muscle.

He looked up at her, gaze hot and unapologetically

sexual. His pants had ridden low, revealing the way his obliques were cut at his hips. She wanted to taste him there. So she did just that, humming in pleasure while he gave a low growl.

At the sound, Kevin bounded over and thrust his huge head between Jack's and Leah's, trying to see what he was missing. "Lay down," Jack commanded.

If he'd used that voice on her she would have done anything he commanded, but Kevin only whined.

"Horse factory," Jack grated out.

Kevin heaved a sigh and trotted off.

"Do you have birthday plans?" Leah asked Jack softly, unbuttoning his pants. She ran her fingers down the center of his chest and lower abdomen, following the line of dark hair to where it vanished into his opened pants.

"Yes," he said, his voice sounding as strained as the waistband of his boxers. "I have plans to make you scream my name."

"I'm not much of a screamer."

"I have my ways."

Leah shivered because she knew it to be true. She'd seen firsthand what happened when Jack was...determined. Her body quivered again as she took in the sight of him beneath her, taut, ripped, waiting with mock patience. "Ah," she said, "but it's *your* birthday. Maybe you'll scream *my* name."

He slid his hands to the backs of her thighs and then up her skirt to cup and squeeze her bottom. Then he tore away her panties.

"Jack!" she gasped in shock.

"Hmm. That's a good start." He nudged her bra straps from her shoulders. "Take this off," he said, then put his attention to shoving up her skirt. His gaze followed his fingers, and at the sight of her, he growled out her name.

She unhooked her bra and let it slip down her body, and then kissed him again, a soft touch of lips to lips before pulling back slightly.

His warm brown eyes were heavy-lidded as he watched her watching him. Reaching for her hands, he guided them down his chest and farther until she'd wrapped her fingers around his hard length.

She squeezed, and a slight tremor ran through him. Practically vibrating with pleasure, she kissed her way down the same path her hands had taken. "Happy…" She gave him a long, slow lick. "Birthday…"

With a low, long groan, his fingers slid into her hair. Not pulling, not guiding…more like he needed a handhold.

Against him, she smiled. He'd been her neighbor. Her protector. Her greatest friend. But her favorite thing was what they were now. Lovers. They fit together as if they were made for each other. Knowing it, reveling in it, she took him into her mouth. Beneath her, hands still tangled tight in her hair, his hips bucked, control slipping. "Fuck, Leah."

"Later," she said, and made him snort. And then she made him sweat. And pant. And swear like a sailor.

And then finally, she made him come, hard.

Afterward, he hauled her up his body to kiss her with enough heat to let her know he'd liked the birthday gift.

Then he flipped them so he was on top, his arms bracketing her body. Every part of him slid against every part of her, and she wrapped her arms and legs around him, anticipation swimming through her.

As she'd done to him, he slid his hands to hers and

slowly guided them above her head to the armrest of the couch. He squeezed her fingers and met her gaze, his message clear. *Leave them there.*

She drew one breath before he took possession of her mouth, and it was like she'd never been kissed before. She'd never even dreamed that a kiss could be so...soul searching.

Perfect.

It was different from their earlier kisses, which had all been just as hot, but also flirty. No end destination.

This was different. This was...intense, demanding everything from her, and her heart started to pound against her ribs.

Lifting his head, he stared into her eyes, trailing his fingers down her jaw, his mouth following, along her throat, where he stopped at the pulse point.

His thumb lightly glided over the spot. "You're either having a heart attack or I'm really doing it for you," he murmured.

"Both. Jack—"

"Shh," he said, his gaze hot enough to scorch. "It's my turn now." And then he lightly nipped her throat before soothing the sting with a kiss. Her collarbone was next, and then her breast. He took her nipple into his mouth and laved, nipped, and teased until she was writhing beneath him. Then he switched sides, taking his sweet-ass time about it too, until she whispered his name. And then said it again in a rather commanding tone that matched the frantic rock of her hips.

This only encouraged further torture on his part. He slid to his knees on the floor as he finally, God *finally*, kissed his way down her stomach.

Her skirt was still shoved up to her waist, and he seemed to really like the look as he stroked a hand over one thigh, urging her to open for him, to hook her leg on his shoulder. His other hand rested low on her belly, so low his thumb could lightly scrape over her. And then not so lightly. "I have condoms," she managed. "An entire box of them. In my purse."

He looked up at her, his eyes dark and intense with concentration, though now there was also a light of humor. "That's a big box."

She felt herself flush. "Well, I thought maybe we weren't done yet."

Turning his head, he rubbed up against her inner thigh with a day's worth of scruff on his jaw.

She nearly came. "Jack—"

"I bought some too. Also a big box. Because I was *sure* we weren't done yet." He glided his thumb over her again and followed it up with his tongue, eyes still on hers.

A man had never looked at her like that, not in her entire life. And okay, so she wasn't all that experienced, but she was feeling things, so many, many things, and she could tell that he was feeling them too. She breathed more than said his name, and he let his eyes drift closed as he went back to what he was doing—driving her out of her ever-loving mind. He was quite thorough about it too, and she lost it completely, coming with a shuddering cry that rocked her to her very core.

Jack staggered to his feet. "Bed," he said firmly.

"I can't feel my legs."

"I've got you." Bending over her, he stilled when she slapped a hand to his chest.

"You're not going to carry me like I'm some silly

girly-girl in the movies all romantic-like," she said. "It always brings me out of the scene because I worry about his back, and— Hey!"

He'd scooped her up and over his shoulder into a fireman's hold.

"*Jack*." She laughed and squirmed to get free, but then realized that she had a most excellent view of his most excellent backside as he strode down the hall as if she were light as a feather. "Put me down."

"I'm dragging you off to my cave."

Well then. Willing to play, she tried to bite his ass. Since she couldn't quite reach, she settled for low on his back, but the bastard didn't have an ounce of fat on him so she couldn't really get a good hold.

He swatted her butt. "Behave."

She tried to bite him again, but then she was flying through the air and landing on his bed. Before she could bounce twice, he'd pulled a condom from his bedside drawer and was on top of her.

And then in her.

He stilled and pressed his face to her neck. "I'm a dead man," he murmured, and then, holding her right where he wanted, he began to thrust, pulling out with each stroke, rolling his hips, and then grinding back in. She could feel him hot and hard, deep inside every time he moved. He gripped her thighs and pushed them forward slightly so he slid in more, pressing a spot deep inside of her. She'd never experienced anything like it. When he groaned her name, she knew neither of them were going to last. Everything about him was causing sensations in her body that she didn't even know what to do with. Squeezing her legs around his waist, she clutched him, crying out.

They came together. Or at least she thought they did.
She couldn't be sure because she lost track of all her
senses.

When she came back to herself, they were damply entangled and she was breathing like a lunatic. Holy cow...
She tried to roll free and found she couldn't move. She
was pinned by one-hundred-and-eighty solid pounds of
muscle, and he was breathing just as hard as she, the
small of his back slick with sweat. And her only coherent
thought was, if they kept at this whole naked friends
thing, they were going to kill each other...

Eventually Jack got up to get them some water and
sustenance, and Leah managed to roll over and shove her
hair from her face. His bedside drawer was open, the box
of condoms torn into and spilling out over a colorful stack
of envelopes—

Leah went still, then reached out and brushed the condoms away, even though she didn't need to. She knew
what that stack of cards was.

Her own cards, sent to Jack when she'd first left Lucky
Harbor. Christmases, birthdays, Valentine's Days...she'd
used them all as excuses to keep in touch, her own way of
hoping he would keep her in mind.

He still had them. Every one of them, by the looks
of things. Her throat tightened as she wondered what it
meant. But she knew. It meant that she'd been important
to him.

And she'd hurt him.

She could have had something here with him, something real. Instead, she was now stuck in this...*fake* relationship that was quickly turning not so fake at all.

And it was all her own doing.

* * *

The next morning, Jack knew the minute Leah woke up because, like Kevin always did, her entire body tensed without moving a muscle.

He wondered if she expected him to do what he did with Kevin: point to the floor and say, "Get down." The truth was, he was far more likely to roll over and expose his vulnerable underbelly.

Instead, he let her have the moment of pretense as he watched her in the early morning light. God, it felt good to wake up with her, which begged the question—how long was she sticking around? She seemed to be settling into Lucky Harbor, though this didn't make any sense at all if she'd won *Sweet Wars*. And surely she had won. This meant she had the prize money to start her own pastry shop and was financially stable, probably for the first time in her entire adult life.

Maybe she'd continue to revamp her grandma's bakery. Surely she wouldn't have started this thing between them if she'd been in a hurry to go anywhere. He tried to figure out what that might mean but couldn't. "Morning," he said quietly.

She didn't move.

This didn't surprise him. If he knew her, and he sure as hell did, he knew she was panicked right about now and reviewing her options.

And most likely the closest exit.

He could feel her heart kick into high gear, and he had some sympathy. She wasn't alone in this. This whole new lover intimacy they had going between them now was going to affect their friend intimacy, no matter what they said or did.

"I know you're awake," he said.

She cracked open one eye. "How? How do you always know?"

"You stopped breathing."

She sighed. "What time is it?"

They'd called in for pizza late last night, ravished it in the same manner in which they'd ravished each other, and then fallen asleep, the heavy sleep of the dead—or two people who'd fucked their brains out. "Eight," he said.

"Eight…" With a gasp, she sat straight up. "*Eight*? Omigod, we fell asleep? The bakery—"

"I thought today was your day off."

"No! I told Grandma she could have the day for herself. I've gotta go." Rolling to her feet, she staggered until she got her sea legs, and then she whirled to look for her clothes.

Jack tucked his hands beneath his head and enjoyed the view of her, all naked and rosy and… "Damn," he said, sitting up. "Sorry about that whisker burn."

She glared at him and then strode—still bare-ass naked—to the mirror over his dresser. She took in the sight of her reddened neck and growled. "Is it too hot for a turtleneck?"

He bit his lower lip to hold in his grimace.

She looked at him, narrowed her eyes, and then looked down at her body.

The whisker burn extended to her breasts, belly, and inner thighs. "You suck," she said.

"Actually, you're the one who—"

"Stop!" She clapped her hands over her ears but did let out a low laugh that pretty much made his heart swell too big for his ribs. "Where the hell is my bra?"

He got out of bed, tripped over Kevin, and headed down the hall to the living room. The dog happily trotted along after him, thrilled to have his people awake, even more thrilled because he could tell time and knew it was *way* past time to eat. To remind Jack, he put his icy nose on Jack's ass, goosing him.

Jack picked up Leah's clothes from the living room floor and handed them over. She began to jerk them on, doing that whole not-quite-making-eye-contact thing that he recognized. It was what she did right before she did something stupid, and some of his glow faded. "That was quick," he said.

"What?"

"The regret."

"Don't start." She whirled for her shoes and purse. "This is all your fault."

"Mine?" He laughed. "You gave me a birthday blow job, which started the whole thing. How was that my fault?"

"Because you came home looking edgy and rumpled and…hot. And then I took your clothes off and…and you looked even hotter."

He grinned. "You think I'm sexy."

"The entire female race thinks you're sexy." She sighed. "Okay, Mr. Rules, Mr. Gotta Be In Charge… we're going to have to renegotiate some things."

"Such as?"

"That," she said, and pointed to the bed. "What the hell are we going to do about *that*?"

"If you're referring to the amazing orgasms, then I vote for more as soon as possible."

"At least that part isn't pretend," she said.

He frowned at her. "What does that mean?"

"Look, forget it. But we need to remember your first rule: this isn't real and there are no hurt feelings." She whirled away and began digging through her purse for her keys. "When people are bitching that I don't have any fresh bread or donuts available today at the bakery, I'm going to blame you."

"Sure," he said, a little distracted by her reiterating his own rule. Which was ridiculous of him. "My reputation could use the boost."

She rolled her eyes, headed to the door, then stopped, sighed, and came back to him. "You're still naked."

"Yeah," he said. "Just in case you want to give me any more birthday presents."

"Look, Jack," she said and then paused.

Uh-oh. "You going to dump me on my birthday?" he asked softly.

"It's the day *after* your birthday." She closed her eyes. "And I don't know what I'm doing here, Jack. I feel antsy. I feel like…"

"You have to run?"

Her silence was answer enough, and he felt the age-old temper for her father rear its ugly head. "You're letting your past rule you again. It's your life, Leah. Own it. Do with it what you want."

"It's not that."

They both knew it was a lie. She sighed and put a hand to his chest and then dropped her head to it. "I'm having trouble with this pretend thing."

His heart kicked hard. "What do you mean?"

"I mean, dammit, you're messing with my head." She lifted hers. "We *have* to go back to pretend, Jack.

All pretend. It's a rule! And it's for my own mental health!"

He thought of what they'd done to each other in the name of sheer lust over the past twenty-four hours, how she was saying what he already knew. They were skating on thin ice. Thin, cracked ice. "What about for *my* mental health?" This came out completely unbidden, and if he had a do-over card, he'd have taken it back. He didn't want to discuss his mental health, or lack thereof. Hell no.

"What are you saying?" she asked.

"Nothing. Forget it." He turned away, stopping to look down when he felt her hand on his arm.

"Jack," she said softly.

"Throwing in the towel now makes sense," he heard himself say. "My mom's getting better. The treatment's working."

"Oh, Jack, that's wonderful. I'd hoped…"

He nodded. "She's still got some treatments left, but the bottom line is that it's working." He paused, his throat feeling like he'd swallowed broken glass. "So I suppose it's best to break her heart sooner than later and tell her the truth." Feeling hollow, he took a step back. "You're late," he reminded her.

"But…are we…okay?"

"Aren't we always?"

She looked at him for a moment, then nodded and headed toward the door, and he let her go.

Had to.

She was in denial, and he wasn't going to call her on it because…well, hello, Pot, meet Kettle.

Still, he hauled her back against him, using the stolen

moment to adjust the collar on her sweater so it covered as much of her throat as possible. For her.

And then he kissed her one last time, long and wet and deep.

For him.

Chapter 20

♥

Leah raced home, changed, then continued on her rush to the bakery, definitely *not* thinking about all that had just happened in the past twenty-four hours: being in Jack's bed—and then later on his couch, his table, his bathroom counter… Everything about it had been magical.

And then the not-so-magical morning after.

She had to park down the street, and she ran to the back door and the bakery, only to skid to a shocked stop.

Her grandma was in the middle of the kitchen, surrounded by the day's baked goods.

"But," Leah said, staring around. Fresh bread. Muffins. Pies… "You made all this?"

Elsie grinned and poured Leah a big mug of burn-the-hair-off-your-tongue, straight-black coffee.

Leah took a few gulps and let the caffeine sink in. But she was still boggled. "Did the pastry fairy visit?"

Elsie laughed, soft and musical. "Funny thing about not having to get up at four in the morning to start baking every day…you don't mind doing it once in a while. In fact, I had the time of my life this morning." She gestured to the recipes Leah had been working on, spread across the counter. "Your stuff is amazing, honey. Utterly amazing."

"It's all in the hands of the baker," she said.

"No," Elsie said. "It's all in the heart of the person putting together the recipes."

Leah didn't know what to say. The praise, coming from her grandma, meant so much and embarrassed her at the same time, and she checked her watch.

Elsie laughed softly. "You can just say thank you."

"Thank you."

"You never did learn how to take a compliment."

Leah thought of how Jack had looked at her when he'd told her she was beautiful. How she'd wanted to close her eyes from the look in his warm gaze, the one that told her he meant it, down to his soul. She *had* closed her eyes, even as she'd wanted to hear him say it again…

But she'd blown that, hadn't she?

Lord. She needed therapy.

"So…," Elsie said. "Big day yesterday?"

Leah winced. "Sorry I didn't come home. I—"

"Don't you dare apologize. You have a life. I'm so happy for you, Leah."

"It's not what you think, Grandma. Jack and I are…" She broke off, not sure how to continue.

"Honey, anyone with eyes can see exactly what you and Jack are." She smiled. "Now I'm going up front to see to our customers."

Alone, Leah worked in the kitchen. She was nearly done when her phone rang. She jumped for it, hoping it was Jack. But of course it wasn't, she'd made sure of that.

"Hey, Sweet Cheeks." Rafe. "Finally able to give you a call. Got your email a few weeks back. Thought you'd forgotten about me there for a little while."

"Not likely, since you're on my TV every week."

He laughed softly, an easy, contagious laugh. If one could make a mold of pure infectious charm and charismatic wit, it was Rafe. He knew how to make you forget everything but him. He knew how to get the best out of anyone. He knew how to get what he wanted.

And he had no soul.

"I thought about your offer," she said.

"Which offer?"

He knew damn well which offer, so she remained quiet.

He laughed again. "Aw. You miss me. Who'd have thought?"

"I want the job."

"But maybe it's no longer available."

Leah ground her teeth but kept her voice light. "Okay. Then I'll go to the Food Network. They were interested as well."

"Well, there's no need to get your panties in a twist," he said. "I was just messing with you. You used to have a sense of humor."

"And you used to at least be a good guy."

"I still am," he said, a little more stiffly now. He had great illusions of being the perennial boy next door and didn't like his faults pointed out to him. "The job offer stands."

"You're going to let me have my own reality show, following a group of fledgling pastry chefs in their final semester of school?"

"I'm going to let you have your own reality show, following *you* in *your* last semester of school."

She stared at her phone. "That wasn't the deal."

"It's been six months. The deal changed."

"Rafe—"

"Look, Leah," he said, not quite as jovial and friendly as before. "The ratings have been pouring in. You're the little media darling now. The camera loves you, and the viewers love you. They all think you're about to win this baby."

She grimaced. "I haven't said a word—"

"Of course not, or we'd have sued your sweet ass off."

"I can't just go back for my last semester," she said, feeling a little panicky at just the thought of it. "I left there. They don't take people back."

"Of course they do. For a price. And we're willing to pay it. Yes or no, Leah?"

You never finish a damn thing, Leah. Not one damn thing. And you never will...

Her father's words echoed in her head and gave her an instant jaw ache from clenching it so tight. It used to be that her father's words were in her head all the time, but she'd managed to block them more and more. Now she heard a different voice in her head. She heard Jack, brave, confident Jack.

You're letting your past rule you again. It's your life, Leah. Own it. Do with it what you want.

Oh how she wanted to be more like Jack, strong of body and spirit, sure of herself. But her mind raced. Leaving here would be leaving him.

You've already done that.

Besides, she knew the truth now. She had to make

something of herself. She had to prove to herself that she could before she could let him in.

But going back to school in front of a camera? Good God. Failing herself was one thing, but failing in front of an audience? Torture.

So don't fail...

"I'm in," she said.

"Good." She heard some clicking, as if his fingers were racing over a keyboard. "The semester starts October first."

Her heart clutched. Was she really going to do this? "That's in three weeks."

"Don't be tardy, Sweet Cheeks. Or you won't be the teacher's pet."

Somehow she went through the motions for the rest of the day. She baked. She sold. She took Elsie shopping for some "hot shoes." She'd planned on an early night to crawl into her bed and crash, but Ali and Aubrey dragged her to the Love Shack, during which she managed to avoid any and all questions about her personal life by keeping her drink near her mouth.

"She's deflecting," Aubrey noted.

"Think that's a bad sign?" Ali asked.

"I know it is," Aubrey said.

"I screwed up," Leah admitted.

"Oh good," Aubrey said. "I love to hear stories of other people's screwups. It's such a refreshing change from reliving my own hundreds of screwups."

"You have hundreds?" Ali asked.

"Maybe thousands," Aubrey said.

"I've just got the one for now," Leah said. "But it's a biggie."

"We're all ears," Aubrey said, and waved for another round of drinks.

Much later, the three friends left the bar together. "Am I the only one who's on a merry-go-round?" Leah asked, world spinning.

"Yes," Ali said, hugging her. "But that's because you did all the drinking." She looked at Aubrey. "Who's driving Tipsy Girl home?"

"I can," Leah said, raising her hand.

Aubrey rolled her eyes and snatched Leah's keys. "*You're* Tipsy Girl," she said.

"Oh." Leah sighed. It was true. Her tongue was numb and her toes tingled, and she wasn't entirely sure but it felt like she had two heads.

She was more than tipsy.

They said good night to Ali, and then Aubrey shoved Leah into her car. Leah looked out the window as Aubrey drove through a quiet and sleeping Lucky Harbor. The shops were dark, the streets deserted. After traveling around the globe, this place should have seemed far too…quiet.

But the opposite was true. She felt like herself here. She was happy here.

And now she was leaving…

A pang hit her right in the center of her chest, but she knew it wasn't a heart attack. Nope, nothing as simple as that.

It was the thought of walking away. Again.

And yet she hadn't given herself much of a choice, had she? She'd been in such a damn hurry to get the hell out before she could prove that she was nothing but a screwup. And now she'd broken up with her pretend boyfriend—

The pang hit again. It might have been indigestion from the chili cheese fries she'd inhaled at the bar along with the alcohol, but she was pretty sure it was a certain tall, dark, and sexy-as-hell firefighter.

Yeah. This was all Jack's fault. Leah pulled out her phone.

Aubrey reached over and snatched it from her fingers.

"Hey," Leah said.

"Trust me, when it's this late and you're toasted, the only call you ever make is to do something monumentally stupid. You can thank me tomorrow. Where do you live?"

"Maybe I just want to see what time it is." Leah sighed. "Okay, so I was going to do something monumentally stupid." She gave Aubrey the address.

Aubrey didn't speak, just drove, for which Leah was grateful. She really needed to go to bed. After all, she had only four hours before she had to be up again...

Aubrey pulled up to the address Leah had given her and parked.

"You don't have to walk me in," Leah said. "I'm not that drunk."

Aubrey gave Leah a long look. "Yeah you are. And this isn't your grandma's house."

Leah bit her lower lip. "How did you know?"

Aubrey didn't answer for a long moment, just stared at the duplex. "Let's just say you're not the only one who's done something monumentally stupid in this lifetime."

Leah's stomach sank. "You and Jack...?"

"No," Aubrey said. "No. Not Jack."

Which meant… *"Ben?"*

"It's not what you think," Aubrey said cryptically and got out of the car.

Leah knew she wanted to follow this conversation, but at the moment she didn't have the brain capacity. So she got out of the car. "I'm good from here," she said.

"Oh, I know."

Leah watched Aubrey head toward the porch. "Then what are you doing?"

"I don't want to miss the monumental mistake."

Leah sighed and followed. She knocked softly on Jack's front door in case he was sleeping and was startled when Ben's front door opened instead.

Ben stood there in faded jeans, a T-shirt, and bare feet.

"Sorry," Leah said. "Did I wake you?"

His hair was rumpled but his eyes were sharp and on Aubrey. "No."

Aubrey met his gaze evenly. "Hello, Ben."

Ben didn't say a word, but his eyes were saying plenty. Leah just couldn't tell *what* they were saying plenty of, though the tension was thick enough to cut with a knife.

Then a *huge* shadow shoved its way past Ben.

A bear.

A bear that was white with black spots and looked like Kevin, greeting Leah with a snuffle and a warm, wet nose that he pushed into her belly.

She fell backward to her butt on the porch.

"Shit," Ben said. He scooped Leah up and set her back on her feet, pausing to peer into her eyes. Still holding on to her, he turned to Aubrey. "She's drunk."

"Tipsy," Leah said.

Aubrey shrugged. "Not her keeper."

Ben shook his head, eyes accusatory. "You okay?" he asked Leah.

"Yep." She put her hands on her butt. "I've got plenty of padding. Where's Jack?"

"Out back in the hot tub," Ben said. "Take Kevin the killer guard dog here. He just drank my last beer, and we're no longer friends."

Kevin burped.

Leah smiled at the dog, then turned to Aubrey. "Thanks for the ride—"

But Aubrey was halfway back to her car. Ben was watching her go, eyes dark and unreadable.

"I'm going to go visit Jack now," Leah said. But her feet didn't move.

Ben sighed as he took her hand and began to lead her around the back of the house.

"You don't have to walk me," she protested. "I can find my own way—"

"Humor me."

"But I don't want to intrude." She paused. "And I'm not at all sure why I'm here. He's not going to be happy to see me, you know. He's tired of pretending."

Ben smiled in the dark. She could hear it in his voice. "You think he's pretending to like you?"

"I think he's pretending that he doesn't want to wring my neck."

This gave her the rare pleasure of hearing Ben laugh. By this time they were around the side of the house and coming up on the back deck, Leah could hear the drone of the hot tub's jets running. Ben guided her up the wood steps to the edge of the tub.

Jack was in it; big body sprawled out, an arm on the

edge on either side of him, head back, eyes closed. There were ear buds in his ears, leading to an iPod on the bench behind him.

Also on the bench—three empty beer bottles.

"He's probably tipsy too," she whispered to Ben.

"You two are a pair," Ben agreed.

"No," she said. "That's the thing. We're *pretending* to be a pair. Or we were. I screwed that up too."

Ben shook his head and let out a sound of amusement. "Like I said, you're a pair."

"A pretend pair," she said. Jeez. And she'd always thought Ben was so smart. "And I don't want to really be his girlfriend anyway."

"No?"

"No. He's bossy. And he likes to have his way. And he thinks I'm just playing with him." She sighed, not taking her eyes off Jack's form.

Jack's very fine, very built, very wet form.

She couldn't see much below the bubbles, and she wondered if he was wearing a bathing suit. She hoped he wasn't. "Can't blame him," she whispered. "I've played with him before, you know. Just last night in fact."

Ben laughed again. "And I'm sure he hated every minute of it. Listen, Leah, you have to wake him up before I leave. I can't leave two drunks out here alone."

"Tipsy. I'm just *tipsy*."

"Right," he said and gave Jack a nudge. Actually, it was more like a shove.

Jack didn't jump. He didn't react at all except for the one eye that cracked open.

"Drunk Goldilocks here wants to crash your party," Ben said.

"*Tipsy*," Leah said, irritated.

Jack's other eye opened, both landing unerringly on Leah.

Leah gave him a little wave, trying to look like the best thing to happen to him that night. She wasn't sure she was successful, but he did reach up and pull out his ear buds. "You got her drunk?" he asked Ben with a hint of disbelief.

"Not me," Ben said. "She managed that all on her own."

Leah sighed. "Tipsy!" Though why she bothered, she had no idea. She kicked off her shoes and dropped her purse to the deck.

"What are you doing?" Ben asked.

She pulled off her sweater. "I'm about to seduce my pretend boyfriend. Go away, Ben."

Ben turned to Jack, who'd risen to his feet in the hot tub. "You need to stop her."

"I'm going to exercise my right to remain silent," Jack said.

Which worked, because Leah had no intention of stopping. She let her sweater fall. She was disappointed to note that Jack was indeed wearing black swim trunks, but at least they clung to his every inch. She *really* liked his every inch... "Go away, Ben."

"Jack," Ben said warningly.

"You heard the woman." Jack never took his eyes off Leah. "Go away, Ben."

Ben tossed up his hands. "You two deserve each other," he muttered and walked away.

When they were alone, Jack looked at her. "What are you doing here?" He sounded wary, which in a distant part of her brain she recognized was probably wise of him.

But she kept stripping. "I'm just realizing that the only time my pretend boyfriend and I get along is when we're not pretending. I want to not pretend, just for a little while." She pulled off her top.

"Leah...seriously. *What are you doing?*"

"Seriously? You're the investigator. You figure it out." She shimmied out of her denim skirt, letting it fall to her ankles. She took a peek at herself and sighed in relief. *Not* her laundry day underwear this time, thankfully. A red lace thong.

Jack's gaze raked down her body, slowly and thoroughly. "Stop."

She shivered at his commanding tone and then stepped right into the tub and plastered herself against his big, wet, warm body. "You sound all official and in charge."

"In charge?" His arms closed around her, and he sank with her into the deliciously hot water. "I have no delusions of being in charge of you."

She smiled. "You saying I have all the power?"

"You always have," he murmured and nipped at her throat, working his way south. "What are we doing, Leah?"

She let her head fall back to give him room to work as steam and bubbles and Jack surrounded her. "I thought we'd wing it."

Chapter 21

When Jack woke up, he knew without opening his eyes that Leah was gone. She had to get up early for the bakery, but he hadn't even heard her leave. Still, he reached out to the spot where she'd been in his bed and…came in contact with fur.

Kevin lifted his head and panted a happy smile. Not quite the smile he'd hoped for.

"We've had this discussion." Jack gave him a shove. "You have your own damn bed."

Kevin licked his chin.

Definitely not the kiss he'd been hoping for.

As for what that meant, both that he was disappointed to be alone and that Leah had sneaked off, he had no idea.

He got up, made Kevin run with him, then spent the entire day digging through the rubble of the Town Hall fire. By dinnertime he was filthy, exhausted, and ready to eat his left arm.

Not officially on duty, he stopped by the station to

shower off the ash and filth and was surprised to find an off-duty Tim at Jack's desk. "What are you doing?"

"Research. Hey, can anyone take that arson certification that you and the deputy chief have?"

"You have to be recommended."

"So…" Tim flashed a grin. "Recommend me?"

"Why?"

"Can't let you have all the fun." He logged off, gathered some papers off the printer, and headed to the door.

Jack put a hand out to stop him. "Why do you want to take the class?"

"Maybe I'm aspiring to take your job." Tim waggled a brow. "Come on, man. Don't be a TBBD."

"TBBD?"

"Typical big boss dick." He paused and smiled again. "No offense intended, of course. So…can I take the class?"

Jack met Tim's earnest gaze. "It's not up to me. I'll check with the deputy fire chief."

"You and he go way back. He was your dad's BFF."

"It doesn't work like that."

"No? How does it work?"

"You earn it," Jack said.

Tim nodded. "Earn it," he repeated. "I can totally do that."

He left, and Jack stood there a moment, wondering if he himself had earned anything at all, or if once again, he'd simply followed the career path laid out for him.

The bakery's new ovens came that afternoon, and it was quite an event. It required a handful of really big installation guys, which brought their neighbors out of their shops to watch.

Elsie had accepted the change and seemed excited, handing out free cookies to all the workers. The ovens were still being set when Max Fitzgerald came by. The guys had just opened up the wall to install the new ventilation hoods, and Max just about had a seizure.

"You're tearing down a hundred-and-fifty-year-old wall like it's nothing." He leaned on his cane, a hand on his heart like he was having a heart attack.

"The wall's going right back up," Elsie told him. "You know it is. You represented the historical society as a part of the permit process Leah got from the building department." She smiled. "And hell, maybe the wall will even be plumb this time around."

Max didn't smile. He was staring in horror at the broken bricks at his feet. "Do you have any idea how *old* these bricks are?"

"One hundred and fifty years?" Leah asked.

He pointed his cane at her. "No one likes a smartass, missy."

Elsie's good-natured smile faded. "Actually," she said slowly, linking her arm in Leah's, "I do."

Max narrowed his pale-blue, rheumy eyes in her direction. "I'm disappointed in you, Elsie. Very disappointed."

"So am I," she assured him. "I'm disappointed that I spent eighty bucks on a hot new dress for the Firemen's Ball since I won't be going with you after all."

Max shook his head and left, and Elsie sighed. "Damn, I really wanted to wear that dress."

"You will," Leah said. "You'll get another date."

Elsie laughed. "Honey, in my world, men don't just grow on trees."

There came a knock at the opened back door. Mr.

Lyons stood there with a small bouquet of lilies. "Hello, ladies. Elsie…" He hesitated. "Ah, hell. I'm no good at this. I was next door at the florist shop collecting the rent when I heard you yelling at Max."

"I'll get you our rent too," Leah said.

"No, I— That's not why I'm here." He thrust the flowers at Elsie. "I bought these for you from Ali. Or I *will* buy them. I sort of just grabbed them and ran out of there, so hopefully she doesn't call the cops. Elsie…"

"Yes," she said firmly, taking the flowers. "Most definitely yes."

He blinked. "Yes?"

"Yes, I'll be your date. That is what you were going to ask, right?"

He blushed to the top of his bald dome. "To start."

Leah watched her grandma beam at him. Mr. Lyons was two inches shorter than her, and twice as round—not that Elsie seemed to notice as she smelled the flowers and then leaned in to kiss him.

There was a sweetness to them that tightened Leah's heart. Happiness always seemed so…mysterious. So elusive. But looking at Elsie and Mr. Lyons, it didn't seem so elusive at all. It seemed as simple as just choosing to be happy. She could do that, right? She deserved that. Didn't she?

Baby steps, she decided. One thing at a time. Getting her grandma set up so everything would run smoothly in her absence was one of those steps, no matter what Elsie decided to do.

Getting her own life in line would be step two. Whichever direction that step took her…

By the end of the day, the ovens were in, the wall

patched, and the kitchen cleaned up. Leah looked around with a huge sense of accomplishment. The place had really turned around, and business was up. Way up. She'd had a big hand in that, and she felt pride. And relief. She could really go and things would be okay.

Everything would be okay. The bakery. Elsie. Lucky Harbor. Jack.

And if she wasn't so sure about herself yet, well, that would come.

Jack spent the morning hours scouring the evidence gathered so far on the Town Hall fire. He pulled out everything they had on the other possible arsons. His gut said he'd missed something, something big.

When he couldn't find it on the page, he hit the fire sites again. He walked each of them as if it were the first time. Nothing stuck out at him.

What were they missing?

He pulled out the notes again. The footprint at the convenience store site didn't match any footprints at the other two sites. Which, if the vagrant had been wearing "acquired" shoes, didn't necessarily mean a thing. Jack turned to the tread forensics and realized they'd never gotten any back for the auto shop fire. He called Ronald.

"Doing my job again?" Ronald asked.

"No." Jack blew out a breath. "Okay, maybe. We're missing forensics on—"

"The auto parts fire. I know, it's coming. I'll forward it as soon as I get it. Also, I'm sending a recommendation for you to be my replacement."

"What?"

"I have a bucket list."

Jack felt his heart stop. "You're sick?"

"No. I'm healthy as an ox. I just want to get to my bucket list while I can still zip-line in Costa Rica and eat the spicy food in Thailand. And I want to be fit enough to walk through Scotland. There's some castles there that someone in my life wants to visit."

His mom. He was talking about Dee.

"I'm not asking your permission," Ronald said. "But it'd be great if you didn't object."

"My mom isn't in a good place, Ronald."

"No shit. But she's getting there. And I intend to help her. To be there for her. To love her. For real, Jack. None of this *pretend* bullshit."

Jack grimaced. "You know?"

"I'm an investigator, as you're about to be. And if you're half the man I think you are, you'll fix things up right with your girl. She's a cutie, and she's good for you. It's been fun seeing you knocked off your high and mighty horse for a change."

"What the hell does that mean?"

But Ronald had disconnected.

Chapter 22

♥

The next day, the town came alive as it prepared for the annual arts and crafts fair at the pier. Every year Leah's grandma set up a booth and sold goodies for people to eat as they walked the fair and made merry.

This year, Jack's mom had a booth right next to theirs to sell her scarves and blankets and other knitted wares. Knowing Jack was working and unable to help, and that Elsie wanted to run their booth and had Riley to help her, Leah went to be there for Dee.

"How are you?" Leah asked, always the first question of the day.

Dee smiled. "I'm better today."

"Today?" Leah's senses sharpened. "What happened?"

"Oh, it's silly," Dee said. "A few weeks back one of my meds got changed, and I like to read all the paperwork with each prescription. Anyway, one of the side effects was paralysis, of all things. And I swear to God, my legs and arms just stopped working."

Listening to the story, Leah felt like her heart stopped working. "Oh my God. What did you do?"

Dee laughed softly. "Well, Jack has picked up my meds ever since, and now all the paperwork is always mysteriously missing."

Leah's throat tightened, even through the urge to laugh along with Dee. *Jack...*

As she worked on setting up Dee's booth, she caught sight of him a few times in his uniform and dark sunglasses. He was standing in for Ronald today, walking the length of the booths and checking out everyone's setup.

As if he felt the weight of her stare, he turned and met her gaze. They hadn't spoken since she'd left his bed the other morning after the Jacuzzi event, and it most definitely *had* been an event. Even now, flashes of Jack holding her, his hands tight on her hips as he thrust into her, his head back, face in a mask of pleasure, gave her a hot flash.

Dee sighed dreamily. "You two are so romantic."

Leah tore her gaze off Jack and went back to work setting up Dee's canopy. It was a collapsible thing, and it did not want to work. "You've been reading too many romance novels," she said, struggling.

"Careful with that. It'll catch your fingers. And I like the happy endings. We should all get a happy ending."

"Those are illegal in some states, you know."

Dee laughed. "I'm serious. Would an HEA be so bad?"

Leah stopped and looked at her. "If you want one, all you have to do is get it."

"Oh. Well." Dee brushed that off with a wave of her hand. "I'm too old. But you're not. Your HEA is right there in front of you."

"Hmm." Leah fought with the stupid canopy for a moment, then realized Dee was sitting there smiling widely at her. "What?" she asked. "Am I doing it wrong? Do I have toilet paper on my shoes? Something disgusting in my teeth?"

"No, you're perfect. You're perfect for him."

"Perfect?" Leah laughed. "Dee, I'm just about as far from perfect as a woman can get."

"You're warm, caring, smart, and you always put him first."

"I—"

"You'll make a great wife, you know."

Oh boy. This had been all Leah's idea, this whole her and Jack façade, but every day that it went on made her feel worse and worse. Now, with her heart pounding dully, it was hard to speak, but she knew she had to find the words. She had to tell the truth because she wasn't going to be Jack's wife anytime soon.

Or in this lifetime. "Dee."

"I know, I'm just a silly old woman. But it makes my heart soar to see my son look so happy. It just seems like a wedding should be the next step. And then..." Dee laughed musically. "Grandkids." She clapped her hands together. "Can you imagine?"

All too easily... Oh God, this was bad. How could she do it; how could she crush Dee and tell her that they'd only been pretending? The answer was simple.

She couldn't.

"Look at you," Dee said to someone behind Leah. "You look just like your dad. So handsome."

Leah turned and came face-to-face with Jack.

Reaching above her, he took over her hold on the canopy.

"I could have gotten it," she said.

"I know." Then he locked it into place with annoying ease, smelling ridiculously amazing while he was at it. "Just trying to help," he said, and leaned in and kissed his mom on the cheek. "You doing good?"

"Yes, sweetheart, I'm great. Thanks for the cookies. The nurses all think you're the sweetest thing. They actually believe you made those cookies." She flashed a smile at Leah. "Even though he can't bake to save his life."

"I can so," Jack said.

"Yeah?" Leah asked. She'd never seen him cook anything. "What do you bake?"

"Frozen cookie dough."

Leah burst out laughing.

Dee laughed too. "Well, now the nurses want you to make some for *them*, whatever they were."

Leah eyed him. "You going to make the nurses cookies, Jack? Up the numbers of your fan club?"

"It'd help you out on that Facebook poll," Dee said. "You're still lagging behind Ben, Tim, and that TV cutie. What's his name? Rafe?"

Jack swore beneath his breath, something about "damn options" before turning to Leah. He rubbed his jaw, looking a little unsure of his welcome. She sighed and gave him a smile. "You going to be in the firemen's dunking booth today?"

He glanced in the direction of where the booth was being built just across the pier and grimaced. "I'm first up, actually."

Leah pulled a ticket from her pocket. She'd gotten it with her entrance fee and could have used it to ride the Ferris wheel or play an arcade game. But she was saving it to dunk Jack. "I'm all ready."

"Good thing you throw like a girl."

"You're going to eat those words," she promised him.

He leaned in and put his mouth to her ear. "Make me." Then he swatted her on the ass and strode off.

Oh, hell no. "Dee," she said. "I've got to—"

"Go dunk him." Dee nodded and handed over her free ticket. "Get him for me too."

Leah stalked over there and got in line behind Ben.

He turned and looked at her, and his mouth quirked. He handed her a string of five tickets and then nudged her ahead of him.

"You don't mind?" she asked.

"I'm only going to mind if you miss."

She stepped up to the white line and met Jack's gaze. He'd stripped out of his BDUs, beneath which he wore navy board shorts. His legs were so long that his toes nearly touched the water of the tank as he sat there looking relaxed and at ease, swinging his feet. Not a care in the world.

He didn't think she could dunk him.

Determined to prove him wrong, she wound up and threw. The ball went wide.

"Shake it off," Ben said from behind her, and she adjusted her stance.

From inside the dunking booth, Jack narrowed his gaze at Ben.

Ben didn't look concerned. "You see the thing you want to hit, right? That round target that's like fifteen feet wide?"

"I see it," she grumbled. *Jeez.* "And it's only a foot wide, max."

"Pretend it's your almost fiancé's face."

"Thanks, man," Jack said.

But Leah did just that. And missed again. She went through two more balls, and then her last, and someone tapped her on the shoulder.

Aubrey.

Leah narrowed her eyes. "You're on my Do Not Acknowledge list after letting me go to Jack's house inebriated."

"You weren't inebriated. You were shit-faced." She handed Leah three more tickets. "Truce?"

"*You let me go to Jack's house*," Leah repeated.

"You were…determined."

"You did it for your own amusement," Leah said.

"Well, of course I did," Aubrey said. "It's Lucky Harbor. It wasn't like I had any other entertainment available. And how'd it work out for you?"

Leah met Jack's gaze and sighed. It'd worked out pretty damn good. She used Aubrey's tickets and… missed some more.

In the tank, Jack leaned back, hands behind his head now, definitely relaxed.

"Jesus," Ben muttered, and pushed Leah up past the throwing line, halfway to the dunking tape.

"Hey," Jack said, straightening up. "Cheating."

The crowd behind her cheered. They didn't care. They loved Jack, but they definitely wanted to see their favorite firefighter dunked.

Leah wanted Jack dunked too. She wound up and threw the ball. No one was more surprised than her when it found its target, and with a loud splash, Jack hit the water.

Leah took a lot of fist bumps and pats on the back, and

then, before Jack could get out of the tank, she hightailed it out of there, racing back to Dee's booth. Breathless, she scooped up her purse. "Gotta go, Dee."

"I know." Dee grinned. "You'd better run fast, honey. He was all-state track, remember?"

No one knew better than Leah just how fast Jack could be when he put his mind to something. She headed straight for Ali's booth, where she found Ali and Luke kissing. And not just any little kiss either, but a full-bodied lip-lock. She waited, glancing at her watch, tapping her foot. Finally, she tossed up her hands. "Hello! On a schedule here."

Ali tore her mouth from Luke's and grinned at Leah. "You're not on a schedule. You're running scared because you dunked Jack."

"Oh and nice job, Ace," Luke said, an arm slung around Ali. "You can play on our baseball team anytime."

"Really?" Leah asked, pleased.

"Hell no," Luke said.

Leah sighed and turned to go, and she ran smack into a brick wall.

A brick wall that was Jack's wet chest. Big hands closed on her arms and held her there. "Going somewhere?" he asked smoothly.

She gulped. "Well, I have to—"

"Later," he said and tugged her along with him.

Both Ali and Luke grinned and waved good-bye. Big, fat lots of help there. "Hey." Leah tried to dig her heels in, but Jack was determined. And she already knew that trying to deter a determined Jack was about as easy as trying to stop a train in its tracks. "Jack—"

"Shh."

Oh no. He didn't just— But before she could even finish that thought, Jack had pulled her down a set of stairs
and onto the beach. He was a sight, standing in front of
her with his board shorts riding low on his hips, making
him look dangerous, alluring, and hotter than sin as he
tugged her under the pier.

"Jack—"

He pressed her up against a pylon. Water slapped
against the wood and on the rocky shore. Somewhere a
seagull squawked, and another answered.

All of that barely registered, nothing mattered except
Jack's hot, hard body up against hers. "You're all wet,"
she complained, feeling her sundress getting soaked from
his drenched board shorts.

"Whose fault is that? You were playing with me." His
mouth was near her ear, and he nipped at it. "Dangerous."
He sank his teeth into the column of her throat, and she
gasped.

"You c-can't take it personally," she managed. "It was
for a good cause."

"Yeah? What cause was that?"

Yeah, Leah, what cause was that? "Well…it made me
happy," she said.

Lifting his head, he met her gaze. "I've got other ways
to make you *happy*." Proving it, he threaded his hand
through her hair and tilted her head back for his kiss. Part-
ing her lips, he slowly stroked her tongue with his own
until she couldn't remember her own name. And then he
kissed her some more, until all her bones were gone, and
certainly her resistance.

From up above, the sounds of the fair drifted down to
them, music, laughter… It surrounded them like a bubble,

their own intimate bubble, and as Jack groaned and tightened his grip on her, she knew she was in trouble. "Okay," she murmured, all hot and damp and ready. "But we have to be quick."

He pressed a kiss to her temple and sucked in some air. "We're not doing it beneath the pier, Leah."

"Dammit, you always do that. You get me all revved up and say no. You can't just leave me like this."

"I never say no," he said, his thumb rasping over a nipple. "And I can't leave you like what?"

She arched into his touch. "All hot and bothered. It's rude, Jack."

He laughed softly against her hair and slid his free hand down her body. "Just how hot and bothered are we talking?" That hand snaked beneath her sundress. Up the inside of her thigh.

"Very hot and very b-bothered— God!" she stuttered when his fingers slipped into her panties.

He let out a low groan, a sexy sound that pushed her to the very edge. "You remember what I told you, Leah?"

"Um—" She gasped when he nuzzled the sweet spot beneath her ear at the same time his fingers grazed over her heated, wet flesh. "I'm not sure—"

He stopped stroking her.

She wanted to cry. "Jack—"

"Think about it."

She was thinking about his fingers, those work-roughened, callused fingers that were driving her slowly out of her mind. "You said it was dangerous to play with you—" One of those fingers slid into her, and her knees buckled.

"And yet it didn't stop you," he said against her collarbone, nipping her.

Oh God, those fingers. "Oh, Jack. *Please*—"

He dragged his mouth back to hers and took her lips on the exact right side of rough as he worked her with his fingers until she was grinding against him, panting for air. "Jack." Her toes were curling. "Jack, we have to stop, I'm going to—"

"Come," he murmured, absolutely not stopping. "I want to feel you come for me." He kissed her again, absorbing her cry as she burst, shuddering wildly in his arms.

"I never get tired of that," he said, slowing his fingers, softening his hold, bringing her down gently until she sagged against his chest.

She could feel him hard against her and reached for him just as he pulled his hand away and stepped back. While she stared up at him in a dazed afterglow, he lifted his fingers to his mouth and sucked them clean.

Her knees wobbled.

He gave her a smile that was so wicked she nearly came again, and then he was gone.

Leah sagged against the pylon, still trying to catch her balance in a world that was spinning more and more out of control every day.

She'd assumed they were done with this. Apparently not. In any case, whatever they were—or weren't—Jack knew her body even better than she did.

And, she was pretty sure, he also knew her thoughts. Which meant that he knew her feelings were becoming real. She thought maybe his feelings were just as real, but the problem with that was she'd had her shot at his heart. A long time ago. She'd had her shot, and she'd blown it.

Jack had a lot of really great qualities. He was smart,

and loving, and strong of both mind and body. He would do anything for someone he cared about.

Anything.

Including going along with a hare-brained plan like pretending to be in a relationship just to please his ill mom. But unlike her, Jack actually learned from his mistakes and rarely, if ever, repeated them.

Which meant that for him, loving her was off the table.

This left her hanging out here with these emotions all on her own. And it was time to face the facts. There were emotions, lots of them, because she'd gone and broken yet another promise to him. She wasn't pretending.

This *was* real, and she *was* hurt.

Chapter 23

♥

After the arts and crafts fair, when everything had been broken down and hauled off, Jack ended up at the Love Shack with Ben.

Ben ordered while Jack checked his email and then stared down in shock at the forwarded message from Ronald.

DNA results had come in, adding a hard fact to the arson case. The DNA from the cigarette butts found near the convenience store and Town Hall fires matched. The same person had stood within watching distance of the fires and...watched? Unfortunately there was no known ID or record, which meant that their arsonist was either new...or smart enough to not have gotten caught.

Yet.

Ben came back to the table with a basket of chili fries and two beers, and Jack didn't even look up. "Must be good porn," Ben said.

"It's work. DNA came back on the cigarette butts found at two of the three questionable fires."

"And?"

"Smoked by the same person."

"Son of a bitch."

"We'll nail him."

"We?" Ben asked. "You on the arson team now?"

Jack shrugged. "I've been working with Ronald. I like this end of things." He paused. "A lot."

"You going to give up firefighting?" Ben asked. "The job you were pretty much born to do?"

"Actually," Jack said. "I think I was born to do this."

Ben looked at him for a long beat and nodded. "Then do it."

"You're relieved," Jack said, surprised.

"Fuck, yeah. Don't get me wrong, taking over as deputy fire chief and fire marshal is going to be hell on wheels, and in some ways much harder than the firefighting, but…"

"But what?" Then he read Ben's expression and leaned back, shaking his head. "Jesus, not you too. I'm not going to die on the job. Tens of thousands of firefighters are on the job at any given moment and most of them manage to stay very alive."

"Your dad didn't."

"I'm not my dad."

"You're kidding me, right?" Ben asked. "'Cause the apple's practically still on the tree, man."

"Look who's talking," Jack said. "Your job takes you to third-world hellholes for months at a time. When you're gone, the rest of us can only hold our breath until we see or hear from you again."

Ben lifted a shoulder. "Guess you're not the only one influenced by your dad's hero complex."

"Yeah." Jack nodded. "But I'm making this choice to get off the front line based on my own needs for the future. It has nothing to do with my dad's influence or memory."

"Nothing wrong with that. What does Leah think of your new job?"

"Haven't told her yet."

Ben stopped with his beer halfway to his mouth. "Why not?"

When Jack didn't answer, Ben swore and set down his beer. "Don't ask me how you can be the smartest guy I know and the most stupid at the same time."

"You know we're not a real thing."

Ben gave an impressive eye roll.

"You thought it was stupid that we pretended," Jack said.

"No. I thought it was stupid that you didn't just go for it."

Jack took a long pull of his beer. "You're going to have to repeat that because I think you just suggested I should be with Leah for real. *Leah*."

"Yeah, you keep saying that. Yeah, it's Leah, who you've had a thing for since...well, ever."

Jack shook his head. "What is this? It's not like you're exactly a relationship king. You haven't been in a relationship since Hannah died five years ago. You're no better at getting yourself into this shit than I am."

Ben shrugged. "At least when it came my way, I went for it."

Jack stared at him and then laughed. "Let me get this straight. You're saying if the right woman came your way, you'd take a shot at another relationship?"

Ben's attention drifted to the bar. Jack followed his cousin's gaze to a beautiful blonde sitting there alone, nursing something clear out of a shot glass.

Aubrey.

"Well, there's a bad idea," Jack said with a shake of his head. "Tangling with her."

"Yeah?" Ben asked lazily. "Why's that?"

"She's got claws." Jack looked at him. "You know this. Remember how she was in school?"

"I also remember how we were."

"We were wild, not mean."

Ben didn't look concerned as he rose, dropped cash on the table, and headed out into the night.

"Gee," Jack said, getting to his feet as well. "Guess we're done here."

He left the bar too, but Ben was nowhere in sight. This wasn't so unusual when it came to his cousin, but it was still irritating. Jack grabbed Kevin from where he'd been happily sleeping in the truck. Kevin's favorite thing—after eating or taking a shit on the neighbor's lawn—was going for a walk on the beach.

After that, inexplicably, they ended up standing in front of the bakery. It was closed, of course. But Jack could see a light on in the back, and with a frown, he walked around to the alley. The back door was ajar, and he stepped close to hear a voice muttering softly.

Leah.

She had her back to him as she stood at the cooking island whipping something into a froth. "Okay, cookie dough," she said, "listen up. Just because I'm giving you to Jack doesn't mean I'm giving a piece of *me* to Jack." She added something from a smaller bowl and went back to whipping. "Because I'm not. I might be a little broken, but no one's getting any of my pieces. Not even if…" More from yet another bowl. "A piece of me—or two—really wants to be given."

Jack wasn't sure how to acknowledge the emotion that went through him at her words, uttered with good humor but also with a sort of grim truth. He'd known she cared about him deeply. Just as he'd known that she didn't know how to deal with those feelings. He'd known all of it, and he'd even known why. He'd accepted it. Hell, he was responsible for the rules in the first place. But hearing her talk about her broken pieces killed him. "Leah."

With a shriek she whirled around, her whisk held out in front of her like a weapon. "Jack!" she gasped. "You scared me."

"Stay," he said to Kevin, and to make sure he did, Jack tied the leash to the back porch railing before entering the kitchen. "What are you doing here this late?"

"Making black-and-white cookies." She paused and then shrugged. "For your mom's nurses."

Again emotion swelled, and he stepped into her, taking the bowl from her hands and setting it aside. "Why?"

Leah met his gaze. Her heart was still pounding, but not from fright. "That's what people who care about each other do," she finally said. "They help each other out."

"People?"

She drew a deep breath and let it out. She wasn't exactly sure what was wrong between them, but she knew it was her fault. "Friends," she said.

Jack expressed polite, doubtful surprise with one quirk of his dark brow.

"We are friends," she said, then hesitated. "Aren't we?"

"Naked friends."

"We're more than naked friends," she said and then bit her lip, because why had she said that? Why had she gone there?

Jack studied her for a long moment, and she knew he could see her nerves. "Talk to me, Leah."

"I'm a bit of a mess. No surprise there though, right?" She turned from him, and wiping her hands on her apron, walked to her purse hanging on a hook by the door. From it, she pulled out the stack of cards she'd sent him throughout the years, the ones she'd found in the night-stand by his bed.

He looked down at them for a beat. "What are you doing with those?"

"The question is, what are *you* doing with them?"

"You sent them to me," he said simply.

And to him, it *was* that simple.

In fact, the only person who'd ever complicated this, the most important relationship in her life, was herself. She ran her fingers over the envelopes postmarked from all the places she'd been. She could still remember where she'd bought him each and every card, how she'd felt when she'd signed it and sent it off.

Homesick.

For him.

In the past she'd always shrugged that part off because *she'd* left Lucky Harbor. *She'd* been the one to go. So how could she get homesick for a place, a man, she'd willingly walked away from? "You missed me," she said.

He shrugged, and her gaze flew to his, catching the light of teasing in his. "Maybe a little," he said.

"I missed you," she admitted. "More than I wanted to."

He gave a slow head shake. "Leah, you don't have to do this."

"I don't want it to be pretend," she whispered in a rush, the words tumbling out of her. "I know I said I did, that I promised that it was just that, but I lied. When I'm here in Lucky Harbor, it all feels right. I love it here. In this place, in this bakery. I love it here with you."

He closed his eyes. "Leah—"

"I was just a stupid teenager, Jack. Too immature to know what I was running away from."

He let out a long, slow breath. "You weren't the only one."

"What did you run from?"

"What I want. I always have." He paused. "Ronald's retiring."

She blinked. "What?"

"Yeah, and he's recommending me as his replacement. I have a formal interview for the job next week."

She stared at him and felt a slow smile curve her mouth. "Oh, Jack," she breathed. "It's perfect for you. Just what you've always wanted."

He stared down at her for a long beat, saying nothing, then he laughed real low and quiet. "Hell if you don't drive me absolutely crazy, even as you get me like no one else."

She still held the whisk. Her other arm wound around his neck. "I drive you crazy? In a good way, right?"

"No," he said, but he smiled a little, hooked an arm around her waist, and pulled her in.

"Hi," she whispered.

"Hi." Lifting her up, he set her on the counter. Holding

her there, he reached out and dipped a finger into the bowl of batter at her hip.

"You want some chocolate?" she whispered.

"Yes." He sucked it into his mouth and then took the whisk from her hand, setting it aside. And then he grasped the hem of her sweater and lifted it up over her head.

"What are you doing?"

Instead of answering, he dipped his finger back into the chocolate. Just as she might have said something about him double-dipping, he painted a streak of chocolate across her collarbone.

"Uh—" she started, but then he flicked open her bra and finger-painted her already hardened nipples.

And then he licked every inch of the chocolate off her, by which time she was attempting to tug off his clothes.

"Not here," he said, holding her off.

"Oh my God," she said. "You and your *not here*." But he was right; they were in the bakery kitchen, for God's sake. Panting, she looked around. "The office."

Lifting her up, he walked with her wrapped around him to the office. He set her down on the desk, right on top of the stack of bills she had to pay. "Lift up," he said, and tugged down her leggings, taking everything off, including her boots and panties.

"Jack—"

He cupped her face and tipped it to his for a hot kiss as he nudged her legs open. Then he dropped to his knees and slid his palms up her inner thighs.

She could feel his breath against her and she slid her fingers into his hair, unable to look away as he put his mouth on her. When he did something cleverly diabolical with his tongue, her breath hitched and her head fell back.

Jack never failed to take her right out of herself, out of everything she knew, detonating the careful distance she liked to put between herself and what she was experiencing.

With Jack, there was no distance. He didn't allow it. He had her right where he wanted her, legs splayed by his broad shoulders, hands gripping her possessively, his tongue making her writhe. She couldn't be more vulnerable to him, and in that moment, on the very edge of a steep, slippery precipice, she couldn't care.

"You taste better than the chocolate," he murmured against her and gently sucked in exactly the right spot at exactly the right rhythm, essentially flinging her off a cliff. As her release washed over her, she felt him press a kiss to her inner thigh before rising to his feet. Towering over her, he scooted her back a little and crawled up her body, making her moan as her achingly sensitive nipples grazed his chest. She clutched him to her and kissed him. Somewhere along the way he'd lost his clothes and put on a condom. Taking over the kiss, he slid inside her. "Leah."

She opened her eyes and looked into his, feeling his heart pounding in tune with hers. She knew there wasn't much that could make Jack's heart race and felt a rush of feminine power.

And then, as he began to move, his hips pushing against hers, she felt the rush of another power entirely as the earth moved.

A few beats later, the earth moved for him too.

They lay there on the hard desk in the small, hot room,

breathing hard, working at getting their pulse back from near stroke levels, when her phone rang startlingly loud in the quiet night.

It'd fallen out of her pocket and was on the floor.

"Late for a phone call," Jack said, and they both peered over the desk and looked at the screen.

The ID said: *Dickhead.*

Jack raised one dark brow.

"Rafe," she said.

He stood up and offered her a hand to do the same. "You should answer it."

"Oh, I don't—"

Jack crouched low and hit SPEAKER, and Leah grimaced, reaching for her discarded clothes. "Rafe," she said, self-consciously, scrambling into her leggings and top sans underwear. Ridiculous, since he couldn't see her.

Clearly feeling no such self-consciousness, Jack still stood there butt-ass naked.

"Way to call me back, babe," Rafe said.

"I've been..." She met Jack's gaze. *Why wasn't he putting on his clothes?* "Busy."

"Doing what? Making donut holes because no one in Podunk knows the difference between *pasticiotti* and *tarte au citron*? Whatever, babe. Lucky for you, the network still wants you back. We've agreed to your terms. You said you wanted out of there before the finals, and your wish is our command. I've emailed your flight confirmation."

She'd closed her eyes halfway through this, and when she opened them, Jack had pulled on his jeans and shrugged into his shirt. "Rafe—"

"Oh no," he said. "Hell no, babe. You're not backing

out. You set these plans in motion. You're playing it cool, but I know you're desperate. My favorite state. The tickets, Leah. Use them." And then he disconnected.

Without a word, Jack headed to the door. Leah caught his arm. "Jack, wait."

He paused. He hadn't buttoned his shirt. His hair was tousled from her fingers. He looked big, bad, and ticked off. "Why?"

"It's not what you think."

"Really? Because I'm experiencing a painful déjà vu here, Leah. A minute ago you were telling me Lucky Harbor feels right. I think you were also telling me that I felt right."

"Yes," she said. "I was."

He shook his head. "And yet you were planning to go. You wanted out before the next show aired."

"I made that call to him weeks ago, Jack."

"When?"

"I don't know exactly."

"Yes, you do," he said. "*When?*"

She couldn't tear her eyes off his. They were filled with things, things she'd dreamed of seeing from him, but she was blowing it faster than she could gulp in air.

Nothing new there.

"Before or after you told my mom we were together?" he asked.

She hesitated. "After."

"Are you kidding me? The whole façade was your idea!"

"I know." She paused again. "It's not you, Jack. It's me."

He laughed harshly. "Oh, Christ. Really? You're going

to use the breakup line, Leah? The one *I* taught you? What's next? You have to 'work on yourself'?"

Her throat burned with shame and misery because it was true, it was happening, her biggest fear—screwing this up with him—was coming true right before her eyes. And the worst part? She'd done it all herself. "This time it's actually true. I'm not good at this stuff. You know that."

She could see that he wasn't buying this. "You don't have to be good at it, Leah. Jesus. Do you think I care what words you use to show me how you feel? I don't need words. I have the actions. You watch out for me. You watch out for my mom. And my oversized, drool-manufacturing dog. You care so much about everyone else and their life, but when it comes to yours, you give up. I know your dad made you feel that you were never good enough, but he was a dick, Leah. And he's gone, so why do you still let him do this to you, let his memory keep you from finishing...everything?"

"That's not what I do."

He ticked items off on his fingers. "Our relationship the first time, college—all four times—culinary school—"

"Okay," she said tightly. "I get it. So I have a little follow-through problem."

"Little?" He spun her around to face the steel refrigerator, where their reflections stared back at her. Her own face, pale, pinched with strain. And Jack's, his expression serious, so deadly serious.

"Your parents didn't deserve you," he said, "but at some point you have to grow up and realize you're not a product of your environment. You are who you want to be. You're *you*, Leah. You're a daughter. A friend. A lover. A sweet, warm, smart, beautiful, talented, successful pastry chef. You're anything you want to be. Figure it out and then own it."

She desperately searched her reflection for the woman he saw. "I don't see me that way," she whispered, throat tight.

"Why not?"

It was a most excellent question, one for which she did not have an answer.

"When do you leave exactly, Leah?"

"I don't—I don't know exactly."

"You always know."

Touché. "Soon," she admitted.

He turned her to face him. "How soon? Truth, Leah."

"Truth?" She forced the words out. "I should have left already."

"Why haven't you?"

"You know why."

He shook his head. "Don't. Don't say you stayed here for me."

She bit her tongue rather than say exactly that. And then she gave him the truth he wanted. "I'd planned to go before the finals."

"Were you going to tell me?"

She wanted to turn away from the look in his eyes. The recriminations. The hurt. But she couldn't tear her eyes from his. "I'm going because I need to. I want to finish school. I want to finish something to prove to myself that I can. I was going to tell you, yes, but I didn't know how," she managed.

He gave one curt nod and reached for the door.

She ran after him and slipped between him and the wood, arms spread as if she could really stop him if he chose to leave.

He scrubbed a hand over his face. "Move, Leah."

"No."

"Listen," he said, a grim set to his mouth. "New rule."

"Jack—"

"No big, drawn-out good-bye." At the look on her face, he let out a long breath. "All my life, you've been my Almost." He softened slightly, his gaze touching over the features of her face as if memorizing her. "I want you, Leah. I've always wanted you. But wanting isn't enough. You have to fight for it too, and you're not going to."

"Jack—"

"I'm cutting my losses on this one, Leah. Pulling the plug. Call it another rule if you want. No more intimacy. I'm ending this now before either of us gets hurt."

And then he gently set her aside, walked out the door, and was gone.

She stood there in shock. "How is walking away fighting for it?" she asked the night.

The night didn't answer.

"Dammit." She searched for her usual state of denial, for her temper, for anything that might allow her to rationalize what had just happened as not being her own fault.

Nothing came except pain.

And guilt.

And more pain.

There was no way around this. However it had happened, it had happened. And worse, for the first time in her life she hadn't been the one to walk away. Jack had beaten her to the punch.

Chapter 24

♥

Jack left the bakery, hitting the highway at one in the morning at speeds designed purely for adrenaline. He got halfway up to Beaut Point before he saw the red-and-blue lights whirling in his rearview mirror. "*Shit.*"

The cop turned out to be Sheriff Sawyer Thompson. Sawyer had been about five years ahead of Jack in school, but Sawyer's wildness was still legendary. How the guy had ended up on the right side of the law was a mystery to Jack, but one thing about Sawyer—he didn't sugarcoat anything.

"Christ, Harper, I clocked you at ninety-five." The sheriff leaned in past Jack to pat Kevin on the head. "The paperwork's going to piss me off."

"So don't do it."

Looking disgusted, Sawyer went hands on hips. "I'm only out here tonight as second-string because the flu's hit the station. I didn't hear a fire call go out."

"There isn't a fire." Except the one in his gut. "You could pretend you didn't see me."

"Or you could slow the fuck down." A full moon was just peeking over the inky black silhouette of the Olympic peaks in front of them, and Sawyer gestured to it. "See what happens when you slow down? You get to enjoy shit."

They both watched the moon. Kevin went back to sleep.

"Yeah, that's real pretty," Jack said after a minute or two. "We going to make out now?"

"Temperamental," Sawyer noted. "And pissy too. You know what temperamental and pissy plus a lead-foot equals? *Sorry-ass dumped.*"

Jack slid farther down in his seat.

"Got it in one," Sawyer said. Clearly enjoying himself now, he leaned against the truck like he had all night. "I haven't been keeping up with your social calendar, Harper. Who dumped ya? That cute flight nurse? Or the teacher? Oh wait. I know. The cutie pastry chef who moons over you when you're not looking."

"Maybe I was the one who left."

Sawyer nodded. "Good. Go with that. That bitchy 'tude works. So…who was it?"

Jack sighed.

"Aw, come on. You know how quiet it's been tonight? I'm bored. Tell me, and maybe I won't ticket you."

"Just give me the fucking ticket."

Sawyer grinned. "It's the pastry chef. Right?" He pulled out his ticket pad and started writing.

"Hey. You said you wouldn't give me a ticket."

"I said *maybe…*"

Twenty minutes later, Jack was in possession of a speeding ticket to go along with his stupid broken heart. He pulled into his driveway, waited for Kevin to do his business, and then headed straight to the fridge for a beer.

He was on his second when Ben came in the back door. Without a word, he took the third and last beer in the fridge and tossed it back. Setting the empty down on the counter, he swiped his mouth and looked at Jack. "What are we drinking to?"

"Women. They suck."

The smallest of smiles appeared on Ben's mouth. "If they're very bad they do. Or very good…"

"Why are you here?" Jack asked. "It's two in the morning."

Ben shrugged. "You seem like maybe someone kicked your puppy."

From his huge bed in the corner of the kitchen, Kevin lifted his big head. "Woof."

Jack craned his neck and stared at Ben. "You're not that good. How did you hear?"

"Maybe I *am* that good."

"No you're not."

Ben flashed a rare smile. "Okay, I'm not. Sawyer told his wife, Chloe, that he wrote you up, and Chloe happened to be at the Love Shack with her sisters, one of whom is friends with one of the ER nurses. Mallory. She's married to Ty Garrison, who's on flight care with…wait for it…Danica. It's all on Facebook," he explained.

Jack just stared at him. "It's like a bad sitcom."

"Except it's your life." Ben's amusement faded. "You okay?"

"Is that concern or gruesome curiosity?"

"Definitely the latter."

Jack swore and moved toward the door, but Ben shoulder-checked him. "Okay, Jesus. It's concern. Put your vagina away."

"Fuck you."

"We're related, so that's illegal in most states." Ben put his hand on Jack's chest when Jack started to push past him. "So it's true then? You and Leah? You're done?"

"We were never *not* done."

"Bullshit," Ben said. "Admit that much at least. It was never a pretend game, and we both know it. What the hell happened?"

"She took a job with that asshole producer."

"Rafe Vogel," Ben said, and at Jack's narrowed-eyed look, shrugged his shoulders. "So I like trash TV; sue me."

"She's going back to school in France, and it's being filmed for a new show," Jack said.

"Nice gig."

He gave Ben a long look.

"And...I'm missing something," Ben said. He thought for a moment. "When did she take it?"

"Shortly after telling my mom that we were dating."

Ben let out a low whistle. "And you think she's running."

"Again. She's running again."

"Maybe she didn't think she had an option."

"There's *always* an option."

Ben studied him. "Oh Christ. She didn't dump you. *You* dumped *her*. You love her and yet you dumped her." He shook his head in disgust. "You sure have a God-given talent for pushing people who really care as far away from you as possible."

"Yeah?" Jack asked, getting pissed off all over again. "Then why are *you* still here?"

"Because someone has to be in your corner, even when you're being a complete dumbass."

"Thanks."

Ben clapped his shoulder. "Anytime." He headed to the door.

"And I don't love her."

"Okay. But you totally do."

Well, hell. It was shockingly, horrifyingly true.

Sleep didn't come to Leah until somewhere just before dawn, when she was woken up by a call from Dee. "You okay?" Leah asked quickly, her heart racing, thoughts jumbled from both the lack of rest and being startled awake after what felt like only a few minutes of sleep. "What's wrong?"

"Oh sorry, honey. Did I wake you? I figured you got up at this time to get to the bakery."

"It's okay; I do need to get up." She shoved a hand through her hair and sat up, flicking on the light. "What's wrong? Are you—"

"I'm fine."

"Jack—"

"Is fine too. Or so I assume," Dee said. "You know what today is, right?"

The first day of the rest of her screwed-up life. "Uh…" She struggled to remember.

Dee laughed. "It's Firefighter Car Wash Day."

Firefighter Car Wash Day was practically a national

holiday in Lucky Harbor. It occurred monthly during the summer and early fall and was more highly attended than the Fourth of July parade.

"I want to get my car washed," Dee said. "But I'm not really okay to drive. I was hoping you'd drive my car to Jack for me."

"You want to make Jack wash your car?"

"I want to contribute to the cause. If I tried to just hand him money to put into the till, he wouldn't take it."

This was undoubtedly true, but Leah wasn't going to be high on the list of people Jack wanted to see today. She kept picturing the look on his face after Rafe's call.

I want you, Leah. I've always wanted you, but you have to fight for it too...

She wanted to hate him for that, but how could she when it was the truth? She'd never fought for anything in her life.

She'd always walked away. Or run. She'd always been a quitter, doing her damnedest to prove her father right. That was going to change.

"You don't mind, do you, honey?" Dee asked.

"Of course not," Leah said, which was how later that day, after eight hours at the bakery, she ended up with Dee—and Grandma, who "didn't want to miss the hotties"—waiting in line at the fire station lot for a car wash.

All three shifts of firefighters had shown up for the gig and were good-naturedly out there doing their part in dark-blue swimsuits and little else except charm and charisma.

Grandma Elsie pulled out her phone to access her camera.

"Grandma!"

"It's not my fault," she said unperturbed. "Lucille pays us for the really great shots."

"Oh my," Dee said and put a hand to her chest. "Look at them all."

But Leah's gaze was on only one. Jack. Unlike most of the other guys, he wore a dark-blue T-shirt as well as his board shorts, with his official badge on a pec. He was standing in front of a Vespa, which had a beautiful redhead in it. She was talking animatedly to him, her hands moving as she told some story that made Jack burst out laughing.

He'd gotten wet at some point because his shirt was clinging to him. His hair was tousled, like he hadn't bothered with a comb. And when he laughed, Leah's chest ached.

"He looks tired," Dee murmured. "Poor baby."

"Yeah," Leah said, watching him lean into the redhead for a good-bye hug before she rode off. "Real tired."

"You know who that is, right?" Dee asked. "Chloe Traeger. Well, she's really Chloe *Thompson* now that she married the sheriff. She and Jack are just friends, honey. You don't have to be jealous—"

"I'm not," Leah said. "Of course I'm not." But she totally was. "Jack can do whatever he wants."

Dee turned to her. "I hope you two aren't going to have some sort of new age open relationship—"

"Dee." Leah blew out a breath and knew it was time to face the music. She reached for Dee's hand. "Jack and I, we're not a thing. I lied to you. I'm sorry. So sorry. I was just trying to help, but I ended up making it worse." She hesitated and then admitted the rest. "I did it to try to make you feel better, or that's how it started anyway. But the truth is, a part of me wanted it to be true between me and Jack. I shouldn't have ever said it though, or tried to deceive you."

"Oh, Leah," Grandma Elsie murmured from the back-seat.

Dee was quiet a moment, taking in the emotion in Leah's eyes. Then she leaned in and hugged Leah hard.

Leah squeezed her eyes shut and squeezed her back. "I never meant to hurt you. I—"

"I know." Dee pulled back, keeping her hands on Leah's arms as she looked her in the eyes. "And I *know*. I always knew."

Leah stared at her. "What?"

Dee sighed. "I was so touched, *am* so touched, that you wanted to help so badly. I'd hoped that you wanting it as much as you did would make it true."

Leah felt her eyes fill and she covered her face, but Dee gently pulled her hands free. "You weren't the only one in on the subterfuge, Leah. Jack isn't a man who bows to pressure. He doesn't do anything that he doesn't want to. He went along with it, and that brought me great hope." She paused, laughter in her voice. "And great amusement as well. Goodness, you two are fun to watch."

Leah groaned in misery.

"I wish you could have seen the way you two danced around each other, slowly coming to realize that it wasn't pretend at all."

"But it's not real," Leah said. "Last night we— He—" She shook her head. "It's not happening, Dee. It's over. Whatever it was that we were doing, it's over."

"Oh, honey," Dee said. "Running isn't the answer."

Leah opened her mouth to tell her that this time, this

one time, it was Jack doing the running, but the simple truth was she'd let him go. She'd taken the easy way out before he could discover her real secret—she loved him.

Hopelessly.

"It's my fault," she said. "I should've told him—"

"What, baby," Dee said. "That he's the one? That he's always on your mind?" She smiled, a wealth of knowledge in her gaze. "I remember what it's like, you know. Being afraid to let go. It's like that silly game you play when you're kids, falling backward and letting your friends catch you. It's all about trust, isn't it? Such a hard thing to do."

"So how did you finally do it?" Leah asked.

"My mom told me that I should trust the man who could see the sorrow behind my smile, the love behind my anger, and the reasons behind my silence."

Elsie was nodding. "Those are good ones. And you had that with Jack Senior, Dee. You surely did."

"He was the one and only," Dee agreed, and her gaze tracked across the parking lot to Ronald.

He met her gaze and lifted a hand.

Dee blushed and returned the wave.

"Dee," Leah said softly. "It's been so long. Don't you think maybe it's time for another one and only?"

"Oh, honey. No one's going to be interested in my old bones. Look at me." She gestured to the kerchief she had on her head, covering up the fact that she'd lost her hair. "I'm a mess."

"Dee Harper," Elsie said sternly. "You're thirty years younger than I am. I'd trade this old body for your skinny ass any day of the week, you just say the word."

Dee pulled down the visor to look at herself just as

Ronald knocked on the window. "Oh!" she said, jumping.

Leah powered the window down for him, and he nodded politely to Elsie and Leah. "The finals run tomorrow night," he said to Leah. "You going to win?"

"She can't tell you," Elsie said. "But yes, she's going to win."

"Grandma," Leah said and sighed.

Ronald smiled and turned back to Dee. "You look beautiful today."

She blushed some more. "You look busy out there."

"It is busy," he said. "Which is great. The money we're collecting today goes to the teen center." He was leaning on the car door by now, and craned his neck, taking in their bird's-eye view of the firefighters working hard. "You enjoying the scenery?"

Dee shocked Leah by looking right into Ronald's eyes. "Yes," she said.

And then it was Ronald's turn to blush a little. He cleared his throat and straightened. "You know, I've got two New York steaks in my fridge. Planning on barbecuing them tonight. Thought maybe you could use some protein."

"Are you asking her out?" Elsie wanted to know. "Because you might have to be more forward than that, Ronald. Our girl here is slower than a three-legged turtle in peanut butter when it comes to these things. You can't be obtuse."

"Grandma," Leah said again, but Ronald just nodded. And didn't take his eyes off Dee. "I'm asking you out," he clarified. "To my place."

"Yes," Elsie said. "She'd love to."

The corners of Ronald's mouth twitched. "Dee?"

Dee's smile had faded. "I...can't," she said and un-hooked her seat belt. "Excuse me." She pushed open the door and headed to the stands, where others were gathered, waiting for their vehicles to get washed.

Elsie got out and patted Ronald's hand. "You did good. Real good," she said gently. "She's just gun-shy."

Leah helped her grandma to the stands to wait with Dee.

"I can't believe you passed that man up," Elsie said to Jack's mom.

Dee shook her head and made herself busy cleaning out her purse.

Elsie sighed and rose to her full four feet, eight inches. "It's a sad day when *I'm* the risk taker."

"Grandma," Leah said. "Where are you going?"

"To the seniors." She jabbed her cane in the direction of the other end of the stands, where a group of seniors sat together, joking and laughing. "They might be old, but at least they know how to kick it."

Chapter 25

♥

At a lull in the car washing, Jack pulled Ronald aside. "I wanted to talk to you about the forensics."

"Never mind that," Ronald said. "I've got something more important."

"There's something more important than the only serial arsonist in Lucky Harbor's history?" Jack asked.

Ronald blew out a sigh. "Said a guy who still has his entire love life ahead of him."

Jack paused. "Huh?"

"I want to retire, goddammit!" Ronald burst out. "I want to retire so I can spend some time with someone I care about while sex is still more fun than bingo, or before I need a little blue pill to—"

"Jesus! I get it, okay?" Jack resisted the urge to cover his ears like a little kid and go running.

"I want that with your mom, Jack. I'm in love with her."

Jack shoved his fingers through his hair. "I don't know what to say to you."

"How about that you'll talk to her and tell her that she's been a widow longer than she was a wife. That it's time to look around and see there are other fish in the sea. That she should keep the smile you put on her face with the whole you and Leah thing. That she could have it for herself if she wanted, and it sure as hell wouldn't be pretend."

Jack looked into Ronald's eyes. He was solemn and quite serious, and…not at all nervous. Ronald was a steady, stand-up sort of guy who didn't do things frivolously or without merit. If he said something, it was so.

And he wasn't asking for Jack's opinion on his feelings, or for Jack to necessarily approve. "You know she's not…well."

"You're enabling her."

"She's been through a lot," Jack said tightly.

"And she's survived. She's going to keep surviving." He gave Jack one last long look and moved off.

More cars pulled into the lot. Jack washed two cars on autopilot, then looked up when he realized Danica was standing there talking to him. "I'm sorry," he said, shaking his head. "What?"

She was in a skimpy little white sundress that showed off her curves to perfection, and she sent him a smile that said she knew it. "I said I heard that you and Leah are over, and that you should let me help you commiserate."

"I can't."

"Aw." She hugged him before he could stop her. "You're so brave," she said. "So hurt. You call me when you're ready. I can help, Jack. I promise."

Jack caught sight of his mom and managed to disentangle himself. "Sorry," he said. "I've got to go," and he strode over to Dee. "Hey," he said.

"Son."

Not a happy tone. But then again, other than when Leah had told her he was in a relationship, he hadn't heard a happy tone from her in so long he'd nearly forgotten what it sounded like. "You okay?" he asked. "Why are you here?"

"To support my son," she said and lowered her voice. "The one who felt he had to lie to me."

Having no idea how she'd found out, he pulled her aside for privacy. "Mom—"

"Oh no. Don't you 'mom' me in that tone. Jack—" She cupped his face. "I didn't want you to make my mistakes. I didn't want you to wallow. I'm so deeply ashamed that you saw me give up like I did. And then to make you feel like you had to fake a relationship to make me happy… No." She inhaled deeply. "This isn't about me. It shouldn't be about me. It's your turn, Jack. Your turn to be happy."

"I *am* happy." Or he had been, until about 0100 hours last night.

She stared up into his eyes. "You aren't. Lie number two. Good Lord, Jack. What else have you lied about?"

"Remember that time Jack told you that someone hit-and-ran your car? Not true. He ran over Mr. Lyons's mailbox."

They both turned to face Ben, who raised his hands in surrender. "Not funny yet? Sorry, my bad." He started to back up, but Dee reached out and snagged him by the front of the shirt. "Did you know?"

"Uh…" He slid a glance at Jack. "Hard to tell. Did I know what exactly?"

"That Jack and Leah were faking their relationship just to make me happy."

"Uh…," Ben repeated, shoving his hands in his pockets and hunching his shoulders. He'd faced hell itself with a shocking fearlessness, but his beloved Aunt Dee in a mood simply terrified him.

"Benjamin Matthew Kincaid," she said sternly. "Look at me."

Ben met her gaze unflinchingly. "Yes, ma'am."

"Don't you 'ma'am' me!" Dee threw her arms around him. "I love you so much, you big, cranky, adorable sweetheart. So much more than your idiot cousin."

Ben had winced at the "adorable sweetheart" but his arms closed around Dee, as over her head his amused gaze met Jack's. "Of course you do," he murmured to Dee.

Jack flipped Ben off.

Ben returned the gesture without letting go of Dee.

Dee pushed free and looked up at Ben. "Thank you."

"You're welcome," Ben said.

"You have no idea what I'm thanking you for."

"None," Ben agreed.

Dee laughed and smacked him lightly on the chest. "For letting Jack pretend to be with Leah. Thank you."

"Let?" Ben asked. "Dee, no offense, but no one lets Jack do shit. He does whatever he wants, when he wants."

Dee beamed. "Exactly."

When both Jack and Ben just stared at her, she shook her head. "Honestly, do I have to spell everything out? You don't see? Neither Jack nor Leah pretended anything."

Jack shook his head, seeing where she was going with this. "Mom, listen—"

"No, Jack. _You_ listen. You've been so good to me. And

I've had a good life. All I wanted for you is the love of a great woman, someone who would treat you right and take care of you. And then I could die happy."

Jesus. "Mom—"

"And when I'm gone," she said. "I—"

"Mom. Stop."

"I'm not done, Jack."

"Hell no, you're not done. You're not dying."

"But—"

"You're *not*. I'm not going to let you," he said very seriously.

At his side, Ben nodded just as solemnly. "No one's dying," he agreed. "Especially you. You're the glue, Dee. We need the glue."

"Oh." She breathed and sniffed noisily, searching her pockets, presumably for a tissue. "Oh, you boys are just the sweetest things."

Again Ben winced at the "sweet" moniker but offered her the hem of his T-shirt for her to swipe at her eyes.

"And as for Dad," Jack said. "You've waved the widow's weeds for long enough. I know you loved him; we all know it. And I know you miss him, but that doesn't mean you're half human. Live, dammit. It's worth it."

She stared at him, and then, horrifying him, her eyes filled with tears again.

"Ah, Mom. No." He pulled her in and hugged her, pressing his jaw to the top of her head. "I'm sorry."

"Don't you dare be sorry." She sniffed and pressed her face to his chest. "I shouldn't have let everything overcome me as much as I have." She lifted her head. "I taught you boys better than that."

"You did," Ben said quietly. "You taught us to go for what we wanted, and we each did."

Jack didn't say anything because in Ben's case it was absolutely true. Ben had wanted to design and build stuff, and he had. He'd wanted to fall in love and get married, and he'd done that too, until it'd been taken from him.

But Jack had let his future be guided by his past. Exactly what he'd accused Leah of, which made him a hypocrite.

He wasn't much for regrets, but that one was starting to weigh on him now.

"Jack," his mom said, cupping his face. "If I have to get over myself and go for what will make me happy, promise me you'll do the same." She pulled Ben in by the hand as well. "Both of you."

"Mom—"

"Promise me," she said fiercely.

Jack nodded. Ben did the same.

And then Dee smiled her queen bee smile, squeezed them both one last time, and pulled back. "Now, if you'll pardon me, I have to RSVP to a steak barbeque."

They watched her walk toward Ronald with great purpose.

"Imagine if she harnessed her powers for good," Ben said.

Jack started to respond, but then Dee went toe to toe with Ronald. Putting her hands on his, she pulled him to her and kissed him like she meant it. "Shit."

"Yep," Ben said. "She's tonguing your boss."

Jack grimaced and then rubbed a hand over his face. When that didn't clear his head, he gave Ben a shove. That helped only marginally.

"Your maybe, sort of, pretend ex-fiancé is next in line, man." Ben shoved him back. "Time to get to work."

Jack turned and looked. Sure enough, Leah was in his mom's car. She'd come around to the hoses and buckets of soapy water and had just hefted one of the hoses in her hand.

Leah stood there in white short shorts and a dark-blue LHFD T-shirt that he was pretty sure was pilfered from *his* closet. It was tied at her belly button, and she looked like a cross between his greatest fantasy and his biggest heartache.

She met his gaze, her own hooded.

Jack handed Ben his sponge and headed toward her. "You're not supposed to be here," he said when he got close.

Her eyes flashed. "Look, you might be right about everything you said last night. I am a complete screwup. I'm a lot of things. But I am still a contributing member of society here in Lucky Harbor, so—"

"I meant you aren't supposed to be *here*, behind the line, with all the gear." He gestured to the madness around him. "It's some sort of insurance liability."

"Oh." In the bright sunlight she blushed. "Right."

He caught her arm just as she turned away, not sure what he planned on saying, only knowing that seeing her was like a punch to the gut. But the next thing he knew, he was doused with water right in the face.

"Whoops," Tim said from the next car over, where he was hosing off the soap. "Sorry, kids!"

He'd also managed to hose down Danica, who was standing next to her car behind them. That snug, thin white sundress was now turning the family car wash into an X-rated wet T-shirt contest. She turned on Tim and nailed him in the face with a soapy sponge.

And just like that, the water fight was on. No one escaped unscathed. And in fact several people ganged up on Jack, including Tim and Ian, and he was pretty sure that it was Danica who'd jumped on his back and smashed a wet sponge in his face. The craziness went on for a while. People were soaking wet and having a good time. Lucky Harbor residents were nothing if not opportunistic and resilient.

When Jack finally pried free and swiped his eyes clear, Leah was gone.

Chapter 26

♥

On the night of the *Sweet Wars* finals, it was Elsie's turn to make dinner. "So," she said over meatloaf and potatoes. "Back to school, huh?" She smiled. "I'm so happy for you."

"It's only for one quarter."

"And then you'll go run a pastry shop, probably somewhere really exciting like Paris or New York, right?"

"I don't know," Leah said. She hadn't gotten that far in her head yet.

Elsie laughed a little. "Why am I asking? Three months out is about as far as you ever plan."

Leah went still, then reached for her grandma's hands. They were dry and callused. A baker's hands.

They matched Leah's.

"Grandma, you knew this was temporary."

Elsie nodded. "Of course, honey. I knew. I understand. If I were thirty years younger and half as talented as you, I'd be off making the most of it too. You have a lot out in front of you. I hope you know that."

"I know it," Leah said. "And I know it because of you."

"Oh. Well." Elsie's eyes filled, but she shook her head. "You'd have figured it out sooner or later."

"No, Grandma, it was all you. You and Jack." Her own eyes filled. "Always loving me unconditionally. Beating me over the head with it all until it sank in."

The doorbell rang.

It was Max Fitzgerald. Leah stared at him in surprise. "Mr. Fitzgerald. What are you doing here?"

"I need to speak to your granny."

"She's busy."

"I'm right here," Elsie said, coming up next to Leah. "What do you want, Max?"

"You convinced Lyons to pull out of escrow? You can't do that."

"Can and did," Elsie said and went to shut the door on him, but Max stuck his foot in it.

"Why?" he asked. "Why the hell would you get him to back out of a deal like that?"

"Why do you care?"

"Because believe it or not," Max said, "I care about you. It was a great offer. He would've gotten good, fair-market value on that piece-of-shit building. So what the hell?"

Leah stared in shock at Elsie. "You talked Mr. Lyons into keeping his building?"

"Yes." Elsie tilted her nose up to nose-bleed heights. "Yes, I did."

"Why, Grandma?"

"Because…" Elsie turned to Leah and softened her gaze. "Because you've reminded me how much I love that damn shop. I made that place, from the bottom up.

I know it's nothing fancy, and I'll probably have to hire some more help after you leave, but..." She shrugged and broke eye contact with Leah. "I'm not ready to let go."

"You didn't have to let go!" Max said. "No one was going to kick you out."

"But the new guy will be making changes. Updating, renovating. At the end of the year, the lease will go up. Everything will change."

Max couldn't deny this. He sighed. "Look, one thing I've learned...it's the way of things, Elsie. Change happens."

Elsie looked at Leah as she answered. "But I know," she said softly. "Except this at least, this one thing, didn't have to."

"You don't think Lyons will raise the lease?" Max asked. "Because he will."

"Not mine," Elsie said confidently, causing Max to toss up his hands and stomp off.

Leah parked at the bakery. She'd made her excuses to Elsie, and to Ali and Aubrey as well.

She didn't turn on any lights as she let herself into the kitchen and hopped up on the counter with a tub of left-over cookie dough and a wooden spoon.

And there, with her iPad and her impending sugar rush, she watched the *Sweet Wars* finals.

Alone.

The challenge had been deceptively simple. Make a five-tiered wedding cake large enough to serve two hundred people.

Except a cake that size was never simple, as Rafe so cheerfully pointed out to the camera. Unlike a smaller cake, frosting wasn't just spread onto traditional wedding cakes. Rather fondant covered each cake tier to give a smooth look. Fondant was made from a sugar syrup that took up to forty minutes of constant stirring to get to the correct consistency. And then after applying it to each painstaking layer, there were still many hours of decoration needed.

Leah could remember the buzz of the adrenaline flowing her through her veins as she'd worked fast and steady, tuning out the sounds and scents and overwhelming air of panic around her.

Now in the quiet kitchen she watched, as with twenty-five seconds left on the clock, the enormity of the situation caught up with her. She could see it so clearly on her own face. The self-doubt reaching up and grabbing her by the throat as she carried her beautiful, perfect, five-tiered wedding cake to the judging table and…

Dropped it.

She watched as it hit the floor with a splat, watched herself go pale and bring shaky hands to her mouth. Watched as everyone else on the cast turned to take in the disaster, shocked horror on their faces.

Each of them had been playing for second place, and everyone had known it.

Except Leah had dropped the cake.

The show cut to an ad break, and there on the counter, Leah closed her eyes. *What had she been thinking?*

But she knew what she'd been thinking. She'd stood there on the set, the win literally within her reach, and it'd hit her like a ton of bricks.

It was hers. The win was hers. She was about to be given everything she needed to open her own pastry shop—with the world watching.

You're never going to amount to a damn thing, Leah.

The anxiety had ridden up and grabbed her by the throat.

And suddenly the very best thing that could happen had become the worst.

The commercial break ended. The show came back on, and Leah forced herself to watch. Forced herself to take in her own misery at being sent home when she knew damn well she'd had first place if she'd only been brave enough to take it.

But she wasn't brave.

She let out a careful breath and turned off her iPad. And since her phone was buzzing like it was having a seizure, she turned that off as well.

That's when the bakery phone started going off.

"Oh my goodness, Leah," came Dee's disembodied voice from the answering machine. "Honey, I'm so sorry you tripped and dropped the cake."

Click.

The phone immediately rang again.

"Leah?" It was Ali. "You tripped? Do you need me? I mean, I realize you've known you tripped for six months, but…damn. Call me."

And so on.

Leah closed her eyes and tuned it out. It wasn't hard to do when the messages were all the same. Lucille said it looked like she'd been tripped by another cast member. Aubrey offered to drive the getaway car.

Leah dug into the bowl of cookie dough with renewed energy, inhaling the rest of it—which was delicious. Gee, maybe she should do this for a living…

Why hadn't she left already?

She hadn't left because of Elsie, she reminded herself. In spite of her grandma's assurances, Leah wasn't at all sure that she could go back to handling the bakery by herself.

And then there was the fact that Leah was all Elsie had.

No, wait. That was backward. Elsie was all *Leah* had. Leah had nearly forgotten what it felt like to be with family, to be unconditionally loved...

And that wasn't all, a little voice inside her head reminded her. There was more holding her to Lucky Harbor, and she knew it.

There was Jack. He was family too, in a very different way. Jack was...

Everything.

As if she'd conjured him up, he appeared at the back door looking superficially neutral. Letting himself in, his gaze settled on hers as he shut and locked the door behind him.

He was in a T-shirt that said JUST DO IT and a pair of old Levi's that lovingly contoured his body, intimately cupping parts of him that she missed. He smiled at the sight of her on the counter, bowl under one arm, wooden spoon in her other hand. But the smile didn't meet his serious eyes.

He'd seen the show.

"I'm not going to talk about it," she warned him. "So if that's why you're here, go away."

He didn't respond to this.

"I mean it, Jack. You said no big good-bye. You said it. It was your rule. I'm leaving tomorrow. Let's just let it go."

He came closer, until his thighs bumped hers. He looked into the bowl and then ran a finger along the bowl's edge and sucked it into his mouth.

"Double fudge," he said.

"You're good."

His eyes met hers, and the things she saw in them dried up her mouth. Because he was also bad. Perfectly, wonderfully *bad*. Not wanting to acknowledge the tightening in her gut—God, she hated knowing she'd let him down along with everyone else she knew—she licked the wooden spoon and said nothing.

He leaned against the counter and waited her out. He always could.

"Still not going to talk about it," she finally said.

He just looked at her.

Dammit. "Listen, just being on that show was a big deal for me, okay? Who could have expected me to get as far as I did, much less win it?"

More nothing from the big, bad, attitude-ridden firefighter, and this pissed her off. "Your expectations for me have always been too high," she snapped.

"You dropped the cake. You fucking *dropped* the cake."

"I know," she said. "I was there."

"Leah, you could make a wedding cake when you were thirteen years old. I know it. I ate it. You'd carry it across my mom's kitchen to the table with pride and grace. You never dropped it."

"Well I did this time."

He shook his head. "Why?"

In the heavy silence, her breath caught audibly. "I don't want to discuss it. I screwed it up, that's all. I'm not going to be a star pastry chef and that's that. Get over it."

He closed his eyes and dropped his head to his chest for a beat before looking at her again, his eyes filled with exasperation and frustration. "I don't give a shit about what you do for a living, Leah. It's not about that. It's about you."

The storm that had been brewing inside her broke open. "I'm not perfect, all right? We both know it. So you, and everyone else who thinks I should be, need to back off. I'm only me."

"Well finally," he said, his voice not quite as low and controlled as usual. "Something real out of your mouth."

She pointed her chocolate-covered spoon at the door. "Get out."

"Oh hell no. We're just getting somewhere."

She clamped her mouth shut. She'd chosen to stay here in Lucky Harbor until the bitter end, so she had no one to blame for this confrontation but herself. She was going to own it. "I lost, okay? I'm not going to make excuses for not being the best."

"Are you going to make excuses for not letting yourself be happy? For thinking you don't deserve it?"

"I'm not going to open a pastry shop in New York City. Big deal. How many people get to do that anyway? I've got other stuff going on. I'm happy."

"If only you believed that," he said very seriously. Way too seriously.

"Don't start with me, Jack. I am happy."

"Are you?"

"Yes."

He looked around, and she followed his gaze, taking in everything he saw. Elsie's favorite bowls stacked up along the counter. Elsie's utensils and cookery. Elsie's everything.

"There's nothing of you here," he said.

"It's Grandma's bakery. Not mine."

"I've been at the house. There's nothing of you there either."

"Again," she said. "Not my place."

"Yeah? Well then, where *is* your place, Leah?"

"You know I don't have one right now. I've been a little busy. And now I'm leaving anyway, so—"

"Bullshit." He caged her in with a hand on either side of her hips. "I'm calling bullshit, Leah."

"No, it's true. I leave tomorrow night."

"Not that," he said. "Yeah, you're leaving. No one knows it better than me. I'm talking about you not letting anyone too close or they'll see your flaws."

Her breath hitched. Dammit. He knew her far too well.

He ducked a little to look into her eyes. "But I've always seen you, all of you, flaws and all. I know you, so I can say this. You're not perfect. But you're perfect for me. And it pisses me off that you won't let that happen. Let us happen. I'm tired of watching you implode, Leah. Tired and done."

"Then get the hell out," she said. "I've asked you twice now."

He did just that. He got the hell out.

Leah covered her face and tried to tell herself he was an ass. A pushy, unforgiving ass. But she knew exactly who was at fault here.

"Knock, knock."

Leah jerked and opened her eyes.

Aubrey stood in the doorway holding a flask and a bag

of potato chips. "Thought one of these might be of some help about now."

"Alcohol and chips?"

"It's my emergency 'Just Fucked Up Again' kit."

Leah sighed. "You heard."

"Everything," Aubrey agreed. "Thin walls." She came in and helped herself to two glasses. She poured a splash of something amber into each and then handed one to Leah, keeping the other for herself. "Cheers."

"Cheers?" Leah choked out.

"You're right," Aubrey said. "How about...to fucking up? I mean, let's face it, we're both pretty good at that."

"What have you ever fucked up?"

Aubrey laughed a little coldly, and yet somehow the sound held volumes of loneliness. "You grew up here. You know my rep."

"You have a rep for being unflappable and gorgeous."

Aubrey took another shot. "And..."

"Okay," Leah said. "And maybe a little untouchable."

"Bitchy," Aubrey corrected. "Mean. Cold."

"I don't think you're mean or cold," Leah said.

Aubrey laughed again, this one much more real. "Just bitchy? Okay, I can live with that."

There was a soft knock, and Ali appeared at the doorway. She saw the glasses and immediately her mouth went into a pout. "Hey. I want to join."

"Can't," Aubrey said. "*You* aren't a fuckup."

Ali paused a beat, taking this in, clearly thinking hard. "You're wrong. I've been a fuckup before."

Aubrey smiled. "Is that the first time you've ever said fuck?"

"Maybe," Ali said. "Let me join the club and I'll say it as much as you want. Look— fuck, fuck, fuck—"

"Stop," Aubrey said on a laugh and got out a third glass, filling it with a few fingers straight up.

Ali knocked it back, coughed, and swiped at her mouth. "So are we drinking to the *Sweet Wars* final or something else?" She divided a gaze between them, clearly assuming it could have been either of them equally to be the screwup.

Leah raised her hand. "The finals. I'm this week's idiot."

"No you're not," Ali said, loyal to the end, but she bit her lower lip because she loved Jack too. "It can't be un-fixable, it can't. You both care so much about each other."

"And isn't that just it," Leah said softly and scrubbed her hands over her face. "How can you fall for the person who knows you better than anyone else?"

"The question is," Aubrey said just as quietly, "how can you not?"

"He knows everything about me," Leah said. "All my secrets. There's no hiding with him, no holding back." She stood up, restlessly turning in a circle before coming back around to stare at her friends. "Do you have any idea how terrifying it is to be laid bare before someone like that?"

Both Ali and Aubrey were looking at her with eyes that assured her that they knew exactly, and she sighed. "I'm afraid," she whispered.

"Jack wouldn't hurt you," Ali rushed to say. "He'd rip off his own arm first."

Leah nodded. She knew this, she did. "It's just that I've never needed a man before to make my life complete. Never. But…"

"But what?" Ali demanded when Leah trailed off, a little overwhelmed by her own epiphany. "But what?"

"But…I need *that* man," Leah said. "I need Jack."

Jack lost himself in his drug of choice—work. It was late, and he was off duty, and yet he was at his desk staring at his computer screen. Around him, the station was quiet and dark.

Inside him, there was no quiet to be found as he picked up the phone.

"Do you know what time it is?" Ronald grumbled.

"And do you know that Mr. Rinaldi, that new developer in town, isn't new at all?"

Ronald blew out a long breath, sounding like he was struggling to come awake. "What are you talking about?"

"He's Max Fitzgerald's brother."

"Well, hell," Ronald said.

"Yeah. Well, hell."

The next morning, Leah was surprised to find her grandma already up and dressed to go to work.

"I'm baking with you this morning," Elsie said. "Our last day. No sadness," she said at the look on Leah's face. "And anyway, yes it's an ending, but it's also a new beginning as well. I'm feeling great. Turns out, having a man's better than Metamucil."

"I'd have to agree," a man said, and to Leah's utter shock, Mr. Lyons walked into the kitchen using his cane, looking as dapper and cheery as Elsie. He gave her a smacking kiss on the lips, winked at Leah, and then limped to the door. "I'll see you soon, chickie," he said to Elsie, and was gone.

"Isn't he the sweetest thing?" Elsie asked.

Twenty minutes later, they were at the bakery. And Leah had a bitch of a headache, which she tried to ignore. It was her last day, and she was stressed. That was all.

It had nothing to do with the hole in her damn heart.

An hour passed and she was elbow deep into the early morning baking when it happened.

The power flickered and went out.

"Dammit," Leah muttered. She had a searing hot poker of pain behind one eyeball. Her headache had upgraded to migraine level, and she was feeling lightheaded to boot.

Not enough sleep.

Dawn hadn't quite broken, so she felt for the junk drawer and fumbled for the flashlight and some new fuses. "Grandma," she called to the front room, where Elsie had been cleaning the display shelves for the new day's goods. "Have a seat for a few minutes; I'll get this."

"Already sitting," Elsie called back. "I might have been a little overzealous on the knee."

"You shouldn't be bending down and cleaning those displays."

"That's not what I got overzealous about," Elsie said.

Leah winced and rubbed her temples. "TMI, Grandma."

Elsie laughed in delight. "Go. I'm fine."

Leah paused to flick the beam of light into the little glass window of the new oven.

Her soufflé was going to be ruined. And hell if it hadn't been one of the most amazing batches ever too. Frustrated, she left the heat of the kitchen and stepped outside, closing the door so she didn't let out the bought air.

Ali wasn't in yet, and the bookstore was closed like

always. Dawn was breaking, the light a brilliant kaleido-scope of oranges, reds, and purples. The air was chilly and seemed to clear her head. There was a tang of salt from the ocean and…

She went still and sniffed again.

Sulfur?

In the alley, she turned in a slow circle, something crunching beneath her shoe.

A scattering of cigarette butts.

That was odd. Extremely odd. The only reason for anyone to be back here was if he belonged in one of the three shops that made up the building.

But no one who did belong here smoked.

She glanced at the back door to the bakery and at the glass window there. Right now, with the sun's rays stab-bing through the early morning, the reflection on the glass nearly blinded her, and she couldn't see in. But as of only a few minutes ago, it would have still been dark outside. Inside the kitchen, she'd have been like a fish in a fish-bowl to anyone in the alley, and knowing it, goose bumps rose on her skin.

Someone had stood right here in this spot, smoking and watching her.

Hugging herself against the chill that raced down her spine, she reentered the kitchen and shut and locked the door. And then bolted it. "Grandma," she called out. "Make sure the front door's still locked, okay?" Her headache was killing her, and adding that to the exhaus-tion of not sleeping was making her dizzy. All this broken heart stuff was hell on her immune system, she thought, realizing she felt weak too. And…sick. Dammit. She sat. Just for a minute, she told herself, and set her head on her arms. Whew. She was seriously woozy. In the back of her mind, it occurred to her that her grandma had never responded to her.

She heard footsteps. Not her grandma's uneven, shuffling gait but someone with a more steady stride. A man, she thought. But her head was too heavy to lift, and her eyelids wouldn't open…

Chapter 27

♥

Jack was deeply asleep, dreaming of being smothered when someone started banging on his door. By the time he sat up and shoved Kevin off his chest, Ben had let himself in and stood in the doorway in a pair of unbuttoned jeans. "Get up," he told Jack, shrugging into a shirt. "Now."

There was little that ever made Ben rush, and knowing it, Jack immediately rolled off the bed and reached for pants.

"Luke called," Ben said. "There's a problem downtown."

Jack knew damn well that Luke wouldn't call about just any problem. "What is it?"

"The bakery. Someone called in a report of seeing an older woman unconscious inside the closed bakery. He didn't know more; the call had just come in. Let's go."

Jack was already out the door, calling dispatch while Ben drove. Emergency responders were just arriving on scene. Nothing to report yet.

Jack ended the call and leaned forward in the passenger seat, like that could get them to the scene faster.

"You think it's Elsie?" Ben asked.

"Don't know." Jack hit Leah's number.

No answer.

If it was Elsie in trouble—and who else could it be—then he wondered what she'd been doing alone at the bakery. Where was Leah? Under different circumstances, she might have been in Jack's bed, but he'd screwed that up pretty good.

He tried her cell again but it still went straight to voice mail. "Leah," he said. "Call me." He disconnected and stared at the road. Had she avoided a good-bye altogether and left town early? He had to work on not having heart failure when Ben went straight instead of left at the pier. "What the hell are you doing?"

"Driving you to the bakery," Ben said.

"By way of Africa? Why the hell didn't you turn on Harbor Boulevard?"

"They're tearing up Harbor. Repaving."

When they got caught at one of the only three stoplights in town, Jack could actually feel a stroke coming on and had to put a finger to his twitching eye. "There's no one in the intersection. Go through it."

Ben didn't move.

"Ben."

"You already have a ticket this week."

"But you don't!"

The light turned green, so in the end Jack didn't have to kill his cousin. And twenty-five hundred years later, Ben pulled up behind the ambulance and fire unit. Both men got out of the car and ran toward the scene.

Luke stepped away from a group of uniforms and into Jack's path. "Tim was driving by before dawn and saw the front light on in the bakery," he told them. "He said he got excited that Leah had opened early and parked. But the door was locked, and through the window he could see Elsie slumped at a table. He knocked but got no response. He broke in and hauled her out. She's come to briefly, but she's woozy and confused. Incoherent. It's a possible CO_2 poisoning, so we're testing for that now."

Carbon monoxide poisoning was known as a silent, viciously fast killer, and he got cold to the bone. "Leah?"

Luke shook his head. "Haven't seen her, but you're literally only two minutes behind us. Still clearing the building."

Hunter and Cindy were rolling the gurney toward the ambulance, where an agitated Elsie struggled with Hunter, who was trying to fit her with an oxygen mask. Her hands were fluttering, her eyes wide with confusion and shock.

"Shortness of breath and chest pains," Hunter told Jack.

Jack leaned over a confused Elsie, taking her hands in his. "You're safe, Elsie." Gently he placed the oxygen mask over her nose and mouth. "Lie still a minute. Just breathe."

Her hand came up, clutching at his wrist. She tried to say something, striking terror into his heart with one word.

"Leah," she whispered.

He gripped her hand. "Is she inside?"

Elsie's head lolled, and her eyes drifted shut.

"Elsie," Jack said firmly, watching her try to snap back into focus. "Elsie, is Leah still in the building?"

"Leah. Get Leah."

Jack whipped around and bumped directly into Luke. "Leah's here," Jack said. And then he ran toward the building, heading around the back via the alley. He got to the porch in time to see the back door crash open and Tim step out, Leah in his arms.

Chapter 28

Leah."

At the low but commanding male voice, Leah startled. *Jack*. She tried to look at him, but it was dark. Very dark.

"Leah, stay with us. Don't you dare leave me."

Oh, how she loved that tone, the way he could be demanding and so alpha she just wanted to eat him up.

His familiar grip settled around her hand and held on like a lifeline. "Open your eyes, Leah."

Oh yeah, she liked that tone too, the one he used when he was letting his emotions get the best of him. Like when he was buried deep inside her, telling her all the things he planned to do to her.

But she wanted to see his face, so in spite of a bitch of a headache, she struggled to open her eyes.

That's when she realized she was flat on her back. Jack stood by her side, his expression grim as he clutched her hand. She was on a gurney, with an oxygen mask on her face, but she did her best to give him a faint smile.

It was enough to bring some light to his gaze. "You're okay," he said.

"What—"

"Possible CO_2 poisoning."

She struggled to sit up. Jack wasn't alone. Tim and Ben and Luke were right there too, and a sea of others. Behind them, there were flashing lights and a crowd gathering.

And it started to come back to her. Being in the bakery, feeling sick, so sick— "Grandma," she managed. "Where's—"

"Being transported to the hospital," Jack said. "She was coming to as they pulled away. She's okay, Leah. Stay still."

She pulled off the mask, shaking her head as Jack started to object. "I'm fine. I…" Whoa. Her world swam, and there was a little man with an icepick behind her eyes, hacking away. An inch from throwing up, she decided maybe Jack had a point and went very still. "I want to go see her."

"Take another minute," Jack said firmly, holding her down when she would have hopped off the gurney. "Dammit, Leah. Give yourself a minute."

"How did I get out of the bakery?"

"Me." On the other side of the gurney, Tim smiled grimly. "I found you unconscious in the kitchen. You were crumpled right at the door on the floor, like maybe you'd crawled there to get out but hadn't made it. I had to break the door down."

"The power went out," Leah murmured, struggling to remember. Everything felt so confusing and fuzzy. "And I got tired…" She trailed off, images coming back to her.

Jack's face when Tim had brought her to him—not his usual calm, nothing even remotely close.

He'd been afraid. For her.

"If I hadn't driven by," Tim said, "God knows what would have happened."

Leah shuddered, and Jack squeezed her hand. She met his gaze, the both of them knowing exactly what would have happened. She and her grandma would've gone to sleep and never woken up. She sucked in some oxygen, and after a few minutes, she retained all her faculties. She insisted on being released at the scene, promising everyone she'd go straight to the hospital and get herself checked after seeing Elsie.

"Hell no," Jack said, taking her arm when she turned to her car. "I'm driving you."

"I'm fine—"

"I'm driving you to the damn hospital, Leah."

They didn't speak on the ride over. Jack was in his zone, and Leah's ice picker had graduated to using a jackhammer inside her head, rattling her brain. She drifted off a little bit, not stirring again until she felt a warm hand cup her face.

"Leah."

She opened her eyes to Jack's concerned ones. He was crouched low at her side in the opened door of his truck. She sat up. "I'm fine."

Reaching in, he clicked open her seat belt and then held her in place a moment. "You know, for a minute back there, I thought—" He broke off and closed his eyes, dropping his forehead to hers.

It was one thing to think the worst, another entirely to have the nightmare come true. He'd had that happen too many times in his life. "I'm okay," she murmured, cupping his stubbled jaw. "Really."

"I'm not." He drew in a long, unsteady breath, his eyes shadowed. "I'm not ready to lose you, Leah. Even when you're pissing me off."

She gave a little laugh and pressed her face against his throat. His arms immediately came around her, pulling her in. "We're still friends, right?" she whispered, needing to hear it. "You still love me, forever?"

He let out a barely there sigh. "Forever."

Her eyes burned. "I'm sorry I'm such a pain in the ass," she said against his warm skin, squeezing him tighter.

"You are a pain in my ass," he agreed. "I just want you breathing, Leah. For a damn long time."

He helped her out of the car, then tightened the grip he'd retained on her when she wobbled. Just outside Elsie's hospital room he stopped her, waiting for her to catch her breath. She could hear his phone vibrating, but he gave no sign that he cared about anything other than being here with her. He had her back. Always. No matter how much either of them screwed things up, they'd still have this. Each other. It was enough, she told herself. It was.

All she had to do was learn to believe it.

"Don't expect much," Jack said to Leah before letting her go into Elsie's room. "She's sedated and drowsy."

Leah nodded her understanding. Even with his warning, he could tell it was a shock to see her grandma prone on the bed, still as stone, eyes closed, skin waxy and pale. Elsie looked tiny and entirely too vulnerable, and Leah put a hand to her mouth.

Jack slipped an arm around her waist and nudged her in.

Tim was taking a chair bedside, clearly having just arrived. He was looking quite serious but also still in cocky hero mode. Next to him was Max. And next to Max was Mr. Lyons.

Leah let out a breath and a reluctant smile. "I hope she knows you're all here because she'd love this, three men at her beck and call."

Elsie's eyes fluttered open and they landed first on her audience, then on Jack. She struggled to say something to him, but Leah rushed to her side. "Shh, Grandma," she murmured softly. "It's okay. You're okay."

Jack pulled out a chair for Leah and gently pushed her into it. Then, feeling the tiny tremors wracking her, he pulled off his sweatshirt and wrapped it around her. Delayed shock. He wanted to get her warm and looked at, and then he wanted to pull her in and hold on.

And never let go.

Leah picked up Elsie's hand. "That was way too close of a call, Grandma."

Elsie let out one light chuckle but her eyes drifted shut.

"I love you," Leah whispered to her, her voice soft. "I love you so much."

Elsie's other hand came up and pulled the oxygen mask from her face. "Ah, honey, and you didn't even choke on it."

Leah let out a half sob, half laugh and dropped her head to her grandma's bed.

"No worries, it gets easier each time now," Elsie said, and over Leah's head she gave Jack a look that had him moving to her side.

"You're going to be okay," he said. "They want you to stay quiet for a little while and rest—"

"Yeah, yeah." She stared up at him. "I hear you, but…sometimes you can't stay quiet. Sometimes…" Her expression was pained, and her eyebrows kept waggling, as if she were having a seizure.

"Are you okay?" Leah asked, straightening to call for help. "Hang on—"

"Oh good Lord," Elsie muttered. "I'm fine. I'm trying to tell Jack something here. I'm saying that sometimes things aren't as they seem. Sometimes people, they act irrationally." She paused, her eyes not moving from Jack. "Do you know what I'm trying to tell you?"

"Oh, Grandma," Leah said, sounding exasperated now. "Just concentrate on getting better. You can go back to meddling into our lives later—"

Jack put a hand on Leah, quieting her. Because he knew exactly what Elsie was saying. He'd put it together the minute he'd seen who'd been waiting at her bedside with anxiety and adrenaline rolling off them in waves.

It made sense, horrible, sickening sense, but he kept his gaze on Elsie. "I do understand," he said, and because the entire energy in the room had changed, he had no choice but to act now. Pulling out his phone, he made a call. "Need backup," he said, and slipped the phone away again.

With clear relief, Elsie lay back and closed her eyes.

Leah craned her neck and stared up at Jack. "What are you doing? What's going on?"

She broke off when Max jerked suddenly to his feet. "Look at the time!" he said, his voice unnaturally jovial. "I've got to go."

Leah stood up and stepped into his path, halting him, eyes narrowed. "You smell like cigarettes."

"Since when is smoking a crime?"

"Oh my God," she breathed. "It was you."

"I didn't do anything!"

"Except maybe try to scare off the new developer from buying up the buildings for sale in town. What I can't figure out is why you were so upset when my grandma convinced Mr. Lyons to pull out of escrow."

Max sighed deeply. "It's complicated."

"Why?" she pressed.

"Because…"

"Because Vince Rinaldi is your brother?" Jack filled in helpfully.

Max looked at him and nodded. "My half brother, actually." He turned back to Leah. "So if what you're really doing is accusing me of setting those fires and then nearly killing you and your granny today out of greed, be very careful, missy."

"You should go, Max," Jack said.

"But—" Leah broke off when Jack slid her a look, and waited with what looked like barely restrained frustration as Max walked out of the hospital room.

Tim was going as well, apparently without a single word, until Jack stepped in his path. "Leaving?" he asked the younger firefighter softly.

"Yeah," Tim said, shoving his hands in his pockets. "Being the big hero really takes it out of a guy."

"Wait." Leah paled suddenly and put a hand to her head. "I remember you being there today," she said slowly. "You were in full firefighter gear."

Tim laughed. "You were out cold, Leah. You don't

know what or who you saw." He started to brush past them, but Jack blocked him.

"Hold on," Jack said.

"Why?"

"You grimaced when you stood up. You hurt?"

"My shins," Tim said. "From running."

"Shin splits?"

"A stress fracture, actually."

Jack nodded. "It's because you don't roll your ankles inward enough. Instead you hit the ground with the outside edges of your feet. Walking or running like that puts a lot of pressure on your legs."

"Okay," Tim said, trying to get around Jack. "That was real informative, thanks."

Jack blocked his path. "Tell me again how it is that you just happened to be at the bakery?"

"I was hungry. The place was still closed, which was weird. I just happened to be there at the right time to help."

"In full gear."

"No. Yes." He laughed a little. "Just my mask. You're trying to trip me up. I was at the front, and then the back." He glanced at his watch. "Seriously. Gotta go."

Sneaky. And cocky. He didn't think he could get caught. Jack leaned in and sniffed at him. "Why do you smell like cigarettes?"

"Dude, that was Max. You getting senile, old man?"

"No, it's you. You stink."

"Aw, you smell good too, LT. Like a fire. It's sexy as hell."

"Thought you quit smoking."

Tim gave up the pretense with easy grace and a shrug. "I quit every day. It doesn't always take."

"Use the damn patches."

"Says the nonsmoker." Tim's affable smile faded. "Doing my best, man."

Jack poked his index finger against Tim's pec pocket and cellophane crinkled.

Tim knocked Jack's hand away. "Knock it off. It's none of your business what I do when we're off the clock."

"We're never off the clock."

"Yeah," Tim said. "As proven by my actions today." He'd been wearing his cockiness like a shield, but there was something new there now, hovering just behind it. An edge of fear.

"Jack?" Leah asked behind him, uncertain. "What's going on?"

Jack held Tim's gaze. "So are we going to do this easy or hard?"

Tim just stared at him, his mouth a little tight now.

Great. The hard way then. "Tim and I are going to go outside and talk."

Leah opened her mouth, glanced at Tim, and then shut it again, giving him a nod that he hoped like hell meant she'd stay put.

Less than a minute later, with her head still spinning and her brain not firing on all circuits, Leah heard a shout in the hallway and then a thump. She let go of her grandma's hand and rushed to the door to find Jack holding a struggling Tim against the wall. They were surrounded by hospital staff, including Dr. Josh Scott and an ER nurse who was on the phone presumably to 9-1-1 because she had one finger in her ear and was yelling about location.

But though it was chaos, Jack's movements were sure

and controlled as he contained Tim. "It's over, Tim," he said. "It's done."

"I want my lawyer," Tim yelled, still struggling. "You can't pin the fires on me, and you sure as hell can't pin the carbon monoxide poisoning on me either. That ancient gas heater they have in there must be faulty."

"No one ever said it was the heater, Tim," Jack said. "But I'm sure that if you're right, a court of your peers will find it interesting that you knew exactly where the leak was."

Tim went still, then dropped his forehead to the wall, no longer fighting. "You fucker," he said. "You think you're better than the rest of us because your dad was some sort of hero. Well, I'm a hero too. I've saved countless people. In that apartment building fire, Sam would have died if I hadn't gotten him out of there. And then the auto parts store fire. Christ, that was beautiful… No one would have gotten there in time to save anyone if I hadn't called it in."

Jack let out a breath. Unbelievable. "Are you kidding me? If you'd managed to start that fire, do you know what would have happened in combination with the gas leak? The whole fucking street would have blown up. People would have died, Tim."

"I wouldn't have let that happen." Tim shook his head, eyes flashing temper. "You should have just let me train to follow in your footsteps. Or let me have a shot at Leah. You have it all, and you wouldn't share. I deserve everything you have, I'm just as good. Hell, I'm better."

Jack stared at him, stunned by the sick and twisted hero complex. "You should shut up now," he said. "Wait for your lawyer. You're going to need him."

Tim turned his head, pressing his cheek to the wall as his gaze locked with Leah still standing in the doorway. "She was next. Your woman was next."

Leah staggered back into her grandma's hospital room and sat heavily in the chair by the bed.

"Leah," her grandma murmured. "Are you okay, honey?"

Before she could answer, Jack strode into the room and tugged her up to her feet and into his arms, as if he needed to hold her every bit as much as she needed to be held by him.

"Yes, Grandma," Leah murmured, gripping him tight, proud that her voice didn't wobble. She tightened her grip and breathed in the safeness and solidity that was Jack. "I'm okay."

Leah was trying to sleep and having no luck when she felt someone slip into bed behind her. Warm, strong arms came around her.

"Jack," she murmured. "You came."

He kissed her shoulder, her neck. "Not yet. You first."

She smiled, then moaned when his hand slid beneath the covers and under the T-shirt she wore. It was his; she'd stolen it years ago and worn it so often it was threadbare.

Jack cupped her bare breast and let out a low, inherently male sound of approval, when she arched into his touch. He didn't say anything but she could feel the tension in him.

Immediately after Tim's arrest, he'd had to go back to the scene. They'd gotten word through Luke that Max and his half brother weren't involved with any of the arsons and cleared as suspects. Max had slunk out of town.

Tim wasn't going to get so lucky. He'd smoked the cigarettes left outside the fire sites as he'd waited for his opportunities. He wore the same size shoes as the footprints found. And, according to what he'd admitted in interrogation, he'd done it all solely for the glory of being a hero.

Leah had been checked out by Dr. Scott—at Jack's insistence, she'd discovered—and then had stayed with Elsie until visiting hours had ended. She'd called Rafe to say she needed a few extra days. Then Ali had taken her home, where she'd showered, crawled into bed, and...stared at the ceiling.

"You okay?" she asked Jack now.

"Tim's being held on evidence that we presented to the judge."

Not an answer to her question. She couldn't imagine how hard it had been, arresting one of their own, and she glanced over her shoulder at him, finding his face shadowed with exhaustion and worry. His hands were touching as much of her as he could reach, gently roaming over every inch of her. "Are you wearing my shirt?"

"Maybe," she said.

When he spoke again, there was a whisper of a smile in his voice. "You stole my shirt."

"Maybe." She tried to turn over, but his arms tightened on her and he buried his face in her hair. "Talked to Dr. Scott," he finally said, his lips brushing the curve of her ear as he spoke. "You were treated for mild shock. How are you feeling?"

He was still touching her. His fingers brushed the front of her panties and she forgot the question.

"Leah?"

His front was plastered to her back. She fought the urge to turn and burrow into him, to inhale his scene and hold on forever. "I just can't believe it was Tim," she whispered with a shudder.

Jack stroked a hand up her arm, the warmth of him chasing the chill that wracked her. "You did good, Leah. You took a bad situation and held it together." He was still tense, but she was pretty sure that was pride she heard in his voice. He was proud of her. He was also hard. "Jack?"

He pulled her tighter, his fingers trailing over her skin. "Yeah?"

"The rule," she said softly. "The one where we're done?"

He paused, clearly choosing his words carefully. "I was pissed off and butt hurt. And I was wrong. You've never misled me or tried to be someone you weren't. Life is short, Leah. Too fucking short. It took me a while to catch on to that. I'm not going to make that mistake again."

"What about the no big good-bye."

His teeth closed over her earlobe and bit down lightly, and heat spiraled through her belly.

And lower.

"I remember," he said.

"So…what are we doing?"

"New rule just for tonight," he said. "I'm going to fuck you until you forget about what happened at the bakery," he said. "And then I'm going to make love to you until you scream my name again. I really like it when you do that."

She nearly came from just the words.

His fingers slid under the edge of her panties. "Still with me?"

"Y-yes."

"I want you, Leah."

Her heart squeezed at the words, given so freely. "Even though I hurt you? Even though I'm leaving? Even though—"

"Even though," he said, voice low. "I don't always agree with you, but I always understand. I want you in my life, Leah. That's never going to change."

Her breath hitched. Unconditional acceptance. It washed through her, heated her.

His cheek brushed against hers, sandpaper rough. "I know you don't want a good-bye, and hell if I do either. So this isn't good-bye. It's an until. Until our paths cross. It's happened before. It'll happen again."

Not a promise, and that was of her own making. She closed her eyes and took in the feel of him surrounding her, his heart beating at her back, his breath on her jaw. Did it matter?

His mouth was on the nape of her neck, his hands gliding over her body, stirring the desire, the all-consuming need. With a moan, she rocked back against him.

No promises. None were needed, she realized, and whispered his name entreatingly.

He dragged her panties down her legs and then his hand slid back between her thighs. She shivered as his fingers stroked, moving in a pace designed to drive her wild.

Or make her beg. Which at the moment she was perfectly willing to do. "Jack."

He pulled free and she heard him open a condom, replacing his fingers with something even better. Sliding into her to the hilt, he bit lightly into the junction of her shoulder and neck, and she came.

"More." His voice was gruff, and he thrust again, deeper. "Again."

She could barely hear him over the rushing in her ears, though she did hear her own whimper when he pulled out. Lifting his weight off her, he rolled her onto her back. "This way," he said. "I want to see you."

"You're so beautiful," she whispered.

"No, that's you," he murmured. Staring down at her, his gaze dark, determined, intense, he tugged her shirt over her head and slid back into her, making her cry out as he thrust right where she needed him. She rocked against him, her eyes fluttering closed with ecstasy.

"Leah, look at me." When she did, he thrust again. His eyes seared into her. "Remember this."

Did he think she wouldn't? He was all she remembered. Always. "Jack—"

His hand slid between their bodies and found her, and she nearly arched off the bed. She met his every move as another wave washed over her, and through it all she kept her eyes open, let him watch as everything inside her peaked and convulsed.

She took him right along with her. His control snapped and he shuddered, groaning out her name. Shifting his hips, he grinded against her, sending more tremors rippling through her. "This, Leah. I'll remember this. You. Always."

Unraveling at his words, she wrapped her arms around him, her legs, and then, she was pretty sure, her heart as well.

Chapter 29

♥

Two days later, Leah stood at her parked car, surrounded by…everyone.

So much for a quiet good-bye.

Jack had spent most of the past two days at work dealing with the Tim fallout. They'd had no private time at all, and now their good-bye was going to be a public deal in front of Ben, Elsie, Dee, and half the town. Nothing she could do about that, she thought, not surprised when Jack took her hand and pulled her aside.

"Not fair," Lucille called out. "We can't hear you."

Jack's amused but solemn gaze met Leah's. "So," he said.

"So." She sucked in some air. "Love me forever?"

"And ever," he said. No smile.

Shaken, she stepped into him for a hug. "It really doesn't matter to you that I didn't win *Sweet Wars*, does it?" she whispered, holding on to him tightly. "Or that I screwed up. You really don't care about any of that. You know the core of me, of who I am, and you still put up with me."

"Leah." He slid his fingers into her hair, cupping the back of her head as he pressed his mouth to her temple. "You know all of my dark places, and you accept them. You accept me. So why is it so hard for you to believe that I know yours and accept them as well? You've been a part of my life for so long, one of the most important parts. That's what I care about. Not you quitting some TV show, but that you don't quit me."

Her breath caught. Her heart hitched. "But I have to go do this."

"I know. It's okay. Whatever you want to do, school, open a pastry shop, or nothing at all... That's not why I love you. And I do love you, Leah. I want you to know that before you leave. Not to change your mind, but to take with you."

The marvel of it washed over her and was better than the straight shot of the oxygen mask had been. That he felt this way was no surprise, not really. He'd been showing her how much he loved her in one form or another since the day she'd moved in next door to him.

Having grown up as she had, she knew the expression of emotions was all in the actions, not the words.

But the words...oh, the words. They were the most amazing words she'd ever heard. Getting into her car and driving off was the hardest thing she'd ever done.

As the dust settled from Leah's car, Lucille patted Jack on the arm.

"I'm fine," he said.

"Of course you are. You're an idiot, but you're fine."

Ben, at his side, choked out a low laugh.

When Jack slid him a look, Ben lifted a shoulder. "She's right, you know. You are an idiot."

"Yeah? And how's that?"

"You let her go."

Jack buried himself in work, and when he wasn't snowed under by all the work Ronald had left him, Luke and Ben dragged him out. They ate and drank so much he had to increase his workouts, which turned out to be for the best.

Exhaustion was the only way to sleep.

Leah wrote him. She sent emails, texts, and even a few greeting cards that made him smile.

He wasn't as good with the written word, so he called. The time difference was a bitch, but they spent hours on the phone talking about...hell if he knew.

He just liked the sound of her voice.

She often asked about his mom, who was doing well, thanks to Ronald. She asked about her grandma, who was also doing well. She asked about Jack's work, and how the transition to deputy fire chief and fire marshal was working out for him, better than he could have hoped for. "Leah," he said halfway through her last semester. "I miss you."

There was a thick silence, and then her shuddery sigh sounded across the airwaves. "Miss you too."

"Wow, you didn't choke on it," he said, teasing her by mimicking her grandma's words.

"Or this," she said, and drew in a deep breath. "I love you, Jack."

He let a stunned beat pass, and then he had to swallow hard. "We pretended to be a couple for an entire town, you nearly died by the hand of a serial arsonist who wanted to date you, and then there was the big, dramatic good-bye we didn't want, and you never said a word. Now you're, what, twenty million miles away and you say it?"

"Five thousand miles." She laughed a little. "And timing was never my strong suit."

No kidding.

Leah did what she'd promised and committed to doing. She finished school. And surprising even herself, she enjoyed it.

She didn't have to be the best to be *her* best. All she had to do was be herself.

Rafe made her an offer.

"I've been asked to get you to renew your contract," he said. "The network wants to keep you on board. You're a natural in front of an audience, and the camera loves you. The network wants to follow you as you open up your own pastry shop."

It was a sweet offer. But the last time she'd truly been happy had been in Lucky Harbor, with Jack. He loved her, and she understood what that meant now.

How had she walked away from that? "No," she said to Rafe. "Thank you, but no."

"No?" Rafe sighed. "Fine. What's it going to take?" A ten percent raise?"

"Again, thank you. But I can't." She had something she wanted to do. Needed to do. For the first time in her life, she had a plan. She had revisited that plan in her mind every day for three months—knowing exactly the life she wanted for herself, and she was going for it.

"Listen," Rafe said. "I get it, okay? We're prepared to double your contract, but that's our last, cold, hard line, Leah. Take it or leave it. And let's be clear, we expect you to take it."

She shook her head, pushed his big, fancy contract back at him, and walked away.

"Where you going?"

"Home."

"You don't have one."

Maybe not. But that was simply a technicality. She knew where home was. Truthfully, she'd always known.

A day and a half later, she pulled into Lucky Harbor. It was dusk. It'd rained, making everything shiny and wet. The strings of white lights on the storefronts and in the tree-lined sidewalks glistened in the fading light like...

Home.

She drove by the senior center and slowed. The lot was completely packed, but what caught her eye was the fire truck, front and center.

She recognized that fire truck and knew exactly who'd be inside. Heart already thumping in anticipation, she parked and entered the building beneath a huge sign: SAFETY AWARENESS NIGHT.

The main room was packed to the gills, and up front stood Jack and Kevin. The former was giving a safety speech. The latter was snoozing at Jack's feet, sprawled on his back, feet straight up in the air like a three-day-old carcass.

Unlike when Leah had once come to the senior center to give a cooking lesson, none of the seniors were napping or playing on their phones. In fact, everyone was riveted. Elsie was there, sitting next to Mr. Lyons.

Leah gave her a big hug. "I'm sorry," she whispered. "But there's something I have to do before I can talk to you."

"Go get him, honey," Elsie said.

Leah realized the room had gone so silent she could have heard a pin drop.

Kevin gave one exuberant, joyous bark and leaped at her, knocking her back a step in his exuberance.

"Good boy," she said, giving him a hug too.

Jack stood still at the front of the room, watching her with an unreadable face.

She waved at him.

His smile came slow and warm, and everyone craned their necks like they were watching a tennis match. "You're home," he said.

Some of the tension left her, but not all, because he still wasn't giving much away. Not that she expected him to in front of their captive audience. Plus, it was her turn to give it all away. To give him everything. "I'm home."

He gave her a finger crook, the universal sign for "come here." She glanced at the crowd avidly soaking up her every move.

"Ignore them," Jack said. "You're only surrounded by fifty of Lucky Harbor's finest gossips. Everything you say here will be repeated and posted on Facebook."

"And tweeted," Lucille called out. "I've found the Twitter."

"I thought 'tweet' was a female body part," one of the seniors said, sounding confused.

Anxious but holding her gaze steadily on Jack, Leah walked up the center aisle toward him.

"Damn," she heard Lucille whisper. "Siri, remind me to download the bride's march song on my iPhone."

"Wait. She's back?" someone else asked, sounding confused. "I thought she ran off."

"She didn't run off, you moron." This from Elsie. "She went back to school. Don't any of you read Facebook?"

Leah stopped at the foot of the stage and looked up at Jack. "I was wrong," she said.

Jack curled a hand around his ear, like he hadn't caught her words.

"*I was wrong,*" she repeated.

"Oh, I heard you." He smiled. "I just like the sound of the words on your lips."

The crowd tittered at this. Ignoring them, Jack reached down and gripped Leah by the wrist, easily lifting her to the stage. "And not that I don't love those words, but what were you wrong about?"

"Walking away from you." She stepped into him. "I'm done with that, by the way. I'm walking straight at you from now on."

Around them came a collective "aww," and Jack's smile spread to his eyes as he finally pulled her into his arms.

Over his shoulder she could see her grandma beaming, and Kevin sitting in Lucille's lap. Lucille was handing over money to Mr. Lyons.

"They were betting on whether you were going to break my heart or not," Jack told her. "The stakes got so high I even put in my own bet."

"Which way did you bet?" she asked.

Mr. Lyons walked to the front of the room and slapped some twenties into Jack's palm and then stomped back to his seat.

"Let's just say I won," Jack said easily. And then he

bent and kissed her to the whoops and hollers of their delighted audience.

"I wouldn't mind a kiss like that," Leah heard Lucille say.

"Me either," Elsie said, and then squeaked in delighted surprise when Mr. Lyons pulled her close and gave her a smacking kiss right on the lips.

Against her, she could feel Jack shake with laughter just as he scooped her up and slung her over his shoulder in a fireman's hold.

The crowd ate this up, especially when Jack turned and flashed them a grin. "Excuse us," he said. "We need a minute in private."

"Well that's no fun," Lucille complained as Jack strode out of the room, down a hall, and into the first room they came to—the dining room.

He set her down on the counter that ran along one wall, pinning her there with a hand on either side of her hips as he looked into her eyes. "Hey."

Everything within her flooded with affection, need... love. "Hey." She cupped his face. Beneath her fingers, his face was rough with at least a day's growth. She wanted to feel it against her bare skin. "Last time I was home you asked me when I was going to realize that I deserve to be happy." She paused. "Now," she said. "I realize it now. I deserve it," she said softly.

The very corners of his lips curved, and what might have been pride came into his expression. "Yeah?"

"Yeah. And I know something else I deserve," she told him.

"What?"

"You. I'm in love with you, Jack. And you're in love with me too."

There was a very slight quirk at the corners of his mouth. "You sound pretty sure."

"I've never been so sure of anything." She gave him a nudge, hopped down off the counter, and pushed him into a chair. "So you might as well give in now."

"You think so, huh?"

She climbed into his lap. "I really do."

Someone knocked on the door.

"Lucille," Jack called out, not taking his gaze off Leah. "This conversation is off limits. Go practice your safety techniques. There's going to be a quiz."

"Oh!" She squealed in delight through the door. "I love quizzes."

And then there was blessed silence.

"So," Jack said. "Back to this you love me thing."

She pressed closer and slid her fingers into his hair. "I do love you, Jack. I don't want to be without you."

"Neither do I."

Hearing the true emotion in his voice, in the grip he had on her, she felt herself begin to let loose of the last of the tension in her gut.

"New rule," he said. "No more rules."

She smiled. "And if I agree to this 'no more rules,' what's in it for me?"

"Me."

She felt the smile burst full bloom across her face. "Well, if that's not the best offer I've ever had," she said.

He was grinning as he kissed her until she was dizzy.

"Come on," he said, and then stood up with her still wrapped around him.

"Wait!" she said, panicked, when he headed toward the door.

"Oh no you don't," he said, tightening his grip on her. "Not now, not when I finally have you where I want you."

"And where is that?"

"With me." He stepped back into the front room, and everyone clapped until he held up a hand for silence, letting Leah slide down his body. "We have an announcement."

"We do?" Leah said, her world spinning out of control, like a dream. The best dream she'd ever had.

"We do." He brought their entwined hands up and brushed his mouth across her knuckles as everyone in the room leaned forward in unison, straining to catch his next words.

"What?" Lucille finally demanded. "What's the announcement?"

Jack smiled at Leah. "We're taking this relationship off the radar."

"Well dammit," Lucille said as the rest of the room groaned.

Ignoring all of them, Jack tugged Leah into his side, kissed her softly, and smiled into her eyes. "Class dismissed," he said.

And then kissed her again.

And again...

Aubrey is setting out to right old wrongs. But Ben doesn't even know he's on her list.

Despite their troubled past, Lucky Harbor could be a hot, new beginning.

Please turn this page for a preview of

Once In A Lifetime.

Chapter 1

♥

There was one universal truth in Lucky Harbor, Washington—you could hide a pot of gold in broad daylight and no one would steal it, but you couldn't hide a secret.

Throughout the twenty-eight years of her unarguably colorful life, Aubrey Wellington had had lots of secrets, and almost every single one of them had been uncovered and gleefully discussed ad nauseam.

And yet here she was, still in this small, Pacific, West Coast town she'd grown up in. She didn't quite know what that said about her other than she was stubborn as hell. In any case, she was fairly used to bad days by the time she walked into Lucky Harbor's only bar and grill, but today had probably taken the cake. Ted Marshall, ex–town clerk, ex-boss, and also, embarrassingly enough, her ex-boyfriend, had just self-published his own tell-all, thoughtfully informing the entire world that she was a money-hungry man-eater.

She'd give him the money-hungry part since she was sinking her savings into a used bookstore, a silly, sentimental attempt at bringing back the one happy childhood memory she had.

But man-eater? Just because she didn't believe in happily-ever-afters, or even a happy-for-now, didn't mean she was a man-eater. She simply didn't see the need to invite a man all the way into her life when he wouldn't be staying.

Because they never stayed.

She sighed. Okay, so maybe she was a bit of a man-eater. Shrugging that off, she walked through the Old West–style bar and grill. It was like taking a step back a hundred years, in a good way. The walls were a deep, sinful, bordello red and lined with old mining tools. The ceiling was all exposed beams, and lanterns hung over the scarred bench-style tables filled with the late-dinner crowd. The air hummed with busy chattering, loud laughter, and the music blaring out of the jukebox against the far wall.

Aubrey headed straight to the bar. "Something that will make my day go away," she said to the bartender.

Ford Walker smiled and reached for a tumbler. He'd been five years ahead of Aubrey in school, and he was one of the nice ones. He'd gone off and had his fame and fortune racing sailboats around the world, and yet he'd chosen to come back to Lucky Harbor to settle down. He ran the Love Shack Bar and Grill.

She decided to take heart in that.

He slid her a vodka cranberry. "Satisfaction guaranteed," he promised.

Aubrey wrapped her fingers around the glass, but before she could bring it to her lips, someone nudged her shoulder.

Ted.

"Excuse me," her ex started, and then his handsome features went still as he realized it was her. He immediately started to move away, but she grabbed his arm.

"Wait," she said. "I need to talk to you."

"Yeah, I got your messages. All twenty-five of them." Ted had been born with an innate charm that did a really good job of hiding the snake beneath. He kept his face schooled into an expression of easy amusement, exuding charisma like a movie star. With a wry smile for anyone watching, he leaned in close. "I didn't know there were that many different words for asshole," he murmured.

"And you still wouldn't," she hissed, "if you'd have called me back even once. What were you thinking? Why did you have to say those things about me in your book?"

Ted shrugged and leaned back. "I needed money. So I wrote a book. What's the big deal? Everyone writes a book nowadays. And besides, it's not like you're known for being an angel."

Aubrey knew exactly who she was. She even knew why. She didn't need for him to tell her a damn thing about herself. "The big deal is that you're the one who wronged people," she said, keeping her voice down with effort. She wasn't as good at charm and charisma as he. "You're the one who two-timed me," she said, "along with just about every woman in town, including the mayor's wife. You even let her steal fifty grand of town funds that you were in charge of, and yet somehow you made *me* out to be the bad guy."

"Hey, *you* were the town clerk's admin," he said. "If

anyone should have known what had happened to that money, it was you, babe."

How had she ever worked for this guy? How had she ever *slept* with him? Her fingers were gripping her tumbler so tightly that she was surprised it didn't shatter. "You said things about me that had nothing to do with the money."

He smiled and gave her another shrug. "The book needed a little titillation."

Of all the humiliations Aubrey had suffered—and there had been many—having everyone know she'd dated this tool took the cake. It was the last straw on a no-good, very bad day, and as she'd been doing for most of her life, she acted without thinking. Almost before she knew it, her arm swung out, splashing her vodka cranberry at Ted's smug, far-too-good-looking face.

But though Ted was indeed *at least* twenty-five kinds of an asshole, he was also fast as a whip. He ducked, and her drink hit the man on the other side of him square in the face.

Straightening, Ted chortled in delight. "Nice."

Aubrey got a look at the man she'd nailed and stopped breathing. Oh God. Had she really thought her day couldn't get any worse? Why would she tempt fate by even thinking that? Because of course things could always get worse. They could *always* get worse.

Dripping her vodka drink, Ben McDaniel slowly stood up from his barstool, six feet plus of hard muscles and brute strength on a body that didn't carry a single extra ounce of fat on him. For the past five years, he'd been in and out of a variety of third-world countries designing and building water systems with the Army Corps of Engineers. His last venture had been for the Department of Defense in Iraq, which Aubrey only knew because Lucky Harbor's Facebook page was as good as gospel.

Ted was already gone, of course, out the door like a thief in the night, the weasel.

But not Ben. He swiped his face with his arm, deceptively chill and laid-back. In truth, he was about as badass as they came.

Aubrey should know; she'd seen him in action. But she managed to meet his gaze. Cool, casual even. One had to be with Ben; the man could spot a weakness a mile away. "I'm sorry," she said.

"Are you?"

She felt herself flush. He'd always seemed to see right through her. And he'd never liked her. He had good reason not to; he just didn't know it. "I wasn't aiming for you," she said, her heart pounding so loudly she was surprised she could hear herself speak. "Are you okay?"

He ran his fingers through his sun-streaked brown hair. His eyes were the same color, milk chocolate streaked with gold caramel. It was hard to make such a warm-colored gaze seem hard, but Ben managed it with no effort at all. "Need to work on your aim," he said.

"Yes." She nodded like a stupid bobblehead. It was all she could do—she hadn't taken a breath since she'd nailed him with the drink. "Again, I'm...sorry." And with little spots of anxiety dancing in her vision, she backed away, heading straight for the door.

Outside, the night was blessedly cold, tendrils of the chilly air brushing her hot cheeks. Lucky Harbor was basically a tiny little bowl sitting on the rocky Washington State coast, walled in by majestic peaks and lush forest. It was all an inky shadow now, but February had hit hard. Aubrey stood still a moment, hand to her thundering heart, the one still threatening to burst out of her rib cage.

Behind her the door opened again. Panicked that it might be Ben and not nearly ready for another face-to-face, she hightailed it out of the parking lot. In her three-inch, high-heeled boots, she wasn't exactly stealthy with the loud *click-click-click*, but she was fast. In two minutes, she'd rounded the block and finally slowed some, straining to hear.

Footsteps.

Dammit. He was following her. She quickened her pace again until she passed a church. The building, like nearly all of the buildings in Lucky Harbor, was a restored Victorian from the late 1800s. It was a pale pink with blue-and-white trim, and lit from the inside. The front door was wide open and inviting, at least compared to the rest of the night around her...

Aubrey wasn't a churchgoer. Her rocket scientist father hadn't believed in anything other than what could be found in his science books. Cold, hard facts. As a result, churches always held a sort of morbid fascination for her, one she'd never given into. But now, with her car back at the Love Shack and Ben possibly still on her trail, she hurried up the walk and stepped inside. Trying to catch her breath, she turned around to see if he'd followed and nearly plowed a man over.

"Good evening," he said. He was in his thirties, average height and build, wearing jeans, a cable-knit sweater, and a smile that was as welcoming as the building itself.

But Aubrey didn't trust welcoming much.

"Can I help you?" he asked.

"No thanks." Unable to resist, she peered out into the night.

No sign of Ben. That was a slight relief, but mostly she felt like the fly who'd lost track of the spider.

"Are you sure you're okay?" the man asked. "You seem...troubled."

She had to grate her teeth. She was sure he was very nice, but what was it with the male race? Why was it so hard to believe she didn't need a man's help? "Listen," she said, wanting to be clear. "Nothing personal, but I'm giving up men. Forever."

If he was fazed by her abruptness, it didn't show. His eyes crinkled in good humor as he slid his hands into his pockets and rocked back on his heels. "I'm the pastor here. Pastor Mike," he said.

Good going, Aubrey, being rude to a man of God for having the audacity to be nice to you. "I'm sorry." It didn't escape her notice that this was the second time tonight she'd said those two very foreign words. "My life's in the toilet today...well, every day this week so far really." She shook her head. "I seem to keep making the same mistakes over and over," she murmured, and shook it off. "Forget this. I'm going home to have another stiff drink."

"What's your name?"

She considered lying but didn't want to further tempt fate. Or God. Or whoever was in charge of such things. "Aubrey."

"You don't have to go be alone, Aubrey," Pastor Mike said, managing to sound gentle and in charge at the same time. "You're in a good place here."

"Well—" But before she knew it, he'd ushered her into a meeting room where there were about ten people seated in a circle.

A woman was standing, wringing her hands. "My name is Kathy," she said to the group, "and it's been an hour since I last craved a drink."

The entire group said in unison, "Hi, Kathy."

An AA meeting, Aubrey realized, swallowing what would have been a half-hysterical laugh with great effort as Pastor Mike nudged her to a chair. He sat next to her and handed her a pamphlet. One glance told her it was a list of the twelve steps to recovery.

What was she doing here? And what could she possibly say? *Hi, my name is Aubrey, and I'm a bitchaholic...*

Kathy had sat down. A guy was standing now. Ryan, he told them. Ryan was talking about how he'd been working on something called his fearless moral inventory, starting to make amends to the list of people he'd wronged.

Aubrey bit her lip. Her list would be long. Horrifyingly long.

The man continued to talk with heartbreaking earnestness, and somehow, in spite of herself, she couldn't help but soak it all in, unbearably moved by his bravery.

She wanted to be that brave.

She didn't realize that she was sitting there, utterly transfixed, until Mike gently patted her hand. "You see, it's never too late," he said quietly.

She stared at him, wondering if that could really be true. "You don't know for sure."

"I do," he said with conviction.

Aubrey thought about that when the meeting ended, as

she walked back to her car and drove home, which was little more than a room above the used bookstore she'd adopted. Her aunt Gwen had run the store up until her death last year, and her uncle hadn't been able to bring himself to lease the space to anyone else.

Until last month, when Aubrey had left her job at Town Hall after the Ted fiasco. Restless, she'd signed a lease, both as an homage to Aunt Gwen—the only one who'd ever been nice to her on her dad's side of the family—and because she was determined to bring the bookstore back to its former glory. She was working on that. And maybe she could be working on other things as well, such as her karma.

Her mind wandered back to tonight's meeting, and the people there, and what they were trying to accomplish with their lives. Could it really be as easy as making a list? Checking it twice? Trying to find out if she could pass on naughty and move on to nice?

Once inside, Aubrey took her first real breath in the past few hours. Most of the postage-stamp-sized area was filled with her design drawings for the layout of the space below and boxes of things she'd been saving for the store. She hoped to open by the end of the month, especially now that the other two storefronts in the building held flourishing businesses, a florist and a bakery owned by Ali Winters and Leah Sullivan respectively. Recent acquaintances, and maybe even friends.

At the thought, she plopped a little dejectedly on the small loveseat. Yes, Ali and Leah were friends, new ones. Which meant that they didn't know the same Aubrey that Ben did, the one who hadn't always been the best person.

She glanced at the pamphlet she still held and then

pulled her small notebook from her purse and began making a list.

People she'd wronged.

It took her a very long time, and when she was done, she eyeballed the length of it and hefted a sigh. Surely it'd have been easier to simply face Ben tonight rather than run into Pastor Mike. Blowing out a breath, she kicked off her boots and leaned back, staring at the last person on the list, the hardest of them all.

Ben.

And he wasn't there because she'd tossed her drink in his face...

Chapter 2

♥

The next morning, Ben walked out of the bakery and stood on the sidewalk taking a bite from his soft, still-warm bear claw.

As close to heaven as he was going to get.

He glanced inside to wave his thanks to the pastry chef, but Leah Sullivan currently had her arms and lips entangled with her fiancé, who happened to be Ben's cousin Jack Harper.

Ben turned his back to the window and ate his bear claw. Eventually, the bakery door opened behind him, and then Jack was standing at his side. He was in uniform for work, which meant that every woman driving down the street slowed down to get a look at him in his firefighter gear.

"Why are you dressed?" Ben asked him.

"Because when I'm naked, I actually cause riots," Jack said, sliding on his sunglasses.

"You know what I mean." A month ago, Jack had

made the shift from firefighting to being fire marshal. He didn't suit up and respond to calls anymore.

Jack shrugged. "I'm working a shift today for Ian, who's down with the flu." He pulled his own breakfast choice out of the bakery bag.

Ben took one look at the cream cheese croissant and shook his head. "Pussy breakfast."

Unperturbed by this, Jack stuffed it into his mouth. "You're just still grumpy because a pretty lady tossed her drink in your face last night."

"It was an accident."

"I know," Jack said. "I just didn't realize that you knew it too." He looked at his watch. "Luke's late."

The three of them had been tight since age twelve, when Ben's mom, unable to take care of him any longer, had dropped him on her sister's doorstep. Luke had lived next door. The three of them had spent their teen years terrorizing the neighborhood and giving Dee, Jack's mom and Ben's aunt, gray hair.

"Luke's not late," Jack said. "He's here. He's in the flower shop trying to get into Ali's back pocket. Guess that's what you do when you're engaged."

Ben didn't say anything to this, and Jack blew out a breath. "Sorry."

Ben shook his head. "Been a long time."

"Not that long," Jack said.

It felt like forever ago that Ben had been engaged, and then married. He and Hannah had been high school sweethearts in a different life. Then, like most teenage boys, he'd been unceremoniously dumped. Two years later, he'd run into Hannah at a party, and they'd become college sweethearts. They'd done the mature thing and hadn't married until they'd both graduated, and they'd had a solid marriage.

Until she'd died five years ago.

Ben went after his second bear claw while Jack looked at his watch. "Shit. I've gotta go. Tell Luke he's an asshole."

"Will do." Ben washed down his breakfast with icy-cold chocolate milk. *You drink too much caffeine*, Leah had told him, all bossy and sweet at the same time, handing him the milk instead of a mug of coffee.

It was early, not close to seven yet, but he liked early. Fewer people. Quiet air.

Or maybe that was just Lucky Harbor.

Either way, he was nearly content, and that in itself was such an odd emotion for him. He shoved the thought aside, uncomfortable with the feeling.

A few snowflakes floated out of the low, dense clouds. At his right, the Pacific Ocean pounded at the shore. The pier was strung with white lights, still shining brightly through the morning gloom. On his left was downtown Lucky Harbor, an oak-lined street of more colorful Victorian buildings strung with the same lights as the pier, still quiet and sleepy.

A month ago, he'd been in another country, hell, practically on another planet, elbows deep in a project rebuilding a water system for war-torn Libya. Before that, he'd been in Haiti for months. And before that, Africa. And before that...Indonesia? It was all rolling together.

He'd seen people at the worst moments in their lives, and at some point, he'd become numb. So much so that when he'd gone to check out a new jobsite at the wrong place, only to have the right place blown to bits by a suicide bomber, he'd realized something.

He didn't always have to be the guy on the front line. He could design and plan from anywhere. Hell, he could become a consultant instead. Five years of wading knee deep in shit, both figuratively and literally, was enough for anyone. He didn't want to be in the *right* hellhole next time.

Polishing off his second bear claw with one more bite, Ben sucked the sugar off his thumb. Turning to head toward his truck, he stopped short at the realization that someone stood watching him.

It was Aubrey, and when he caught her eye, she dropped the things in her hands. "Oh," she said. "It's you."

Her tone suggested she'd just stepped in dog shit with her fancy high-heeled boot. The tone didn't surprise him. She'd been a few years behind him in school, and they hadn't traveled in the same circles much. In those years, he'd spent much of his time either in trouble or on the basketball court—the only reason he'd ended up in college and not in jail. Aubrey had been the Hot Girl, the one with a sharp wit and sharper bite.

Few had ever messed with Aubrey.

There'd been an instinctive mistrust between them, as if they both recognized two like-troubled souls and had made a mutual decision to steer clear of each other.

And except for the rare interaction, they had done just that. So he had no idea where the animosity between them came from. It'd simply always been there, like a limb. He crouched to reach for the things she'd dropped.

"I've got it," she said, prickly, bending low to get her own stuff. "I'm fine."

She certainly looked the part of fine; she always did. Her long blond hair was loose and wavy, held back from her eyes by a pretty pale-blue knit cap. A matching scarf was wrapped around her neck and tucked into a white wool coat covering her to a few inches above her knees. Leather boots met those knees, leaving some bare skin below the hem of her coat. As always, she was completely put together. In fact, she was always so purposely put together, it made him want to ruffle her up.

A crazy thought.

Even crazier, he wanted to know what she was wearing beneath the coat. "Where did you come from?"

"The building." She scooped up her things, and he grabbed a fallen notebook.

"The building," he repeated. There were three storefronts in this building, one of the oldest in town. The floral shop, the bakery, and the closed bookstore. She hadn't come out of the floral shop or the bakery, he knew that much. He glanced at the bookstore.

The windows were no longer boarded up as they'd been the last time he'd been home to Lucky Harbor, and through the glass panes, he could see that the old bookstore was in flux. Shelves were scattered, half empty. Boxes were open on the floor. Someone was cleaning up, packing all the old stuff.

"What are you doing here?" she asked, reaching to take the notebook from him.

Ben didn't know why he did it, but he held it out of her reach. "It's a public street."

Again she reached for the notebook. It was small and like Aubrey herself, neat and tidy. Just a regular pad of paper, opened to a page she'd written on. It was nothing special but clearly his holding on to it was making her un-comfortable. If it'd been any other woman on the planet, he'd have handed it right over.

Instead, he folded his arms.

She narrowed sharp, hazel eyes on him. "I want that back. It's…my grocery list."

Grocery list, his ass. It was a list of names, and his was on it. "Why am I on your grocery list?"

"You're not." She tried to snatch at it again, but one thing living in third-world countries did for you, it gave you quick instincts.

He held it firmly. "Yes," he said, looking down at it. "I am. I'm right here. Number four says Ben."

"It's Ben. And Jerry. *Ice cream*," she informed him.

Bullshit. Straightening, he skimmed the rest of the list. "Cathy Wheaton," he said, frowning. "Why do I remem-ber that name?"

"You don't." Straightening as well, Aubrey tried to crawl up his body to reach the pad.

Ben wasn't too ashamed to admit he kind of liked that. A lot.

Frustrated, she fisted a hand in his shirt, right over his heart. "Give me that!"

"Wait—I remember," he said, wincing since she now had a few chest hairs in a tight grip. "Cathy…nice girl. She was the grade in between us, right? A little skinny? Okay, a *lot* skinny."

Aubrey went still as stone, and Ben went back to the list. "Mrs. Cappernackle," he read. "The librarian?"

With her free hand, Aubrey pulled her phone from a pocket and looked pointedly at the time.

He ignored this because his curiosity was getting the

better of him. "Mr. Tyler." He paused. "Wasn't that your neighbor when you were growing up? That cranky old DA who had you arrested when you put food coloring in his pool and turned it green?"

Her eyes were fascinating. Hazel fire. "Give. Me. My. List," she said.

No way. This was just getting good. But clearly far more motivated than he, she twisted the grip she had on his shirt, yanking out those few hairs she'd caught.

"Hey. Ouch—"

Aubrey got a better grip on the pad so now they were tug-o-warring over it. "Seriously," he said. "What's going on?"

"None of your business," she said through her teeth, pulling on the pad.

He still didn't let go, even though his chest was on fire and missing a few hairs now. "It's my business when you're carrying around a list with my name on it."

"Why don't you Google the name *Ben* and see how many there are?" she said. "Now leave me alone."

The door to the floral shop opened, and a uniformed officer walked out. Luke, with impeccable timing, as always. Eyeing the tussle before him, he raised a brow. "What's up, kids?"

"Officer," Aubrey said, voice cool, eyes cooler as she yanked the pad from Ben's fingers. She shoved it into her purse, zipped it, and yanked it up to her shoulder. "This man is bothering me."

Luke grinned. "Should I arrest him?"

Aubrey slid Ben a speculative look. "Can't you just shoot him?" she asked hopefully.

Luke's grin widened. "I could, but there'd be a bunch

of paperwork. I hate paperwork. How about I just beat him up a little bit?"

Aubrey didn't take her eyes off Ben.

Ben cocked his head at her.

Finally she blew out a breath. "Never mind." Still hugging her purse to herself, she turned, unlocked the bookstore, and vanished back inside it.

The door slammed shut.

"I thought the store was closed," Ben said, absently rubbing his chest.

"It is," Luke said. "Mr. Lyons is her uncle. She's going to renovate and reopen it. She's living in the tiny little studio above it."

"How do you know so much?"

"Because I know all," Luke said. "And because Mr. Lyons called. He needs a carpenter, so I gave him your number."

"Mine?"

"You're still good with a hammer, right?"

"Yeah." Ben's phone rang, and he looked at the unfamiliar but local number.

Luke looked too. "That's him," he said. "Mr. Lyons."

Mr. Lyons opened with a gruff "Don't say no yet."

Ben sighed. "I'm listening."

"I need a carpenter."

Ben slid Luke a look. "So I've heard. I'm not a carpenter. I'm a civil engineer."

"You know damn well before you got all dark and mysterious that you were handy with a set of tools," Mr. Lyons said.

Luke, who could hear Mr. Lyons's booming voice, grinned like the Cheshire cat and pointed at Ben.

Ben bit back a sigh. "Why not hire Jax? He's the best carpenter in town."

"He's got a line of customers from Lucky Harbor to Seattle, and I don't want to wait. My niece Aubrey needs help renovating the bookstore. She wants to reopen next month. I know damn well she can't afford you, so I'm paying. For my sweet Gwen's memory. Don't give Aubrey the bill, and whatever you do, don't tell her how much you're going to cost me. I don't want her worrying about it. She's going through some stuff, and I want to do this for her. For both my girls."

"You should be asking me for a bid."

"I trust you."

Jesus. "You shouldn't," Ben said. "You—"

"Just start the damn work. Shelves. Paint. Hang stuff. Whatever she wants. Can you do it or not?"

Ben started to say no. Hell no. Being closed up in that bookstore with Aubrey for days and days? Surely one of them would kill the other before the month was up.

But he couldn't deny that he wanted to know what she was up to. "Yeah," he said. "I can do it."

Whether he'd survive it was another thing entirely.

When Jill's neighbor decided to have an extension built, she was suddenly gifted with inspiration: a bunch of cute, young, sweaty guys hanging off the roof and the walls. Just the type of men who'd appeal to three estranged sisters forced together when they inherit a dilapidated beach resort . . .

Meet Maddie, Tara and Chloe in

 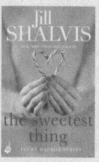 

'Count on Jill Shalvis for a witty, steamy, unputdownable love story'
Robyn Carr

headline
ETERNAL

When the lights go out and you're 'stuck' in a café with potential Chocoholic-partners-in-crime and nothing else to do but eat cake and discuss the mysteries of life, it's surprising just what conclusions women will come to. But when they decide to kick things into gear, they'd better be prepared for what happens once they have the ball rolling . . .

Here come Mallory, Amy and Grace in

'An abundance of chemistry, smoldering romance, and hilarious antics'
Publishers Weekly

headline
ETERNAL

The women of Lucky Harbor have been charming
readers with their incredible love stories – now it's
time for some very sexy men to take center stage.
They're in for some *big* surprises – and from corners
they'd least expect it.

Really get to know Luke, Jack and Ben in

headline
ETERNAL

*L*ucky Harbor is the perfect place to escape to, whether that means a homecoming, getting away from the city or running from something a whole lot darker. Whatever the cause, Lucky Harbor has three more residents who are about to discover just how much this sleepy little town really has to offer.

Escape with Becca, Olivia and Callie in

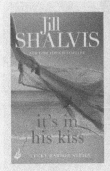

'Clever, steamy, and fun. Jill Shalvis will
make you laugh and fall in love'
Rachel Gibson

headline
ETERNAL